MW01241179

Catch a Falling Star

Book One of The Shooting Stars Series

#1 Amazon Bestseller

★★★★★

—Catch a Falling Star is a Must Read—

"I loved *Catch a Falling Star*! I couldn't put it down. It's hard to believe that this is Leah Downing's first book! She is highly skilled at engaging the reader by developing intriguing characters and creating unexpected twists and turns in the storyline that keep you on the edge of your seat and wanting more!"

— S. McGuinness

★★★★★

—Best Book I've Read in a Long Time—

"This is what a page turner is all about. It has something in it for everyone, a great love story, suspense, thriller and comedy all wrapped into one phenomenal book. I cannot wait to get my hands on the next one!"

—KashP

★★★★★

—Heart Pounding Movement & Intrigue—

"Fast paced, intriguing heart pounding movement that splashes with tactile imagery. Leah commands the scenes with rich detail and authority. It is fun & funny without skipping a beat of juicy detail, weaving in mystery beyond worlds. Bravo!"

—Kesha Engel

★★★★★

—Best Romance Novel I've Read in Years—

"*Catch a Falling Star* is so much more than just a love story. It layers mystery with hope, passion with fear, and adventure with legends of supernatural forces. It draws you into the world of Lauren St Germain and James Bayer. I can't wait to read Book Two: *The Path of Least Resistance*."

—Dr. Cindy Mann

Catch a Falling Star

Leah Downing

Catch a Falling Star

Copyright © 2016 by Leah Downing

Leah Downing Books are available for order through Ingram Press Catalogues.

This book is a work of fiction. Names, characters, places, and incidents are either products of the author's imagination or are used fictitiously. Any resemblance to ac-tual events or locales, or persons, living or dead, is entirely coincidental. Some as-pects of this story fall under the definition of Historical Fiction; whereas, true characteristics of the time period and events have been borrowed, but story and character(s) are fictitious.

Published by Full Net Enterprises

Printed in the United States of America
First Printing: February 2016

For more information on future works, events, and blogs visit:
Facebook: Leah Downing Author
Twitter: @ledowningauthor

ISBN-13: 978-0-9977323-0-6

www.529Books.com
Editor: Lisa Cerasoli
Interior Design: Danielle Canfield
Cover Design: Claire Moore

For Kevin

Praise for

The Path of Least Resistance

Book Two of The Shooting Stars Series
#1 Amazon Bestseller

★★★★★

—AMAZING…ADDICTIVE…and not to be missed—

"Be prepared to immediately pick up *Catch a Falling Star* to read again once you finish *The Path of Least Resistance!*"

— Jesse Neidt
Intuitive Consultant
http://www.jesseneidt.com/

★★★★★

—Outstanding Novel that Instantly Connects the Reader to Story —

"Once again Leah Downing proves her talent for weaving a mystical story that hooks you from the first page, takes you on an engaging ride, and leaves the reader wanting more! Downing has fast become one of my favorite authors. I was so blown away by the ending that I read the last few chapters a second time."

— Laura Kelly
Bestselling Author of *Splintered Reflections*

★★★★★

—The minute I finished reading *The Path of Least Resistance*,
I was ready for Book Three—

"I had the same 'problem' with this book as I did with the first— I could NOT put it down! I stayed up so late the first night reading *The Path of Least Resistance* that I had to FORCE myself to go to bed halfway through! I hope Book Three comes out soon. In the meantime, I'm re-reading Book One: *Catch a Falling Star.*"

—Dr. Kristy Ingebo, MD

yoga terminology

Sanskrit is the ancient language of India. Yoga—a practice developed over 5,000 years ago in a civilization in Northern India—uses terminology for poses (asanas) and concepts in this language.

- o Savasana: Corpse Pose
- o Asana: Pose
- o Ranis: "Queens"
- o Sutras: Meditative discipline of liberation consisting of eight steps.
- o Adho-sukha-svanasana: Downward Facing Dog (down dog)
- o Vinyasa: Movement between poses that strings them together like a dance.
- o Kakasana: Crow Pose—an arm balance.
- o Sirsha-asana: Headstand
- o Bakasana: Crane Pose—almost identical to kakasana/crow.
- o Tadasana: Mountain Pose
- o Namaste: "The light in me sees the light in you." Closing statement for yoga classes.

- Prana: Breath, life-giving force.
- Yin Yoga: Slow-paced style of yoga where the asanas are held for long periods of time.
- Dhyana Mudra: A meditative gesture with both palms facing up on the lap.
- Chakrasana: Wheel Pose—backbend
- Vrscikasana: Scorpion Pose—a difficult forearm balance where the bottoms of the feet connect to the crown of the head via backbend.
- Surya Namaskar: Sun Salutation—a designated vinyasa done as a warm-up.
- Ujjai: A style of breathing.
- Virabhadrasana: Warrior Pose—standing dynamic poses.
- Niralamba-Sarvangasana: Shoulder Stand
- Matsyasana: Fish Pose—a reclined counter pose to arch the spine up.

CATCH A FALLING STAR

p r o l o g u e

F-150

Collin: *Heading in early, f'n haboob* ☺, *burritos and mex-icoke?*
14 MAY 2008, 05:30
Angel: *Think the roach coach will be out in this shit?*
14 MAY 2008, 05:31
Collin: *Yes*
14 MAY 2008, 05:31
Angel: *Alrightee then, my brother, bring it*
14 MAY 2008, 05:32

6:15 a.m. on May 14, 2008
Fort Bliss, TX

Collin St. Germain dropped the food and drinks down on the worktable in his shop before heading right back out. Over the roaring wind, he could still hear the awful knocking sound coming from a decrepit car engine.

Angel Torres-Rodriguez had just pulled up in his wife's beat-down Fiesta. The car's nose displayed a splotchy sunburst design across the center of the hood with tendrils reaching out to the top of the headlights.

Angel cracked his window. "Man, this shit is nasty!" he shouted over the ruckus.

Collin flipped his fingertips back and forth across his neck in a slicing motion to communicate the universal sign—*cut your engine, bro.* The wind that morning was brutal, which would create a realistic training scenario, even though no one would be able to hear shit.

"I bet we need to reset everything," Collin observed as he bent down, with the familiarity of easy friendship, to peer into the window.

Angel nodded as his gaze swept the field. "And brush it all over again." Getting out of the small car was cumbersome for him. Angel had the physique of a weightlifter and walked with the limp of an ex-linebacker. The Fiesta's shocks groaned as they sprang up in relief when he pulled himself out of the car. "Dude, come back in the shop and take a look at this truck I found on eBay, it ends today."

Collin hesitated, there were still several devices in the field that needed to be reset before the SF[1] teams reported for training.

"Quickly," he responded and led the way back into the shop.

Angel ripped apart the foil on his burrito. The charred smell of carnitas mixed with tomatillo sauce enticed Collin into eating his breakfast as well. They stood on either side of the workbench scrolling through pictures of a white F–150 for sale on eBay.

"Hold off on bidding," Collin said as he set his Coke down hard on the steel surface. A burst of carbonated bubbles rose up the neck of the bottle. "Let's check Craigslist one last time before the auction ends."

Collin neatly wrapped the remaining half of his burrito up and turned on a heel toward the door. He had the sole mission of making the deadly scenario outside absolutely perfect for the elite SF soldiers.

Angel slid onto the stool in front of the laptop as he wiped salsa verde on his pant leg. He inserted his CAC[2] card into the laptop drive and gained access to his time sheet. "Right behind you!"

---

[1] Special Forces—Military units trained to perform unconventional missions.
[2] Common Access Card—ID card for active-duty military personnel, Selected Reserve, defense civilian employees, and eligible contractor personnel. Required to be on person at all times when on base.

"Roger that." Collin strode out the door toward the first pressure plate in such a rush he almost stepped directly on top of the IED.[3] Realizing he needed to slow his roll as to not make any mistakes, he carefully backed up and knelt down over the device.

This first pressure plate was buried about ten meters into the field. If all went as planned, it would be the preliminary mock explosion of the morning. Collin visually inspected the wires between the crushed soda can to make sure they hadn't moved away from each other due to last night's wind. Surprisingly, they were intact.

The second booby trap was near a mesquite bush, another twenty meters out. Collin deliberately approached this one. It was easy to spot and only took a few minutes to relocate.

Later that morning, highly observant SF troops would scour the training field for IEDs. It wasn't a live fire type of exercise; the IEDs didn't contain actual explosives. However, if Collin tripped one, a blast of white powder would go everywhere. He reached down and scooped up a handful of mesquite pods. They could be used to camouflage his tracks after he brushed it over again.

---

[3] Improvised Explosive Device—A simple bomb made and used by unofficial or unauthorized forces AKA roadside bomb, booby trap.

The two wires on the third pressure plate had separated from each other overnight. After studying the compromised device, Collin crouched down to feed some copper wire into it. His knees stiffened, but his determination to lengthen the trip wire won out over his aching joints. Dirt started to cake up on his face from the whipping wind, so he dropped the pods and pulled his hand over his cheek.

At this same moment, Lauren St. Germain, Collin's wife, accelerated on a wide turn into the shop parking lot. She pushed open the door of her government-issued Ford Fusion and her nose wrinkled from the smell of burnt rubber. She grabbed Collin's CAC card from her purse. She spotted it earlier on his dresser, just as she was squatting to get her Spanx pulled all the way up to her crotch.

As she stepped out of her car, she lunged deeply, still trying to wiggle the Spanx into place before slamming the car door. Flustered from her hair blowing in her face and sticking to her lipgloss, she burst into the shop a little feistier than usual.

"Hey!" Angel exclaimed as he snapped the laptop lid shut with a crack. "What's up, Ms. Lauri?"

She waved Collin's CAC card up for him to see.

"He's out there." Angel pointed toward the range.

"Okay, Angel." She mispronounced his name calling him an angel like he had a halo.

"*Angel,*" he corrected as she left. "Like An-hell, which is where you can go, puta."

Lauren stumbled as she hurried across the parking lot. She stopped short at the edge, not wanting to stride into the field. Her high heels would get eaten up by the rocks and goat heads if she proceeded. She cupped her hands around her mouth. "Collin!" Her hoarse voice was drowned out by the howl of the wind.

His head swiveled and he stood up to see his wife signaling her irritation with open arms and shoulders up. His lanyard flapped back on her leg in an erratic pattern. Collin momentarily forgot their "discussion" from last night and chuckled. Lauren was kind of cute when she was pissed. He took a step in her direction when he noticed a foreign pressure plate in his peripheral vision. Collin's analytical brain crawled along sluggishly, but his instinctive physical actions shot into place.

Collin wondered why Angel had set up another plate so close to the third target. His boots traversed on a straight course to the misplaced pressure plate when the realization that Angel had arrived late that morning dawned on him. Without fully comprehending what he was experiencing, Collin made the last stride needed in order to get a closer look.

TEN MONTHS LATER

chapter one

THE MRS. ST. GERMAIN

March 28, 2009

I was waiting to go through Customs in the remote Kujjiquaq airport located as far north as one could go in Quebec before crossing the Hudson Bay into the Nunavut Territories. My two mismatched totes served as a footstool while I blankly stared at Tyler and Thom passing through the solo Customs line.

My matching luggage set was collecting dust in a storage unit near El Paso. Before leaving for Malibu, the contract was extended for another six months. I wasn't quite ready to sever all ties. My mind skipped around on this topic; maybe I should just stop paying the bill and let the owners auction off everything. Unfortunately, Collin's military memorabilia was still locked up in that unit and he would want all those medals to be passed down. Eventually.

As if Tyler read my mind as I was floating off into the never-never land of the past, his chin sharply tilted up as he shot me a look. *Buck up.*

My best friend and gay husband, Tyler, had the canny ability to analyze my inner workings before my mouth opened to speak. This perception extended to anyone who crossed his path, which has proven to be the foundation of his hugely successful company—PuraYoga.

His partner, Thom Nguyen, is the mouthpiece of the couple and usually takes center stage. Definitely the more flamboyant of the two, he's known for wearing women's yoga pants that show off his perfectly toned legs (and man bulge). Half Vietnamese and half German, he's a rare mix of eastern compactness but lengthened into a tall frame. His black wavy hair makes the perfect topper. Thom often wears retro-styled glasses with heavy frames circa 1960s beatnik. (He has no prescription, of course.)

Tyler, a white man of Danish descent, has eyes that are such thin slits he can appear to be dozing. His style may be understated, but he's been a proven tastemaker. He would never say it, but he's credited with taking yoga from fringe devotion to national trend.

In the late 1990s, yoga, especially hot yoga, was making its way into the physical fitness scene during our era in Vegas. Tyler and I both had avid yoga practices so much so that it was likened to religious fanaticism by some of his friends. This was a time before every house-wife in America had a five-day-a-week practice and yogis were still considered dirty hippies. *Autobiography of a Yogi* could be found only in obscure New Age bookstores and "down dog" was a command to keep Fido from jumping on guests. It was a magical time; Tyler was on the cusp of something big.

Less ambitious than he, I developed my own yoga practice with equal emphasis on the physical and the metaphysical. I ventured into learning about other belief systems and had even considered changing my lifestyle to a more conservative one with a devout religious prac-tice. But for all my interest in Middle Eastern and Far Eastern practices, I jumped from thing to thing, unable to commit to any particular doctrine.

By 2000, I mainly served Tyler's vision by demon-strating the asanas for his growing classes. Sometimes I volunteered to teach in back rooms of crystal shops...the kind that employed psychics as cashiers. Then I transitioned up to a more mainstream venue, Las Vegas Athletic Club, usually subbing for hungover yoga teachers on Sunday mornings.

Any career in yoga was not in my cards past the Las Vegas Athletic Club. As 2000 rolled into 2001, my rela-tionship with Collin intensified and he urged me to

3

switch my major to Criminal Justice. It was a time of un-
certainty and after 9/11, I was on my way to a Bachelors
in Criminal Justice. The decision to shed my bohemian
lifestyle for a more rigid one came, and Mrs. St. Germain
emerged.

As I was hanging up my Be Present yoga wear for
structured jackets and heels, Thom and Tyler rose to
mega yogalebrity status. After the immense success of
their PuraYoga studio brand, they established a niche
service that trains actors to perform yoga for film, TV,
commercials, and photo shoots. This branch of their
company is called DesignaYoga by Pura. No longer just
exclusive yoga instructors, they catapulted themselves
into the lucrative movie business where they had one-
on-one intensives with celebrities.

Tyler personally guaranteed that he and Thom could
get any actor to perform yoga in perfect form in under
six weeks. All forms of yoga, every asana and all off-
shoots of yoga, were included in their repertoire.
DesignaYoga delivered, and now they could command
whatever type of staffing support they desired.

Less than a month ago, Tyler wrote me in as a contractor to come work with him under the Northern
Lights at the top of the world. A title was discussed with
no conclusion. The suggestion "subordinate" came up,
but Thom snubbed this. Military jargon was still stuck in

my vocabulary and they wanted absolutely no connection to that part of my life. So that word, along with my married name, were banished.

In the end, I was simply Lauren.

"Ms. St. Germain," the Customs agent called, waving me up to his window.

After clearing my throat, I corrected him. "Mrs. St. Germain."

My breath stopped as he scanned my passport. It had been released back to me a month ago, reinstating my foreign travel privileges.

"You should keep an eye out for Arthur Turturro and Janel Rios. They're expected to be on set this week, right?" the agent asked.

"I don't know," I mumbled and turned my back to retrieve my bags once my passport was back in hand. I didn't bother to correct him. There was no set. We were going to be on a *cruise ship*. The phrase sounded ridiculous even in my own head.

As I looked for Tyler and Thom, my thoughts shifted away from the bleak past and onto the upcoming week's adventures in the moviemaking business. *Films*, that's what professionals call them. There were so many nuances in movie production lingo; it's almost a language in and of itself. I grilled Tyler the entire flight up here for the correct verbiage so I'd appear less green when we started the training.

And it was exciting that *the* Arthur Turturro was cast in the lead for this film. Janel Rios was cast as the mother, and wasn't scheduled to attend this week's training. The whole focus would be completely around Turturro. He was about to be transformed into the recently deceased yogalebrity, Bronne de Luca. For the next week, the founders of the globally successful Pura brand were going to do what they do best; turn Academy Award-winner Arthur Turturro into a seasoned yoga practitioner for his upcoming film.

Thom was tapping his foot full out as I approached them.

I shrugged a *"sorry"* and meekly followed my two *ranis* to the van.

After an hour of driving in darkness with the occasional flash of headlights coming from the opposite direction, we reached a crowded strip mall that served as the Pura rendezvous point. From here, sixty or so tourists were negotiating their limited edition, brand-name luggage into the storage areas beneath the public shuttle bus.

Public shuttle may not have been an appropriate description for this vintage double-decker bus with freshly polished brass handles and dark green benches. No expense had been spared to make the embarkation of this wintery voyage match the elegance and mystery of a first-class Orient Express ticket.

The wealth that filled the bus was stunning. There were stylish cold-weather clothes not available in catalogs. As the heaters warmed the bus, gloves came off to display sparkling diamonds that rivaled the twinkling white lights that framed the observation windows. Half of the cabins on board the cruise ship, appropriately named Namasea, were sold to an eccentric jet-set crowd. The remaining cabins were designated for our group.

There were approximately twenty-five of us that made up the entourage on this project, ranging from yoga extras to assistant directors and photographers. Oddly enough, this whole concept (yoga courts the filthy rich) seemed to mesh perfectly with the vodka martinis being served up in frosted glasses while Inuit natives hocked fur hats to the rich tourists.

The Aurora Borealis motif was consistent in every aspect of the ship. It's the second biggest draw for people to pay such exorbitant amounts of money to cruise up to Cape Dorset. The ship's main attraction was the facilities; an all-inclusive detox, weight loss, and elegant party vessel complete with life coaches, large workout areas, and three fully functional PuraYoga studios. At least once per year, Tyler and Thom bring some big celebrity up here for a week-long spiritual retreat and make sure pictures of these stars enjoying the highbrow Zen experience go viral.

The premise of the movie was based on the real life of the late Bronne de Luca. He was a first-generation Italian-American boy who came out to his parents while growing up in Philadelphia. De Luca was beaten by his father and promptly kicked out of the house. Hiding in a population of other disowned souls, he found refuge in a gay commune deep in the slums of Philly. Free yoga classes taught in the basement of a church beckoned, immersing him into a deeply spiritual practice. His story was so inspirational he made the cover of *Yoga Journal* before he was nationally recognized. He became one of the first top-billed (and top-paid) instructors in history due to his massive following.

De Luca was diagnosed with HIV in the late 1990s, which was kept secret until 2004, when he made a public announcement. His status skyrocketed. Worldwide he was anointed into "agnostic sainthood" as he became a beacon for young men everywhere dealing with the illness. Since his death in 2006, the rights to his story were purchased and this bio-pic, *The Purpose*, was being created to honor his work and life.

c h a p t e r   t w o

INTRODUCTIONS

Everyone had to meet first thing in the morning to get the week's itinerary. It was a tight room where fifteen or so extras donning the most recent lines of Spiritual Gangster and Lululemon garb lounged as we waited. They wore perfectly fitted tops layered under soft, slouchy hoodies. A little less than half of this group were men, with half of those dudes sporting man buns.

There were four assistants seated at a table opposite the extras, looking like they were in charge. They methodically tapped away on their tablets, phones, and laptops, like little energizer bunnies all wound up to pound out some yoga.

A man entered and a hush fell over the group. No one knew for sure, but he could have been Arthur Turturro. This slight man looked lost, and had poorly cut brown hair with threads of grey glinting through it. A thinning patch was visible on the back of his head. It looked like a DIY hack job.

No one followed him in.

"The lead has been changed—improved upon, actually. My name is Matthew Czerniawski. Don't worry, you only have to call me Matt or Mattski, if I like you."

It was an uncomfortable introduction at best.

As Matt began to describe the delicate process of casting and contracts, my mind drifted to my hair, which was French braided. It would remain in this style all week since Collin and I used to butt heads about how my hair should be worn while working; the easiest solution was to just wear it up all the time.

With great ceremony, Matt finally announced that Arthur Turturro unexpectedly dropped out and James Bayer would be taking his place as lead. Without skipping a beat, he married that statement with news that Mr. Bayer recently signed on to play Superman.

Sensing an undercurrent of annoyance about the lead, Mattski's delivery, you name it; his eyes darted to Tyler. "Would you care to elaborate?"

"We've had Mr. Bayer on a strict diet for the past two weeks to give him a head start for his physical journey. The timing of this project was rearranged so we can complete his physical transformation before he travels to India for the ashram scenes. Final shots may need to be taken on a sound stage, but that's still to be determined. All shooting needs to be wrapped before Mr. Bayer starts training for his Superman role. Obviously he'll need to bulk back up for that." Tyler could smooth over anything.

An image of James Bayer came into my mind while I tried to put everything I knew about him in order. He's a classically handsome British actor who's more suited to play James Bond, not a sinewy, gay Italian yogi.

Everyone in the room nodded a *yes, Tyler.* Even my head bobbed up and down. I glanced at Tyler's smooth profile, knowing he already had a game plan to get this buff British guy's guy of an actor transformed into a spirited Italian-American living in the armpit of Philly teaching sutras to the poor.

I foresaw the movie showcasing troubled, but beautiful, yoga devotees experiencing emotional journeys while decked out in limited-edition Lulu originals. They'd probably be designed especially for the movie too. *Ugh, "film," Lauren, film!*

Matt was James Bayer's manager. Lastly, he informed us that if we had any desire to communicate with Mr. Bayer outside of professional necessities, we simply should not. No further explanation, just "NOT," he emphasized. Without pause, Matt listed the many attributes of Mr. Bayer's superb feats of physical endurance and transformation for previous roles.

My mind was cataloguing any bits of information I could recall about James Bayer. All I could come up with was a corny sci-fi film from a few years back. There was a steamy scene where he and some sexpot of a green alien got it on. It resulted in an alien-human offspring, I think. Who cares? There may have been a sequel.

I've seen him in *US Weekly* before, but never a full page and always in the back of the issue. I was certain that I wouldn't be the only person rushing to the internet tonight to dissect every bit of information available about this rather unknown actor from Great Britain.

Matt continued to tick off his master's successes while that alien sex scene looped in my head. His sexual prowess was so raw that the viewer excused him for taking advantage of the poor (naked) abandoned alien, who had been unfamiliar with the desires of earthly men. Any woman, green or not, would have traded places with her in a heartbeat. What was the line? "You can trust me to have a great care for your heart?" Or something like that...a total pantydropper. I caught my right hand absentmindedly smoothing down my braid and pulling the tail of it forward over my shoulder. I abruptly shot my hand back down to my side.

"Yes, Miss, um, yes? Did you have a question?" Matt asked.

The group peered at me with a gaze of irritated omness. "What movie was Mr. Bayer in with Alanna Willis?" I managed to muster.

Matt seemed surprised by my question.

God, what if he already told us?

"*Probing Deep Space*," he brusquely replied, eager to move off the genesis of Mr. Bayer's film history.

It was a smart move on my part, referring to James Bayer as "Mr. Bayer." I wasn't up for being dressed down by this Mattski guy in front of a group of people I hardly knew.

With no warning, the door opened in a sweep of confidence and Thom waltzed through as James Bayer in the flesh held it open for him. They were both laughing, no doubt at some Thom-ism.

Matt cleared his throat loudly. "Well, thank you, this is Mr. Bayer."

I crossed my arms under my chest so I could press my cotton shirt under my boobs to absorb the slimy dampness from lotion and sweat.

"James. Hi," he introduced himself in an unassuming way as his hand extended to Tyler.

"Tyler," he said with a firm handshake. "After so much face time on Centrix, it's a pleasure to finally meet you in person." Tyler was always so cool in any situation, even James Bayer couldn't help but to be taken by him.

They released hands and Tyler curved his arm out in front of Matt to pull me up. "This is Lauren."

James stepped and extended his hand just in time to glance down and see a wet spot on my sleeve.

I shrank back into the group feeling like an inflated sponge, so full with fluid that it was literally seeping out of every surface pore. I didn't really know what I was doing there, all dirty and broken among these silky white-feathered swans. Tyler, once again, took me back under his wing after all these years. I was shamed to the core the day he arrived in El Paso to establish his support for me.

I could lie to myself and rationalize that since we were so close and I worked so diligently at my practice, he offered up this great opportunity to me instead of to a thousand other friends. In actuality, I think he simply felt sorry for the shattered shell that was left of me.

As James worked his way around the room, Tyler handed me a schedule face down and whispered, "Take a look."

There was just enough time for me to scan the detailed schedule and see my name peppered all over it. Two of the yoga studios on the ship were being utilized by us so the third one could remain open for paying passengers. I double checked it closely. There were only three instructors listed: Thom, Tyler, and me.

"Let's move to the conference room now that we're all present," Thom announced.

We moved into an impressive meeting room with a long mahogany conference table set up with individual binders at each seat. Name placards were already on top of each one, with bottled water set to the side. Only one was missing a last name, and I sat in that spot.

Keeping the paper under the table while everyone else settled into their spots, I studied the schedule further. I was relegated to be the leader of the extras, while Thom and Tyler devoted all their time to James Bayer.

My extensive vocabulary of yoga had been honed since I spent the past few months in self-imposed reflection by immersing myself in round-the-clock classes at PuraYoga. Avoidance thinly masked as introspection convinced me that I was not hiding, but returning to my yoga roots as a "step in the right direction."

The months of daily exertion in steamy, hot yoga studios left me swimming in my clothes. Tyler insisted that I purchase smaller tops and leggings before we left on this trip; ending his lecture with the statement, "Bag-a-lady-a-lini is not a style."

When Thom called the meeting to order, I snuck a few glances at the star. In real life, James Bayer was as insanely good looking as he was on screen. He's tall, perhaps six feet and change with thick, shiny, brown hair resting in cowlicks that were curled up as a result of the humid sea air. Under the light, a faint reflection of ex-pertly applied caramel colored highlights accented the natural waves of his hair. His eyes had the type of hazel coloring that combined green and deep chestnut. James Bayer had an easy smile, both in his eyes and lips. He gave it freely; flashing his perfectly white, movie star teeth to any girl that looked his way.

Everyone in the room was dressed in some form of athletic clothes and James was no exception. We got a preview of his bare midriff when his T-shirt briefly clung to his fleece when he pulled it over his head. Everyone held their breath as if instructed, myself included.

Halfway through the meeting, James got up and walked over to the coffee station. His shoulders were the broadest part of his body and he moved with exceptional grace. There was no need to see him without a shirt to know there'd be carved out abs framed by defined obliques sloping down and inward from his chest. With coffee in hand, he sat back down and all heads jerked down to their binders.

I inwardly smiled and began to highlight my name in yellow on the schedule. My first class was today after lunch.

chapter three

THE POLITICS OF YOGA

The first line of business was a group evaluation led by Thom. He called it an "objective assessment of the whole," but it was more of a ranking system to designate each person into their caste for the week. Thom made a point to say that once the class began to flow, he'd take the liberty of moving bodies around so he could get a feel for different groupings. He had also pre-determined that the yoga mats were to be set up in four vertical lines across the room, facing front and equally spaced.

As I began to set the mats up for Thom, Tyler asked, "Why don't we put two mats in the front-row slot and then a few clusters near the middle and door? That would be more organic, students don't line their mats up."

"They do in my class. That way everyone can share energy from a place that has equal boundaries. I know there are some yoga teachers who allow their students to put their mats anywhere they choose, but not in my class."

During this exchange, I fidgeted around with the mats, and struggled to contain a giggle. All the extras waiting for this yoga class, *aka* assessment *aka* beauty pageant, were trying to figure out whose lead to follow. It was best to just wait it out.

Finally, Thom hushed Tyler with, "Okay, I have it."

Tyler must have understood his meaning and moved to stand in the same direction as the rest of us, like he was one of us.

Thom began. "Leave the mats lined up, Lauren. We'll go for seventy-five minutes to start. I need to see where everyone is at this stage." Thom pointed to me. "She's here for you to follow. Lauren will be my right hand all week in getting each and every one of you up to the standard Tyler and I expect. She knows how we want everything to look. Even if you're used to doing a pose a certain way, no matter how perfect you think it might be, if it doesn't look the way we need it to look, she will adjust you. And it's best to take her correction. You don't want me to correct you a second time. We are not here to practice yoga. We are here to perform it."

This statement hung in the air long enough for the extras to second guess their capabilities and exchange muted expressions of nervousness.

"Now…" Thom pointed at me again. "Lauren, come here." He opened his palm toward the front row so I would step to the mat just right of center. "Tyler," he called.

Tyler proudly moved forward to the mat just left of center also in the front row.

"James." He pulled the star up to the mat between us. "This way, you can watch either one of them no matter which direction you're facing. The rest of you can go ahead and choose a mat. I may move you around as the class progresses. If I do, just follow me without disturbing the others."

Tyler glanced at me with a telling look. I sensed Tyler was irked since Thom placed him on a mat for the class to follow, a move basically relegating Tyler to the same assistant position I was holding down. Tyler wouldn't say anything that questions Thom's authority in front of the class to keep up with continuity in their leadership, but there was no way Tyler was going to let Thom steal the show in the end. Visions of Tyler's floating handstands were fresh in my mind. No one gets from forward bend into plank into downward dog like Tyler. It looks like Ganesh himself is puppeteering his every vinyasa. Tyler's skills on the mat are nothing short of spectacular; no one would look at me for guidance or listen to Thom once they saw him in action.

There was a slight shift in Thom as he realized this inevitability. He was probably cursing himself for not keeping Tyler up front with him doing adjustments while he called out the sequences.

Once everyone claimed their mats, Thom stated, "Inhale, both arms up...." In conjunction with this, his expressive hands arched high over his head in a commanding gesture telling us to go with the flow. Thus commencing the most challenging yoga class in history.

During the break, Tyler took James and me into the hot studio to show us the upgraded heating and humidity systems. The floor in there was made from a nontoxic, consciously sourced padding that had the spring of a high-end yoga mat; I'm talking 6mm or more. The ventilation system in the hot studio silently sucked all the sweaty stink out and replaced it with fresh air.

"Not just fresh air," Tyler told us, "but air that is infused with a proprietary blend of essential oils that have the same vibrational properties tuned to the crown chakra."

I was pretty sure that James couldn't tell if Tyler was being serious or not.

Most of the group had settled into an easy comfort with each other by the end of the day—a bunch of yogis at summer camp for rich kids. What was there not to be happy about?

My group classes were held in the non-heated room, which doubled as a professional dance studio. It was huge, but there were black velvet curtains on high rods making a smaller rectangle from the ceiling. The size of the room could be manipulated as the mirrors could be covered by one of the great fabric panels. The ceiling showcased a gorgeous mural depicting the Aurora Borealis. With the curtains drawn, the studio became a dark cozy cave perfect for candlelight yoga.

While Tyler and Thom devoted their energies to James that afternoon, I deciphered Thom's written flow sequences to break them down for the extras. The flows had to be taught more like choreography because their movements had to read as yoga on the screen, but still be visually enticing to the average moviegoer. The extras tried to intimidate me at first by showing off their skills, but once they realized I could move them around for the shots they calmed down and stuck to the choreography.

Most of them knew I was a has-been yogini, who used to teach in health clubs before selling out to a less bendy mainstream life. I even overheard one of them say, "Didn't you see her in the news? She was involved in that bombing on an army base last year."

The cupped hands capturing half-secrets and passing them from mouth to ear didn't even do it justice. No one there really knew anything about me.

Aria and Jennifer were both tall, lean yoginis who could easily be in magazines selling all types of yoga paraphernalia. There was a passive-aggressive bitterness between them. The mounting tension enveloped them like a sticky mist, trailing behind for all to notice.

After a particularly grueling session on the third day, Jennifer amped up her level of bitchiness. Aria had fallen out of crow during the last go-round, and another girl didn't even bother to lift her toes for it.

During a brief water break, Jennifer asked, "I know there are so many different ways of doing kakasana. When I teach my classes, I instruct them to start with their knees in their armpits and then lengthen their arms. Your pelvis is supposed to be over your shoulders so your head gently drops to the floor. Then you can glide up into shira-asana with grace."

No one, including me, responded.

"I'm sure balancing on your triceps is okay for some situations, but getting your knees nestled into your armpits in one movement is the advanced way to do the asana." Jennifer's eyes were closed the entire time she spoke. They popped open at the end of her speech.

"What exactly is your question?" I asked.

"I just want to make sure I'm doing it right." Eyes closed.

"If you aren't, I'll let you know. We're doing kakasana not bakasana for this particular sequence though, so keep your knees bent."

There was a snicker from some of the guys in the back.

"Start in tadasana," I instructed.

The whole room stood up a little straighter.

After we finished the same sequence, everyone looked beat. I had them sit on the floor with their legs crossed and initiated a twenty-minute meditation. Once the energy stabilized, I quietly left the room to hunt for Tyler.

Thom was working with James on floating through handstands to land in plank without making a sound when I appeared in the door of the hot room.

Tyler was filming James's attempts with his phone as James effortlessly went up into the handstand. He was still clunky on the landing though. Once James flowed completely through the vinyasa and lifted his legs into down dog, Tyler set the phone down. James's heels were on the ground in the pose. That was impressive.

Without turning around, Thom barked, "What?!"

"I need to get some information about Aria and Jennifer from one of you." The door closed behind me. The

energy in this hot studio was way calmer and more connected than my room. It was just these three men, all
focused on creating a whole new way of moving for
James.

"What's going on there, Thom?" I asked while clearing the length of the room. "They're causing the group
as a whole to look disjointed during the flows."

Thom turned to face me, but it was Tyler who spoke
first. "You tell her. They're your teachers."

"Jennifer has a dedicated following and doesn't like
it when other teachers come take her classes. Obviously
she can't prohibit them from attending." Thom paused
and shooed something away with his hand. "Anyway, Jen
had the sneaking suspicion that her boyfriend might be
cheating on her and that filtered into her savasana lead-
ins...."

Tyler chimed in with, "Remember that no matter
where you are in life and no matter who has let you
down, you can always come to your safe place—the
mat." He suppressed a laugh. "The mat will never disap-
point you and it's only there that you'll find the breath to
support you through trying times. Times when it might
feel like you're being betrayed by those who have sworn
to love you...." He finally cracked up.

Thom glared at his lover. "Yes, Aria told us this was
going on in Jen's classes, so we counseled her on what is

and what is not appropriate to share in front of our clients."

Tyler jumped back in. "Your mat won't find wanton solace between the legs of some born-again slut."

James broke into a laugh, while Thom fumed.

"So?" I asked.

"So, Jen sent Aria a long email banishing Aria from coming to any of her classes again," Tyler said to James more than me. "This could've been handled with just us, but little Jenny copied all the other teachers. Aria got pissed and forwarded it to all Jen's students. They were both reprimanded."

"When did this happen?" I asked.

"About a month ago," Tyler responded with a shrug.

"Why did you bring them both here then?"

"Because we staffed this and signed contracts with both of them before it even happened, Lauren!" Thom snapped. "Now, look, Jesus…I told them they needed to keep their personal shit out of the studio. If they're holding grievances, and it sounds like they are, it affects the continuity of the whole class."

I didn't mean for this to turn into a bitch session. "I'm sorry I had to interrupt you guys. I can figure something out." Thom seemed to be over me, James was every kind of interested, and Tyler was the court gesture. All I wanted to do was go. "Are they both contractually obligated to be in the film?"

"No one is. The contract is about having the *opportunity* to be cast. They're the only two from the La Jolla location. The rest are from the LA store and shouldn't know what went down between them."

"I'm sure they all know," I corrected. "I'll mix it up, and if there're any more problems, I'll let you know." On that note, I skedaddled.

I stopped outside the door to my yoga studio and looked in through the narrow window to see them all inside seated in silence. I closed my eyes and leaned my forehead against the wall. A headache from wearing my hair so tightly braided was on the horizon. The door from the hot studio opened and closed behind me, but I didn't turn around, assuming it would be Tyler.

"Hey," a male voice that was not Tyler's spoke lightly to the back of my head.

I turned around. "Hi. How's everything going in there?"

"Really well," James said.

I tried not to make direct eye contact with him. He was so yummy. My eyes would give my thoughts away.

"They want me in your class for the next segment. I was hoping it would all be worked out beforehand." James motioned toward the door to my class.

"Yes, of course," I assured him, feeling even more pressure. "Are Tyler or Thom coming to watch?"

"I don't think so. Thom said he wants fresh eyes on my flow for tomorrow."

"Okay, well my next segment starts at four. Are you finished with them for the day?"

"Yeah, I'm heading up to take care of a few things with Matt now, but like I said, I hope the issue between these two girls will be resolved before the session starts."

James wasn't exactly being bossy, just firm about the level of professionalism he expected.

"I understand," I conceded, not wanting to expand on the conversation any further.

James continued to stand there like he had something else to say.

I needed to get back to my class, but waited for him to leave so it wouldn't seem like I was dismissive of his request. It was a really long three seconds.

"I'm looking forward to your class," he finally offered and walked away.

I was both flattered and flustered. I knew Tyler and Thom would be exiting the hot studio any minute, so I gently opened the door to my studio and went in before they could catch me in the hall.

I didn't have a solution to deal with Aria and Jennifer. Time was not on my side to mediate a truce between them either. Excusing them from the class would create gossip, but trying to confront the situation would be, well, trying. Neither of them seemed the type to give up the last word.

I smoothly sank to the floor in front of the class and folded one leg over the other. My eyelids dropped down with a deep inhalation. After a few moments, I peeped my eyes open to a striking sight. Fifteen physically exquisite humans sitting like statues in lotus faced me in perfect uniformity. That's when an idea materialized.

I tapped the singing bowl and announced, "We'll break now and meet back here at 4:00 p.m. Get some rest and juice or light snack. Once we start back up, we'll continue through the whole block of time."

A collective groan looped around the room.

"It's really important for all of you to be on your game. Mr. Bayer will be joining us for the next session. We all need to be present."

There were piles of stuff scattered all over. "And no water bottles on the floor," I added.

No one stood up. They were all discreetly looking at each other.

Ah, yes….

"The light in me sees the light in you, namaste." I closed the class and briefly bowed my head.

The class returned the gesture with out-of-sync mumblings of "namaste" before they left.

"Aria and Jennifer, can you please stay back a moment."

Each of them rolled their mats at a calculated pace.

"Ladies," I began once they made their way up to me, "you're both exceptional with beautiful practices. I want to move you both up to the front row during the next session...on either side of Mr. Bayer. Why don't we see how that configuration would look?"

To be in the film? hung silently in the air between them. I could practically see the words.

Their eyes lit up.

"Set your mats in the corner and take a break. I'm going to reset the room anyway."

The line of competition drawn in the sand between them must have worked because, by the end of the day, they executed the vinyasas with the agility of seasoned Cirque de Soliel performers. Their body language read charismatic desire while cementing into the mat and drifting over it, especially when James stopped to watch the class at the end of the session. Perhaps massaging the resentment into competition may not have been the most yoga-esque way to resolve the problem, but it worked.

Tyler was proud.

As with the creation of physical expression, momentum gains speed when people are able to get out of their own egos. Getting over the roadblock allowed the entire group to move with fluidity while they exquisitely danced complicated and challenging repertoires side by side on yoga mats.

That afternoon, another female extra caught my attention. Scarlett was an anomaly in the group, having a soft body with dewy skin. She reminded me of a peach, ripe and succulent. Her face brightened the whole room and her naturally blonde hair hung long and straight. She didn't bind it all up and out of the way like the rest of us. There was a moment when I noticed James Bayer staring at her in lieu of Aria or Jennifer. Not that I could blame him. I made a mental note to put her next to him should Thom want options on our last day.

I was proud of this group, my group, at the end of the day while they did their final run through. The music instructed them what to do and which beat to follow. There was no longer a need for me to give the calls. The whole experience awakened a dormant part of me lost to the previous decade.

Once the session ended and everyone left, I went to turn off the lights and lock up. I had been up here three days since we arrived, and I'd barely thought about Collin. Guilt set in, overtaking the satisfaction. The familiar yearning to succeed that was fostered while on the ship began to wane.

I rolled the dimmer knob back and forth in my fingertips, making the lights go bright then dark over and over.

chapter four

MUSH

There were at least ten eateries with all levels of service and sophistication, but most were crowded with passengers during our lunch break. Even though there was never a wait at the buffet, it tempted overeating with all its lavish pastries. Yes…the buffet was frowned upon. The stairs outside the yoga studios led directly to the upper deck that housed two cafés. These lunch spots squarely divided the cast and crew every day around noon. Not much eating occurred in the cast café with limited menu choices such as vegan gluten-free wraps or kale salads. Every Friday was free-range chicken day, though.

On Thursday, I snuck over to the crew café because I was craving some real food. I was greeted with an appreciative nod by one of the camera guys—who were mainly there to do ad hoc screen tests—but there was no invitation to sit.

With my laptop open on a booth table and a burger in one hand, I spied James Bayer stroll in to get in line at the hostess stand. It surprised me because I overhead Matt saying that he usually ate in a private dining area with the best Wi-Fi connection.

Matt constantly reminded anyone who would listen to him that James had other obligations, promoting his recent Lifetime miniseries and signing headshots for his Japanese fans. He had some kind of teeth whitening strip campaign that was all over Japan. Matt pointed out how crucial it was for James to attend to these building blocks, no matter how insignificant they seemed at this point in James's career.

A moment later, James waved a quick *hello* to me as he sat down alone in a booth nearby. I was in his direct line of sight until a waitress in a Pura baby tee moved in, setting down his burger.

I pushed my plate aside and focused on my task. The second reason for coming to this café was so I could get an hour of uninterrupted time on my laptop. The decision about where I'd go after this week had arrived in the form of a yellow telegraph that was slid under my door late last night.

"I can give you a break on the deposit," Al told me on Tyler's satellite phone earlier this morning. "But I need the full payment for both spots in the next forty-eight hours, okay? I emailed you the link to pay and you can use PayPal since you asked. That's the best I can offer and I wouldn't do this for anyone else. We've already secured food, supplies, and lodging for the couple. I have to cover my losses."

"Can I confirm by way of payment?" I had asked Al since Tyler's satellite phone was so expensive. "Like in the next seventy-two hours? If I don't pay, that means I can't go."

He said I could.

After disconnecting the phone, it left my mind. The morning's schedule was full, and Scarlett needed assistance with getting into the perfect backbend. She and I spent a long three hours alone in painful, upside down positions that needed to look graceful and sexy for the camera. Thom, Tyler, and the other extras were nowhere to be found all morning, making it easy for me to slip away during lunch to get my entire life together.

The high-pitched giggle of the waitress brought my attention back to my laptop. As I scrutinized the photos on Al's website, this unique opportunity became both more and less appealing.

I thought of Pamela, my grandmother's half-sister, an Inuit elder in a remote village on the far eastern side of Baffin Island. Any time spent with her would be cathartic. She insisted that there was some kind of ritual to release my heartache. She was the biggest influence on me as a child, and if anyone could help me really start living my life again, it would be her. Given the circumstance, it seemed to be the next reasonable step in my journey to healing.

Absently, I drummed my fingers on the table, as if the sensation from the varnished wood might inspire an answer.

"Your food is getting cold," the waitress commented as she passed my table.

At the exact moment, as I scooped up my burger and opened my mouth wide enough for someone to see my fillings, James made direct eye contact. His eyes danced with amusement, probably from my caveman-like manners. Then to my horror and delight, he stood up with his plate.

"Want some company?" he asked.

I pulled my napkin up to my cover my mouth and chewed while nodding. Then I said a quick prayer that nothing was smeared on my face. "Sure, um, sit down."

"I hope I'm not taking you away from some important work." He glanced at my open laptop.

"Oh, no." I closed it up. "I was just trying to decide where to go after this week. Anyway, how are you finding the training? You're doing really well."

"It's been much more difficult than I thought it would be. My 'yoga' experience consisted of being stretched out by a trainer after heavy, weight lifting intervals. CrossFit type stuff. Some of Thom's classes…especially the hot ones…Jesus." He took a bite and shook his head in disbelief.

"Eventually you build up a tolerance for the heat. When I started doing hot yoga, I thought I was going to die." I smiled. "I was wondering, why did you take this role?"

He arranged his face in an expression that he might have practiced for reciting a prepared answer during a Q and A as he leaned toward me. "My manager has been trying to get me as a lead in a serious film for two years now. Matt wants to diversify my resume so I'll be considered for more roles, better ones. The kind that really bring in the money."

"And Arturo dropped out of this?"

"Yes, rather unexpectedly." He paused and swept a look around to the surrounding booths before continuing. "Okay, honestly, Lauren, this was the only thing he could get me in."

I heard what he said. But when he called me by my name, the other words fizzled into gibberish. "At what point did you read the script?" I had to keep this professional.

"Less than a month ago. It's a moving story, very motivational, and it plays into my brand as an actor."

"Your brand?"

"Yeah, Matt masterminded this plan to reinvent me as the physical transformation actor…taking roles that require things like extreme strength, weight loss, gain…." He smiled. "Flexibility, as it turns out, for this." His eyes shifted away from me when miss baby tee, I mean the waitress, walked by to check on his meal.

When his gaze turned my way again, he looked so defeated it was heartbreaking.

"It would seem that's my strongest suit as an actor," he mumbled and took a bite of his burger.

This information opened up a new perspective of James Bayer, the movie star. I had never considered what it might be like for him, not wanted for the craft that he had obvious passion for, but to stay in the business solely as an offshoot of that artistry. The conversation sunk in while I tried to think of something enlightened to say. I was at a loss. Tyler would have had the perfect response.

James had a desirous body, making him an obvious choice when casting calls went out for the "sex sells" movies. The skilled actor designation lay by the wayside for those kinds of roles, and even though he was very matter-of-fact about this path being created for him, I sensed his self-confidence had taken a hit.

I resisted the urge to stroke his ego and ignorantly reassured him that everything would be okay, that he's a gifted actor. How would I know that, anyway? As with most celebrities, the chance of a whole entourage already doing that were pretty high. I wondered how disappointed he really felt with the blunt realization that Matt's plan banked on something other than acting as a way to succeed in his career.

"Embodying Bronne de Luca is more than just a physical transformation," I tried. "The physical aspect of yoga, the asanas, are the end result of an understanding you need to have with yourself. In order to get there, the mind, spirit, and prana all need to mesh together and open up space for the body to create the poses. If their plan was to have you play this part for the physical aspect only, then they misjudged the depth of his character— Bronne, I mean. He touched so many people who had nothing. Making the poses look visually stunning for the film has nothing to do with that aspect of his life. It's just a…a…." I was at a loss for the right word.

"A marketing strategy," James finished my sentence cleverly.

I twirled my low-hanging ponytail and nodded in agreement. My fingertips gently rubbed the end of my long dark hair, and, at that point, we held eye contact for longer than a breath. The contact filled up my emptiness despite the brief connection. Some sort of unknown memory existed between us.

"You know," I broke the trance, "I looked you up on IMDb and saw you were in a period drama on BBC at the beginning of your career. Have you thought about doing another one?"

"At the time, it seemed like it would open all sorts of doors for me. As you also probably saw, it didn't do well, and I couldn't get any kind of momentum from it. It's a tricky thing after you play a period character, too; studios don't want you because they think the audience can't see you as anyone else. And directors, God, the directors get it in their heads that you're flat...one-dimensional."

It was mesmerizing how his accent smoothed over the internal despair he was communicating.

Since I didn't respond, James switched topics. "So where were you thinking of going after this, before I so rudely interrupted you? Not home?"

I gave him a brief rundown of the trip, glossing over the whole shamanistic ritual bit. No need to open Pandora's box in this casual conversation.

"That's fascinating, really?" His voice became stronger and rang with confidence again. "What an unbelievable opportunity! That's *really* what you were mulling through when I came over?" Without giving me time to respond, he continued, "You know, I've secretly fancied the idea of training for a dogsled race. There's just no real convenient way to do so unless you make the trek up here and immerse yourself in it."

A younger version of James Bayer popped into my mind. I imagined a boyhood fantasy about mushing may be in there somewhere. "Yes," I stammered, "um, well, there was a Danish couple who backed out."

"May I?" He reached for my computer.

"Go ahead, there's a live feed of the weather up on the desktop. It's been kind of hairy this week, but it's supposed to clear up by the weekend."

As he opened up the laptop and peered to the screen, I glanced down at my burger with one giant bite ruining the perfect circle of the bun. Something about that barely touched burger reminded me of the first time I dumped a full salt shaker over a meal from which I had taken only two bites. I'm not into wasting food...but sometimes self-control takes precedence over practicality. It had been a long time since that dinner with Tyler in Las Vegas when he'd praised my efforts.

I placed my napkin over the plate between James and me while he was clicking away on the touchpad. There was no doubt that he was looking through the website and not paying attention to whether my plate was empty.

Namasea's final dock was the artist community in Cape Dorset, which was located at the edge of a peninsula jutting out from Baffin Island's southwest corner. PuraLife Cruise passengers disembark to this charming town for a day or two before flying down to Quebec to make transfers back home. My plan would be to take a small island hopper to Iqaluit and then go on a run with Al's tribal dogsledding outfit to the remote side of the island to visit Pamela. On actual dogsleds. For three days.

James continued to tap away on my laptop as he made comments about the different sleds and types of dogs from Al's website. "This is really out there, Baffin Island, that sounds very rugged. Sleeping in an igloo? You didn't strike me as that type of girl."

I was surprised at how much he knew on the subject of dogsledding. The exact opposite of how much he knew about me.

As he turned the laptop back, he half-joked, "I'm a little jealous of whoever you're going with, it sounds like an amazing opportunity. You must be very excited, Lauren."

He said my name again.

Since the number of people traveling with me was complicated, I circumvented the topic. "My grandmother's half-sister lives there, she practically raised me. Originally I planned to charter a prop plane from Iqaluit, but she insisted that I travel by dog to come to her. 'The most sacred path,' her words."

"So what were you trying to decide on then?"

I began to tick off the reasons why I shouldn't go: financial hardship, freezing temperatures, the complicated travel plans to get home afterward, all perfectly good reasons, but not the truth. I knew Pamela well enough to realize that this was an introspective voyage set up to strip away the layers of distraction I had built into my daily routine. To truly unearth my reservations about going would be to tell James why I was so fearful to be alone with my thoughts.

When Pamela called a few weeks back, she implored that nature is the end-all be-all healer for all who inhabit the earth. She said I had to let it encompass me so she could clear away the pain and hurt to which I clung. Letting go of control and submitting to the whims of the former Northwest territories and the mysterious mythology surrounding the Inuit culture excited me. But, the reality of spending three days surrounded by icy landscapes would push my sanity past its breaking point. I wasn't ready to exorcise any emotional demons just yet.

Plus, I was craving comfort, not ice beds.

I resisted the temptation to go into all those heavy details with James. He was obviously captured by the adventure of mushing with his go-getter attitude. He might not understand why I was so leery to attempt the trip.

"The thing is," I wrapped up, "I have some obligations back home that would make it difficult for me to pull off another week up here. Honestly, James…" I had been waiting for the right moment to address him by his first name, "I was just entertaining the idea because it seemed interesting. I really didn't give it much thought." With that, I flipped the laptop lid down and turned the light off on our exchange.

"What are the chances you'll ever get up here again and go on a run?" he demanded.

My head snapped up at his sharp tone.

"So many people out there paint themselves up into their own little safe havens and have no chance of growing. It's like they're too afraid to get out of their comfort zone and really live. Really live," he punctuated. He took a deep breath, perhaps realizing he was getting preachy. In a calmer tone, he went on, "It's hard to get out of your comfort zone, I get it, but how else will you grow? Do you want to be on your deathbed knowing you missed this once-in-a-lifetime opportunity?"

"Well," I drew out slowly as I tried to figure out which direction to go with him on this. "Pamela and I discussed that I might come up next year instead, when I have more time." Total lie.

Satisfied with my answer, he sat back and an unfiltered wishful look of yearning splashed across his face.

I picked a direction to steer the conversation. "Listen, why don't you go and take my place? I can give you all the information about the dogsledding part of the trip. Pamela would be happy to host you on her end, I'm sure. Then you could just charter a prop plane back to the Iqaluit airport and transfer down to civilization from there. The deposit's been paid, but it's for a double occupancy since there was a couple who backed out last minute. You would have to pay the rate for two. Perhaps

42

Matt could go with you." As I detailed the offer, my heart lifted. "It would be a shame if no one went and right now, I...we...well, it's just not a good time."

"I'm not due to fly out of the States for Mumbai for a few days."

I saw the wheels turning....

"You never know," I said lightly, "leading a pack in such brutal conditions might come in handy. There could be a movie about mushing right around the corner." *Film! Fuck, Lauren.*

He didn't say anything, so I put away my laptop and stood.

"That's really generous of you," he finally said. "But are you sure you don't want to go?"

"It would make me happy knowing you would get to experience it." I didn't know if I really wanted to go or not. I set Al's card on the table. "If you decide that you and Matt want the spots, you need to call this guy, probably tomorrow. The amount of the supplies they bring on the run depends on the exact weight of the people going."

His words spilled out in a rush. "I've gotta get all this to Matt so he can wrap his head around it. I've been known to jump into things without thinking 'em all the way through." He laughed at his own observation and winked at me a second time. "Can you email the link to

Matt so he can work on this? Oh wait...." His brain finally caught up to his mouth. "It's all on the card, that's right, and you're sure I can go?"

"Yes." It came out bluntly, so I cleared my throat and nodded. "Please, go and enjoy. In all honesty, it's really so much money and I'm trying to eliminate unnecessary expenses right now. Really, go if you can, that would be great." Emboldened by the personal discussion we had earlier, I added, "Perhaps it would be a good time for you to do some soul searching. It could be your chance to get away from the Hollywood bullshit and get out in nature, on nature's terms."

I dropped a couple bucks on the table. "It would be a shame if no one took my spot. Let me know if you have any problems with Al."

The waitress brushed past me while I feebly wished James might watch me go. The waistband of her top was tied up showcasing some very toned abs.

Jesus, Lauren, who cares?

c h a p t e r f i v e

PRE-HEAT

It was the last day of training and everyone was beyond ready to be free for the weekend, just in time for our arrival at Cape Dorset. The last morning's test shots rolled on longer than anticipated and bled over into the afternoon.

There was a lot of waiting around, but no downtime as Thom continually reworked the flow and ran test runs with James in numerous configurations. It was an unspoken game of *Survivor* with Thom playing the part of Jeff Probst. His highness has spoken....

I popped in and out of the studio, taking on menial tasks like getting bottled waters over the more important task of whispering in Tyler's ear. I was leaning toward Scarlett for the coveted spot in the front row for the big studio scene. On my recommendation, Thom moved

Scarlett up into Aria's spot next to James. When he saw her next to James, he confessed that she was growing on him. Scarlett and James made a beautiful pair.

Aria shot me a scathing look to which I remained blank. She had no idea about the looks I'd received from thousands of people last year when I walked down the steps of the courthouse in DC. She couldn't even crack the surface.

When not occupied with Thom, James would meander my way to strike up a conversation. He was able to get in touch with Al, but hadn't made a decision. "Matt's not a real fan of the idea," he confided in me with a chuckle.

Tyler noticed us talking from the other side of the studio just as Thom began to bustle toward James. Tyler caught Thom's arm and leaned in to whisper something while pointing at Scarlett. Thom nodded and beckoned her over to their huddle.

This went on until almost 6:00 p.m. Everyone was trying their best to keep irritation at bay, but the rolling eyes and exaggerated huffs were growing in frequency. Finally, Thom announced we were done and it was time to head to the non-heated studio for the final class.

The non-heated studio had been transformed into a candlelit cave with all the velvet curtains drawn together. The coziness of the room was enhanced by the faint vanilla scent drifting off the ivory candles. LizBeth Starr, a master yin instructor and gong player, sat cross-legged on the floor at the head of the studio with eyes closed. The schedule had her on for leading a two-hour yin class with a gong meditation. It was our finishing ritual and was considered to be the icing on the cake—even by the most advanced vinyasa practitioners.

The purpose of the gong playing is to generate a soothing sound lacking pattern and rhythm, thus prohibiting the listener from anticipating any rhythmic patterns within the resonance. This suspended state of being enveloped by the unknown is the device that tunes our chakras.

Also, one can get away with napping in a yin class, so I set up in a spot near the back.

James made a beeline to the space next to me, which had a curtain brushing the floor on the other side of him that served as a wall. There wasn't any space left for mats to be put down behind us. My hopes were that no one noticed his play. I carefully extended my extremities no further than the boundaries of my own mat for fear of accidental touching.

I rolled my head from side to side, giving the impression that I was releasing tension in my neck. If someone were to study me closely, they would see I had one eye cracked open with the intention of catching a glimpse of James fully reclined.

The thump of Scarlett's mat dropping and unrolling on my other side caused me to rotate my skull in her direction. She plopped down and instantly looked over.

I smiled and winked at her.

She did this cute, little up-and-down movement with her eyebrows as if to say, "Hey, hey."

I momentarily set aside my keen appraisal of James's body so close to mine. Earlier today, the conversation between us replayed in my head about a million times. As much as I tried to analyze it, no hidden meaning could be deciphered. It was time for a blank slate to enter my head.

After a sumptuous ninety minutes of yin, we transitioned into savasana. My being began to absorb the gong's erratic, but pacifying, vibrational chords. This type of mediation brought with it such detachment that my body began to melt away from any and all conversations.

As LizBeth went deeper into her playing, the images in my head transformed into pages being torn from a book and set afloat on the wind. Those pages filled with rhetoric from my bashed-in heart flew away, and the ability to understand what really mattered revealed itself.

I distinctly heard my guru's voice speak. "And it is slightly left to the center of the rib cage under your heart. That is the location in your physical body where you can communicate with God. Go there. Now."

The rabbit hole of shifting dimensions came to take me, the real me, far from that sultry harem den.

Suspended miles above in airy communion with the clouds, my width expanded all the way to the sacred Nunavut shoreline, where jagged, ancient rocks impregnated my lower self's cellular level. The understanding that everything is connected occurred, bringing with it the fleeting bliss of savasana.

Something at my right hand twitched.

I don't want to come back down.

Unwilling to let me remain in my altered state, the pressure on my hand mounted and I was sucked back down into the tight confines of my body. A flood of thoughts dumped into my head while my eyes remained shut. James had moved his entire left hand and forearm close enough to drape over mine. The outer ridges of our forearms pressed together...*and the pressure wasn't coming from me.*

Without moving, I directed my thoughts to him and the sanguine red swirls of living energy penetrated the very point at which our hands connected. First circular maroon, then deep violet tidal waves of vitality initiated from this seemingly simple handhold. Whatever this bond between us was, or would become, it saturated the protoplasm pulsating through my veins.

The gong playing calmed to a still. Silence was the enemy, allowing the thump of my heartbeat to blast on full volume through the microphone of my head. Liz-Beth's distant voice told us to roll over into the fetal position on whichever side felt most comfortable.

Not wanting to embarrass James, I rolled to my left. Not the case, though, because he let his hand slide onto my exposed lower back. The bottom of my shirt had risen up, allowing this intimate contact to continue.

"Push yourself up into a comfortable seated position and stack your palms in dhyana," LizBeth's voice echoed from a faraway place. With this instruction, all physical contact between us ceased.

"Namaste."

I started to stand up and in the most nonchalant way I could muster, I glanced over my right shoulder. "Did you enjoy that?" I asked him, unsure of how to calm the sexual tension between us.

"Very much." Total confidence.

Everyone was rolling up their mat and discussing party plans for the evening while we were caught in this moment.

With reluctance, I stated the obvious. "It sounds like there will be a wrap party tonight." It came out so chunky. I rolled my mat.

"Yeah, there always is." Still total confidence.

Before I could respond, Thom shot down on James's mat and almost snuggled up to him for a one-on-one talk.

I escaped to the bathroom where the blackest feelings of guilt surfaced behind the locked stall. As I sat on the toilet, I placed my palm against the small of my back where his touch exhilarated me. But…a free woman, I was not.

There was no slipping away from the group. Everyone congregated on the landing at the base of the stairs. The mix of voices became rowdy and Matt came down to join the pre-party. There was so much steam to blow off, but a drunken gathering would not reset me from this intense week. LizBeth caught me outside the bathroom and chatted me up on the sidelines until the crowd dispersed.

James crossed and uncrossed his arms while conferring with Matt. LizBeth reigned in the last of the group and herded them up, Scarlett and Jennifer lagging behind. When I reached the step behind James, Matt shot up the stairs and caught up to the girls. James and I were alone and several yards back from them as we ascended to the upper deck.

I kept his slow pace so we wouldn't become engulfed in the thick of the chaos. "I was hoping to soak in one of those outdoor Jacuzzi things over there," I stated with some formality. "The Northern Lights are supposed to be in full swing tonight."

His silence was nerve wracking.

"Thom's obsession with one-legged chakrasanas took a toll on my back." The chatter kept coming. *Stop, Lauren, be cool.* I reached around to give my lumbar a little massage before feeling self-conscious from touching the spot where he had touched me with such intention.

We stepped on the bridge overlooking the public Jacuzzis. There were twenty or so people spread out all over them with red plastic cups littering the cement.

Shit. This was the plan to avoid a loud party because they were talking about going to the nightclub downstairs. Must have been a change in plans though, through the blur of faces, Thom's voice rose above the rest, directing our group to get someone over there "and call a fucking Jacuzzi already!"

I was conflicted. I had always been faithful to Collin, but now I yearned for James to pay attention to me. Alone.

Everyone was jockeying to get a piece of him, especially on our last night of training. The buzz of anticipation rose in an adult game of "telephone," since he and Matt were expected to drink with everyone tonight. Several heads turned to see him and then whipped back around in excited discussion.

"It looks like you aren't the only one with that plan tonight," he observed.

"Apparently." I started to pick back up to a normal pace with the intention of locking myself up in my cabin.

Earlier today, I threw in the towel on the whole dogsledding trip and now wanted to create some distance between me and this entire hemisphere.

Without warning, James stepped so he was out of sight from the throngs of partiers. "You know," he began slowly, "there's one of those Jacuzzis off my cabin upstairs. It's outside."

Curiosity set in, it seemed more likely that he should be heading toward the bubbling yogini soup rather than shuffling his feet around me.

"It's jetted and uses a magnesium salt water solution instead of chlorine. Umm, you could come up and take a soak? I would be there. I mean we could...." He inwardly laughed at his tameness. "I'm sure you'd have a good view of the lights from there, too."

I unnaturally blinked several times, waiting to see if he was finished. "Sure," I replied. Knowing I sounded caught off-guard, I tried to play it off. "Is this some kind of ploy to see me naked?" My left eyebrow arched. His attempt to get me to flirt with him worked.

"Obviously."

The image of him au natural insatiably crept into my head, making it difficult to judge where the conversation was going. Any further efforts to engage in flirtatious banter came to a screeching halt, for I was rusty in my ability to relate to any other man besides.... *Deep breath.* It was time to focus on the man in front of me.

"I'm on the lower level." I motioned to the stairs past all the brouhaha.

He pressed a card key into my hand. "If you show this to the guard at the A elevators, he should let you go past for the lift. I'm in state room 4A." He rattled off the directions so smoothly that, against my better judgment, I fell right into the "hot tub with a movie star" scenario. A betting man would take the odds that this had happened a thousand times before on set and it's sure to happen a thousand times more. The risk of anything further than a secret, one-night stand was impossible.

I slid the card key into my pocket without looking at it. The ease of being so far away from reality enticed my physical desire to jump over the cliff...directly into hot water. I gave him a smile. "I'll be up shortly."

I meandered off, certain that this time he watched me go. The view over the edge of the boat allowed for zero visibility, but I kept looking over the railing as my stomach knotted up. With one hand clasped over my forearm so tightly it was sure to leave red marks, the lack of vision overtook me. I was blindsided by this James Bayer and fumbling into sexual territories with a man other than my husband. Freezing water with little shards of ice flew into my face. I tucked my chin down.

After everything I've been through over the past year, I should have known better.

But if no one ever found out, then no one would get hurt…right?

c h a p t e r   s i x

COMPLETELY CLICHÉ

Thank God my bikini wax from last week has left my skin soft and fresh. All the hair down there was still gone, save for the landing strip. I threw one foot on top of the bathroom counter and examined my shin under the unforgiving fluorescent light. No stubble in sight, but I ran my hand slowly up my leg anyway. I judged myself naked in the mirror. The past year had reshaped me back into my college figure—an enviable silhouette that combined the long svelte muscles of a dancer with full breasts. When I weighed myself at the beginning of the week, I was exactly the same weight that I was when I met Collin. Now I appeared to have lost several more pounds since arriving on the ship.

During my years working as a federal investigator, I constantly beseeched myself to stop overeating and get the body back that I once had. After each cheesy, tortilla-filled lunch, I swore that I'd start the next day off with coffee and fruit only. By 11:00 a.m. though, I was ravenous and stressed, searching for anything to eat on post. The results of which transferred me into the "women's" section of Dillard's. Begrudgingly, I opened a Lane Bryant credit card back then.

But now, my eyes fell to one area of my reflection: the scarring that wrapped around the left side of my torso. It couldn't be overlooked, even from a few feet away. Cauterization, multiple skin grafts, and time finally downgraded the bright, puffy tentacles into a pinkish topographical map. I shifted and twisted in the mirror, trying to get into a position where I could face James head on and not display the trauma branded into my skin.

I forced my gaze upward and abruptly pivoted to the left for a quick boost of confidence. My breasts were even and fell in the C cup range, unlike the flat-chested yoginis who never had to wear bras in class. Since I never had babies, they still sloped up. A flat belly and rounded hips contrasted my long, narrow waist. All of that expertly sculpted area contained doodles of faint stretch marks from before the blast.

The tags were still on the black string bikini shoved into the outside pocket of my suitcase. Once all strapped up, I bent over and pulled each breast up in hopes of containing them. I should have tried it on before I bought it; those triangles were so small. The bottoms hung slightly off my hips from the "post-divorce diet," as my mom called it before realizing how horribly inappropriate that was to say.

I twisted my hair up into a high, loose bun and grabbed the white robe off the back of the door. I pulled on my UGGs, thinking of the stereotype of desert girls wearing UGGs with bikinis. *California girl now, not a desert girl anymore.*

The far side of the bridge allowed me to pass over the public Jacuzzi area without being spotted. The multitude of loud voices came to a hush as Thom's voice rose to a peak that was followed by a roar of laughter. The group was nothing compared to the quiet hall leading to James's room; that trek was far more intimidating.

A line of light outlined his door, which was propped open with the interior lock flipped out.

"Knock, knock," I called lightly, peeping my head in first. "Should I leave this open?" A question with multiple meanings.

James was standing at a drink cart, wearing a pair of board shorts with his back facing the door. He wasn't startled by my voice and looked over his shoulder with an easy smile. "No, I left it open for you in case you got here while I was on the deck adjusting the temperature of the tub. Come in."

The state room door closed, punctuated by a whirr and clank from the automatic locking mechanism. As I walked toward him, I set the card key on the table that ran along the wall. Scattered on it were tiny clusters; things he must have taken out of his pockets each time he returned to his cabin. Curious about him as a private person, my eyes lingered on his trinkets—crumpled receipts, his cell phone, wallet, and Al's business card turned over with my handwriting on it. I had almost cleared the room when I noticed a small mound of rocks piled up in a mini altar. It warmed my heart to think of him bending down to examine a rock that caught his eye. I could imagine him putting a few in his pocket and then forgetting about them until he took off his pants at the end of the day.

My mind dropped the rocks when *that* image crept into my mind.

The closer I came to him, the heavier my legs became, like they were pushing through a strong current. I really needed to get a grip. After all, we had been working in close proximity all week.

"I set the temperature to 38.8 degrees Celsius. It's the recommended temp for magnesium absorption into the muscles. That is, as long as you soak at least thirty minutes."

His accent made my knees buckle. He was speaking straight to me with no distractions. "Did you request this to be put in or was it already on the ship?" I asked.

"They said all the state rooms have them. Isn't it a PuraLife or PuraYoga thing?"

The question stumped me. Since I was there as a PuraYoga person, I should know this. But I didn't, so I just agreed with a nod.

There was no condescending tone in his voice and it dawned on me just how *normal*, how comfortable, it was to engage him in conversation. His ease was the stepping-stone I needed to regain my composure as I approached him to see what he was doing.

He was fumbling with a wine bottle and corkscrew.

"I can open that."

He handed over the bottle with a teasing smirk.

I smoothed down the foil shredded off on one side and rotated the bottle to show him the label in demonstration. "There's a trick to using these. When you peel the top foil off, you scrape in and up with the blade like this." I discarded the remaining, now neatly peeled, foil top on the cart. "You line up the sharp tip of the corkscrew with the center of the cork and keep this top T part fully in your palm." I set the bottle on the cart between us and used my free hand to stabilize it. "Waiters use the table to steady the bottle so they can get the screw down the cork straight."

I motioned to the bottle and he bent over slightly to take a closer look in mock reverence.

"Then," I continued, "you pull the corkscrew straight up, using your thumb on top for leverage." The cork popped out effortlessly and I handed him the bottle to pour.

"You're quite accomplished at that," he noted, pouring two glasses for us.

"Most people use cumbersome wine openers when all you need is a simple tool." I fixated on this wine-opening conversation, worried once it ended I would be tongue-tied. "But screw caps are no longer gauche, so I guess my knowledge is a lost art." *Okay, that was a little overkill.*

He handed me a glass, allowing me to take a sip of wine as an excuse to stop talking.

"Thank you," I said graciously and tilted it toward him.

"Cheers."

"This is really stylish," I commented while looking over the décor in his state room. "I imagine you have a beautiful view of the coast during the day."

"Yes," he responded. Having no interest in continuing with pleasantries, he opened the door to the deck. "Be careful, it might be slippery."

James gingerly lowered himself into the water causing a roll of visible steam to circle his chest as he sat down, making a living frame around his shoulders and face. Like me, James was leaner than he was on that first day. His drop in weight allowed each one of his abdominal muscles to be more accentuated in this three-dimensional image of male perfection.

When my robe slid off, he gave me the once-over. Those forest green and brown eyes briefly indulged in staring at the fan-like design tattooed over my exposed midriff before his gaze shifted up to my breasts. Upward still, his eyes finally reached mine, which was just in time for me to glance away and sit down in the seat farthest from him.

The heat calmed my shivering enough for me to twist back and grab my wine glass. I purposely jutted my chest toward him before I repositioned myself and took a sip. Regaining my confidence, I scanned the deck and said, "This is heaven."

"Which one?" He insinuated toward the wine or the Jacuzzi, but I knew what he really meant.

"All of it." I motioned around the hot tub, including him, and ended by letting my fingertips caress the rim of the wine glass. He was transfixed momentarily by my graceful sweep. With this, we relaxed and the conversation began to flow with ease.

My inquisitiveness took over the sexual tension. First came the pointed questions about the process of making

films. Then an inquiry about the specific physical training he'd done to prepare for past roles. A seamless
switch into more philosophical questions about superheroes as archetypes kept him talking. As I briefly thought
I might be playing twenty questions in order to sabotage
a sexual encounter, the jet pump kicked on, which
caused me to shuffle over to the seat next to him.

With one bottle of wine down, he took the empty
glass from my hand and set it on the deck behind us,
closing the space between us. "I just realized you now
have the unfair advantage of knowing all about what I
do, but your life is still a bit of a mystery to me."

He didn't back off. I was slipping into him; he was
so easy to talk to and so inviting.

"You live in southern California...?" He gave me a
lead-in.

"Yes, right on the southern tip of Malibu. I have an
almost beachfront property, but it's quite small."

"And how did you get into this line of business?"

"I'm kind of a subcontractor for Tyler and Thom,
this isn't my full-time thing. Right now, anyway. I'm in a
bit of a transition period, really, and Tyler, well we've
been friends for years, and I think he wanted to give me
an opportunity to...." I was rambling. I didn't want to
say *"clear my head,"* or *"see if I could work without the crazy
meds."* "...to see if this is a profession I want to become
more invested in," I recovered.

"Are you on your own?"

I looked at him quizzically.

"Are you in a serious relationship?"

I took the plunge and shook my head, holding my breath for that instant.

My head tilted down ever so slightly to place my forehead a slice of air away from his lips. This seemingly off-handed motion was the invitation he needed to fully understand that I wanted to feel his hands on me and get lost in the comfort he exuded.

James shifted his head to bypass my forehead as he grasped each of my shoulders and, with deliberate strength, pulled me all the way into him. One hand stroked up my neck to catch my chin and he tilted my face up to his. As he began to tenderly kiss me, his fingers stroked my jawline, then trailed down and around to firmly cup the back of my neck.

My mouth opened to let his warm tongue press in deeper. The long finish of the wine's passion fruit bouquet remained on his breath.

After a few moments of necking in this half-turned position, I slithered into his lap and straddled him. I rested down onto my knees, open on either side of his thighs, so the base of my bikini could land directly on top of his hardness. His pelvis tilted up and began to steadily rock, creating the pressure that can only be followed by insertion. A mere two slices of incredibly thin, quick-drying microfibers were the only things keeping him from entering me right then and there.

"Look up, Lauren," he whispered in my ear.

It was as if he somehow knew the sound of his voice speaking my name melted all the twisted up feelings inside me.

Seeing the sky was like looking into the opening of a portal. My vision field was encompassed by an onyx sky unable to contain its swooshing coils of colored light. This living maze of saturated jade, lapis, and turquoise danced in full effect across the starry stage above. These precious stones intertwined, as if to ring out permission granting me this *one night*.

And besides, the possibility of an orgasm not created by a battery-operated "boyfriend" would do my soul a world of good.

His long fingers slipped into the top of my bikini bottom and tugged the back of it up so that my ass swelled out the bottom. From there, his hands glided up my sides to the front of my upper abs. His thumbs simultaneously landed at the creases under my breasts. He used his palms to pull apart my upper ribs so I would arch back and present them in the forefront of his view. He scooted the two triangles covering my nipples away from each other over the string like he was guiding two sliding glass doors open. His open mouth found my right nipple, where he immediately applied enough suction to bring both nipples to full attention.

My hips picked up the pace.

He reached up behind my neck and untied the bow. My bikini top unceremoniously fell open.

Instead of letting it fall away into the swirling water, I picked it up and rose to a kneeling position over him. The front of my vagina slid up his navel, over his belly button, and right onto the center of his chest as I bowed over his shoulder and chucked the balled-up top toward the chairs.

It landed, but there was no hurry to sit back down. The top of my ass had peeked up out of the water, which allowed him to get an up-close and personal view of my pussy outlined under my suit.

His palm crept up the back of my left leg while his fingers curved around my inner thigh. He hesitated at the bottom crease of my ass, so I finished the journey for him by sliding down his chest. When the inside blade of his hand pressed the bottom of my pussy, he kept it there.

"Jesus," he whispered with his eyes closed.

There wasn't a chance in hell any woman (or extra-terrestrial) would get out of this scenario without a sore pussy and, perhaps, an even more strained lower back.

"Let's go inside, shall we?"

There was no need to answer. I stepped onto the deck and I wrapped myself in the luxurious warmth of his bathrobe.

James picked up my bikini top in one hand while placing the other one around my waist to lead me inside.

c h a p t e r   s e v e n

A SUREFIRE FANTASY

A few candles had been lit while we were on the deck. The maid? Matt?

"Sit," James said.

My hand trembled fiercely as I leaned on the edge of the dresser facing the bed. I wasn't really sure where to sit.

Then he smiled. "Relax, Lauren. Are you cold?"

I was a lot of things, and yes, cold was one of them. "I'm nervous," I answered before I could think of a better response.

"It's just you and me here, right now," he reassured me and pulled the duvet back. "No wetsuits in the bed." He motioned for me to get under the covers.

I shimmied out of my bottoms while keeping the robe wrapped on. Once safely blanketed, I pulled the robe off and let it drop to the floor.

James did not turn away. He was tall with broad shoulders framing a chiseled chest. The hair on his chest was moderate and a distinct patch of it began at his navel, which drew a dark feathery line down to the top of his board shorts. I imagined that trail turned into a well-groomed patch of pubic hair nestling his fully erect cock, which was clearly outlined thanks to clingy wet shorts.

The board shorts dropped to the floor like a towel.

I gave him an appreciative look as he simmered in self-confidence before climbing into the bed.

"So, I only get to see you *almost* naked…that's okay. The night's not over yet," he joked and gathered me in his arms so we could ease onto our sides toward each other. He stroked my back and I warmed to his chest, which felt like a breathing rock that had soft bristles of hair grazing against my breasts. The sensation was a tactile reminder of how his whole essence was unfamiliar to me. At the same time, his embrace was so caring that I was overwhelmed for a moment at the recognizable emotional surge I was experiencing.

His tongue slipped perfectly into my mouth and made slow circles inside, exploring all the soft pink sections inside my cheeks. Without breaking contact, he guided me to my back and pushed up onto his left elbow.

His right hand skimmed down my ribcage and followed the inward curve of my waistline before taking my hip. First he clenched and then massaged the swell of my hip with such intention that I got the feeling he was determined to pull me apart.

I don't care.

It's okay not to care right now.

Turn off your conscience.

I was virgin territory lying there, completely exposed, allowing this to go beyond some second-base necking.

My hip was released from his possessive kneading, and my clit was captured under his thumb; no hesitation from his end on location or perfect pressure. Then he inserted two fingers deep inside me and curled them back to catch the upper front part of my insides: the g-spot.

Oh. My. God.

His thumb rhythmically throbbed against my clit and I instinctively pushed my pelvis down to his touch. His hand orchestrated the whole area between my legs, gyrating slowly with his deliberate movements that brought me to a quick and easy orgasm. His fingers slowed, pulling the last bit of orgasmic twitch from the depth of my honeypot.

A low moan escaped my throat before I caught my breath.

His face pulled up and his eyes caught mine, while his fingers slowed to a comfortable rhythm.

Maybe he wanted to say something, maybe he didn't, but it was no matter. A lifetime of profound understanding had already happened between us.

His mouth traveled down into the hollow base of my throat. He paused to take in my scent with a deep inhalation that he held in his lungs for a beat. James leisurely exhaled through his mouth, causing his warm, winey breath to roll over my sternum. His tongue lapped a trail to land under my left breast, and while using his right hand, slightly damp from my own fluid, he stroked the outer curve of the other breast. His tongue led him to the pink point of my nipple and he made a little "O" with his mouth to capture it. His teeth scraped the nipple just enough to send an electrifying jolt straight to my pussy, but it also had the tease of a careless chomp that frightened me just a tad. These sensations were almost too much to bear.

Without warning, he repositioned himself so I had no choice but to spread my legs. My eyes closed in anticipation just as he entered me. The slow and sticky molasses sensation transitioned into pounding penetration of mutual pleasure. Each thrust came a little harder, perhaps with a little more meaning. His hands encased my shoulders to steady me and our connection morphed from sex into lovemaking.

"Move back."

Pushing up my elbows, I scooted back and broke contact with his body, but not his eyes.

He navigated to reenter me and yanked my leg up in his palm so he had the foundation to then evenly fuck me.

It was eerily familiar.

The rate of his breath raced as his thrusts picked up and grew stronger until he climaxed. He dropped his face into my cascading, now messy hair and squeezed my ass with his hand that was still wrapped around my leg. He eased out of me and planted a kiss on top of my head before heading to the bathroom.

As his warm semen oozed onto the upper part of my inner thigh, I rolled to my side and nonchalantly reached over to the nightstand to swipe a tissue. After pressing it between my thighs, I pulled my knees up in my arms and relaxed. As tempting as it was to replay the whole scene in my head on obsessive repeat, I didn't. I remained in the moment.

The unmistakable sound of a toothbrush sawing back and forth broke my spell. With no worries of leaving a wet spot on his bed, I swung my legs over the edge of it and sat up.

James strolled out, still naked.

Before he reached the bed, I hopped up and asked if I could take a quick shower.

"Help yourself," he responded warmly. He was so unbelievably agreeable.

I lingered in the shower, contemplating how to exit. I lathered his bar of soap onto a washcloth and as soon as the scent of expensive patchouli and spearmint infiltrated the steam, all thoughts drained away.

There was an extra toothbrush still wrapped in plastic that had been laid out on the counter when I pulled back the curtain. Thoughts of James's impeccable manners juxtaposed mine of trying to come up with an exit strategy while I brushed my teeth. Maybe he would already be asleep and I could just quietly leave. This would be best for us both. Absolutely no press was permitted on board, but there were plenty of eyes that would turn observations from the ship into sensational gossip for the press.

As soon as the word "press" surfaced in my head, I jumped with urgency at the need to leave, stat. My robe was on the other side of the room, so I held my breath as I tiptoed past the bed.

The candles had been blown out and he was under the covers.

"Hey…" he said softly.

I stopped in my tracks and couldn't think of anything to say. I knew how it looked—like I was about to make the walk of shame across the upper decks.

"Lauren?" His head popped up.

"I thought it might be best for me to wake up in my own bed."

He sat up and shook his head *no*. His arms extended out my way.

There was not enough willpower in the world for me to walk away from such an enticing invitation.

"You can go wake up in your own room later if you want, but not now."

chapter eight

CAT AND MOUSE

My eyes popped open at the sound of my own gasp. Then all breathing ceased at the sight of James Bayer sound asleep and naked in bed next to me. I didn't shift from my position as I concentrated on the rate of his breathing. He was snoring lightly and I giggled to myself, wishing I could tell Tyler that he snored.

Actually, I really wished I knew the time. Sunlight peeped in through the outline of the drawn curtains, but that gave me no clue as to the current time of this…the morning after.

James slept peacefully on his back with one arm resting over his eyes and his head turned into the crook of it, away from me. His other arm was still draped across my side with his hand cupping my hip. I studied the back of his head and the slope of his shoulder. His expertly cut, thick, brown hair made an even line across the back of his neck with a minimal amount of new growth coming in to make the sharp edge soften.

I eased out from under his arm and swung my legs to the floor without making a sound. Both bikini pieces were draped over the back of the desk chair and my robe was a heap of soft, white terrycloth on the floor. The UGGs were in the far corner of the room.

Alright, get the boots after the robe and carry them out. I can put them on in the hall in order to make less noise.

Leaving without saying goodbye was so contradictory to the quality of time we had last night. He had such a genuine way with me, but nothing could come from it. It was best to keep the memory of our time together locked in my head for a later date when I might require a surefire fantasy for motivation in the self-love department. In order to avoid the awkward "uh…good morning," I left without waking him. Simplicity won.

March 30, 2009
7:00 a.m.
Back in the safety of my own cabin. Not a state room. Nor with a view.

Tyler: *Come down here, we r on the B deck*
03/29/2009, 9:12 p.m.

Tyler: *Where r u???*
03/29/2009, 10:00 p.m.
Tyler: *Lauren, it's Scarlett, come down here!!!*
03/29/2009, 10:11 p.m.
Tyler: *TnI r heading up 2 room, don't come there;–)*
03/30/2009, 12:56 a.m.
Tyler: *I am tho bahhhaaahhaa*
03/30/2009, 1:01 a.m.

The selfie Scarlett attached to the text she authored was blurry, but adorable.

Email alerts began and one, in particular, caught my attention.

Occupancy: 2
Service: Supply Route
Meet Time: 31 March 2008 at 1200 at South Baffin Island site (see attached PDF for directions)
Length: 3 nights/4 days
Booked and paid for by Matthew Czerniawski with $0 balance remaining.

Brain fog kept me from comprehending exactly what I was looking at on my screen. The booking time showed the reservation being paid for at 3:33 a.m. today, which must have been a couple hours after I fell asleep. Maybe Matt booked this because James was planning to go the whole time, and Al copied me on the email by mistake.

Something about Matt booking it for James shortly after we had sex irked me. Unreasonably jealous, I was now determined to make myself scarce for the rest of the day.

James and Matt (provided Matt was the second person) would need to disembark tomorrow by 5:00 a.m. in order to make the island jumper flight out from Cape Dorset.

I knew this because it's the only mode of transportation I could find when I researched this whole trip for myself.

The "Ship Information" tab popped out from the spine of a binder under a pile of paperwork stacked on the desk. Once I found the extension for the spa, I promptly made a reservation for a facial and massage. Satisfied with my decision, I lay down on the bed to rest my eyes for just a moment.

Tweet tweet.

I drifted back off and rolled toward the wall.

Tweet tweet.

My hand flapped over the device and scraped it across the nightstand.

Tweet tweet.

I gathered my courage.

Tyler: *Meet me n Thom at the cafe for brunch u lazy beeatchh*
03/30/2009, 10:40 a.m.

Unknown number: *I missed saying good morning to u*
03/30/2009, 10:41 a.m.

Questioning whether I'd hoped to cross paths with James created butterflies in my stomach. My brain sighed.

It would be odd if I didn't meet the boys for brunch, so I pulled on my fleece-lined, maroon leggings and a long-sleeved black shirt with thumb holes in it. I loosely wrapped a soft black and cream print scarf around my neck and slipped on my UGGs. A check in the mirror reflected my face was luminous from the steam and sex. After brushing my hair into smooth, loose waves, I smiled at my reflection. It was the most put together I've looked all week. I slid my sunglasses up the bridge of my nose and pulled my shoulders back as I headed to the fancy café.

My stomach had won.

Tyler, Thom, and Scarlett were already on their second round of mimosas when I arrived. Tyler motioned for the waitress to bring me a drink as well, while I took the seat next to Scarlett.

"We really missed you last night." Scarlett leaned into me. It gave her proximity to graze her hand over mine in a sensuous stroke.

The clamor of noise created from the already buzzed crowd in the restaurant was deafening. The bright rays of sunshine began to bore down through the windows, so I unwrapped my scarf.

"You look amazing, just glowing," she purred.

Scarlett had the type of naturally blonde hair that hung straight no matter how high the humidity was. This morning she had it slicked back into an elegant, low ponytail. Her magenta puffy jacket with princess seams hung off the back of her chair. She wore a grey men's Henley, perhaps thrown on in a rush…it was inside out. No bra underneath either.

The waitress set a mimosa in front of me. "They already ordered. Do you know what you want?"

"French toast," I responded without looking at the menu.

"Bring her the kid's version," Tyler instructed with one eyebrow cocked that carried a silent warning for me not to protest.

I should have never given him carte blanche to do that last year, but I didn't have it in me to get into it over brunch.

"It looks like you guys had quite a night," I directed mainly to Thom. "A little hair of the dog?"

Thom leaned in to impart state secrets upon us as if we were a spy ring. "My dear Sleeping Beauty, there's no reason not to start this glorious day off with mimosas. A little pre-party before *Day Dream* would do you some good, maybe even lighten up those artic loins of yours."

Tyler chuckled with a "humph."

"Matt asked for a couple of VIP passes…." Thom held off on the next line waiting for one of us to finish his sentence.

It was Scarlett with her eyes wide and a squeal of excitement. A photo or two of James Bayer lounging in one of the cabanas at the blowout party would presell next season's offerings on the ship.

"They should be down in a minute. We're heading up after breakfast," Thom ordered, like partying all day was a job requirement.

Scarlett touched my hand again. "You're coming, aren't you?"

I smiled without confirming or denying anything.

The three of them filled me in on all the gossip and loosely recalled events from last night at the public Jacuzzis. Midway through the conversation, James and Matt entered. James's head swiveled around, but it was Matt who spotted our table first and pointed.

My head began ringing, overtaking the noisy chatter in the restaurant and my hands trembled, so I folded them tightly in my lap. In slow motion, I turned my head toward them and made direct eye contact with James, even giving him a welcoming smile, no different from any other time this past week. "Here comes James and Matt."

Automatically, the three of them turned their heads to see the pair walk toward us.

James greeted Scarlett deliberately. "Good morning, Scarlicious."

Thom pulled Matt over and produced the VIP badges.

Tyler stared momentarily at me, but was then distracted by Matt and Thom's discussion.

"Are you coming to the party, James?" It was more of an insinuation rather than a question from *Scarlicious* with her eyes intent on his.

James returned her a provocative look. "I don't know, are you going?"

If I didn't exhale soon, I was going to turn purple.

"Yes, of course!" Scarlett gave me an encouraging look. "Lauren too," she added earnestly.

James flicked a gaze my way. "Ah, yes, Lauren dear, did you get up early today and go to a class? You've definitely got that post-yoga glow going on."

I furrowed my brows. *What?*

"Actually, I booked a spa appointment at noon today," I asserted. After a sweep of disappointed faces, I lied and declared, "I'll come over after."

Scarlett enticed me with a sexy pout. "It's the last day on the ship, Lauren. Let's have some fun." She did the same little eyebrow motion from yin class and shot a quick look up to James, then back to me.

James watched this exchange with a muted expression of amusement.

"Well, I already paid for the service, it won't take long." I really wanted to get off this topic.

Her mischievous eyes danced to James with the promise of something naughty. "We missed you last night, too, James, but Matt said you were at the party on the top deck for the backing producers." Scarlett crossed her legs so her foot reached his calf. She pressed her metatarsal against it.

That story came off Matt's tongue and into her mouth so easily that I almost believed it myself.

My eyes shifted from his leg, then to her, and finally they honed in on my lap during that awkward pause.

James leaned down between us with one arm around her and one arm around me. "We're going to get something to eat now." Then shrouded in a throaty whisper, he breathed the next words in my ear, "My appetite seems to be insatiable this morning." His leg was still connected to the top of her foot as he squeezed my shoulder.

The food runner came with our plates and broke up the powwow.

My face had to have been fifty shades of magenta.

"You should cancel that spa appointment and come with us after this," Scarlett said as she openly and wantonly watched James walk away. "I wouldn't miss any opportunity to see him all soaking wet in a pair of board shorts, my goodness."

"He looks like he's lost some weight. They might not stay up."

All three of them died laughing at my cheeky observation. Even the single piece of French toast enjoyed the joke with its orange slice smile and blueberry eyes.

chapter nine

MY NAME IS...

Tyler, Thom, and Scarlett made one more bid for me to come straight to *Day Dream*. I resisted. It pained me more than I wanted to admit—to think about where the day would end up going with Scarlett and James. I didn't want to watch James with everyone else so I could remember him as he was last night; when it was just us.

After disentangling from the parade of tipsy bodies on their way to the explosion of DJ Shadow's rifts, I kept my face forward. The desire to look back for James's head dug deep. *One more day…* was my mantra during the lengthy trek over to the spa. One more day, and this will all fade into the past.

Thick air scented with eucalyptus and cedar, along with the polished teak benches in the sauna, left no room for a feminine vibe. The heady smell of masculinity engulfed me while I tried to relax. As the sex sweated out, the intention to release all concerns of the debauchery taking place on the other end of the ship became pressing. It was a world away.

The sauna door cracked open, followed by a gust of cold air advancing through the space.

"Mrs. St. Germain?" A female massage therapist interrupted my thoughts with her soothing voice.

"Lauren works."

She handed me a fresh robe.

As I swaddled myself in it, I briefly closed my eyes wishing it to be the same one from last night.

"Our esthetician was double booked, so we're going to do your massage first. I hope that's okay." She opened the door to a candlelit cove. "Undress to your level of comfort and get under the covers face up, please. I'll give you a moment."

The soft terrycloth slid across my skin as I tried to examine my naked body in the mirror next to the door. The shadows concealed all physical imperfections. In this light, I was perfect. No signs of scarring on the body or upon the heart. My hand traveled down to the patch of hair between my legs and rested for a moment. Did I feel the same to James as I feel to myself?

The massage was heaven. It deactivated the over-whelming section of my brain that had a tendency to stay on, rolling along the hamster wheel. She massaged my scalp, then shoulders, and finally down to my calves. I flipped over about halfway through and she parted my hair in the middle of my head, like floppy cocker spaniel ears. From far away, I felt her working her way down a hamstring. She bent one knee up to support my shin on her chest while she kneaded the ball of my foot.

"Yousssseeemveryrelackxes," echoed from a distance, causing a crack in my nap.

"Mmmm…." It was all I could manage. My other leg was bent up in her arm. I slept so soundly that I hadn't noticed she had switched sides.

Her knuckles pressed into the arch of my foot in a semi-inappropriate manner, then her fingers opened and encircled my foot. She pulled my shin in tighter to her chest as the fingertips on her other hand glided down the back of my calf.

Is everyone on this fucking ship in heat?

"Does this feel good?" Male. British accent.

One of my puffy eyes peeled open as I looked over my shoulder to see Mr. Bayer himself standing there, cra-dling the shin of my bent leg to his chest while intermit-tently pawing the pressure points of my foot. He wore a robe.

"So does this feel good?" he repeated.

"It does."

The song "Distractions," by Zero 7 started playing. "I love this song," I said.

"I was hoping to talk to you alone." Again, he was not allowing me to find safety in chitchat.

"Are we alone now?" I wasn't actually sure if the massage therapist was still in the room. It seemed a little shady that she would let a man come in and replace her while I was asleep on the table. Given his status, or possibly some direction from Tyler, she must have figured the star would be a welcome intrusion.

"We're alone," he blanketed the words over us.

I rolled over on my back and pushed myself up on my elbows to look at him. "I'm listening."

"I woke up last night and couldn't get that dogsledding trip out of my head. You know, I thought it sounded like such a great opportunity, sooo..." he paused, "so, I had Matt book it."

Jealousy drove a frigid wall up on my end.

"So," he continued shakily, "right, so, I know it seems rather forward, but we had such a connection that...." He broke off, took a breath. "I just really wanted to give you this, that's all. I wanted to go since you told me about it, and honestly, I even wanted to go with you at that point. After last night, I thought...." His hand trailed up my inner thigh.

It finally dawned on me that he booked this trip for us, not him and someone else. "You want us to go together?"

"I know it seems a bit intense," he backpedaled, uncertain by my reaction, "but I thought I'd just take a gamble, you know, move forward with this crazy plan and see if you were up for it. Even with all the ceremony stuff, I'm game."

Led by pure instinct, I sat up all the way to wrap my arms and legs around him with a tug to pull him in close. I didn't know how to apologize for my indifference. "I think I am up for it, actually."

"Good," he sighed. No longer on eggshells, he leaned in to kiss me.

My pelvis tilted up as if we'd been lovers for years and I spread my legs wider to encourage him to enter me. I didn't know exactly how to tell him I wanted him; I could show him, though.

He pulled my bottom closer to the edge of the massage table, which allowed his erection to press into the crease of my thigh. In one fluid motion, he adjusted to thrust inside me and dug his thumbs into the hollows under my hip bones. We rocked to the same pulsating rhythm.

I pulled my ankles tighter around his waist and released my arms from his neck to lie back and give him full access to my body. My spine arched, causing my breasts to present themselves to him, while my shoulder blades systematically rubbed back and forth on the massage table.

The powerful energy generated by his willingness to manipulate my body without asking and my willingness to let him do so turned me on in the most primal way. "I am there," I heard myself say out loud.

He must have been as well, because he reached one hand under my ass and dragged me over the wrinkled sheet to pull me in even closer.

The orgasm initiated from the deepest part of my seat and shot electric waves down my inner thighs and calves before finally squeezing out of the arches of my feet.

He shuddered into my body with a throaty groan before slumping against my chest.

We remained in our blissful silent cocoon until he broke the spell. Like an otherworldly saint, he helped me sit up and palmed my cheeks to face him. "You're lovely," he echoed as his lips brushed over mine.

My eyelids dropped as the energetic vibrations of my orgasm sunk into my chakras in a grounding way.

"We need to pack," James declared suddenly. He pulled out of me and put his robe back on with a quick wipe using the inside of it.

"So," I asked tentatively, "how do we do this?"

"Matt will arrange three seats for us on the jumper. It would be best, uh…." He seemed uncertain how to proceed; perhaps he was trying not to sound like he'd just used me for sex.

Twice.

"Ah, once we leave the ship, there may be people who would talk to the media. Matt, uh, I, I don't think you would want to be reported in the gossip mags. Also, we want to make sure you're comfortable with the travel arrangements."

I understood his insinuation. James Bayer, the movie star with tons of sex appeal, was the keystone of a money making arch dependent upon the suggestion that he's available. There was no doubt in my mind that Matt had a calculated plan in place that would make it seem like a coincidence we were sharing the same flight out. These were the logistics of it; traveling with him while not appearing to travel with him. I wasn't insulted by any of this. After all, I had my own reasons to keep our trip private.

Then a thought occurred. "What about the sledding trip? It's a group."

"We're traveling on a different route from the others. It's actually the supply route instead of the tourist route. We'll be under the care of two Inuit guides, they'll share one sled and we'll use the other. Less people around means less chance for leakage."

My concern hopped to another realization—spending five days with someone I met a week ago. I couldn't make out what he was hoping to get out of our time together.

Another Zero 7 song started up on the XM station piping into the massage room, "Pageant of the Bizarre."

"Matt planned for the utmost secrecy. He's super anal about this stuff and, to tell you the truth, he was relieved to find out I didn't expect him to traipse along in the snow with me."

"Okay." I leaned back down to my elbows. "Perhaps you should leave and I'll wait fifteen minutes or so. The schedule is still the same for the jumper? Do I have a spot?"

"Yes, but Matt will be on the plane as well, under the guise we're heading out to go on a dogsledding trip together before leaving the area."

"And I am...?"

"Transferring at the Ilquit airport to another island jumper heading up to Clyde River to visit your Great-aunt Pamela."

"He's certainly thought of everything." I was relieved. Matt may not realize that I have more to lose than James if we're spotted together.

"I'll catch you on the other side of this." He closed the door as he left.

chapter ten

ALPHA

My emotions ping-ponged between fear and elation as I boarded the eight-person island jumper plane.

Matt rolled his eyes when I said, "Excuse me," to get past him into the minuscule space. I acted like I didn't notice. The twin-engine jumper left Cape Dorset early on the last day of March in 2009. As we gained altitude, I wondered if the whole plan was some kind of early April Fool's joke. The descent to the almost nonexistent runway at the Iqaluit airport was bumpy and sent my nerves straight to the surface.

Matt bid us farewell as he turned around to get right back on the jumper plane, leaving us to find our ground transportation. It was easy to spot the rusty utility van parked behind an older Inuit gentleman, who gave James a curt nod. James had to jerk on the passenger door in order to slide it open, after which he extended his hand to assist me. Now that we weren't trapped under Matt's all-seeing stare, James rested his hand on my knee.

"Nervous?" he inquired.

"To go out into the tundra of the Nunavut territories on a dogsled with a man I met less than two weeks ago? No, not at all."

He laughed.

"I need my son," the driver seemed to say, but it was hard to understand him. His chapped, wind-burnt lips barely moved when he spoke.

We stopped by a broken-down trailer with large parcels of supplies out front just in time to see a lanky Inuit boy bounding out to meet the van. He had shiny, long, black hair and a playful, narrow face. This young man was fully dressed for sledding. He loaded the parcels into the back of the van while his father waited. He bounced into the front seat and turned all the way around to face us. His smile was so captivating that I couldn't help but smile back.

"Pappa doesn't speak English so well," he started, "so I will do most of the talking for him, okay?"

"Okay," I replied, wanting to play along. "What's your name?"

"Genout," he said, taking a moment to help us each get the pronunciation right (Jen-O). "I know you," he proudly said to James, "from the sci-fi movies. You have the British accent." Then he jabbed, "She says my name better."

Our laughter caused Pappa to look up sharply in the rearview mirror.

The staging area consisted of an outdoor roof structure supported by several timber beams over a slab of concrete. All the dogs appeared to be a mix of German shepherd and collie breeds. Several dogs were staked to a beam, sitting at attention or lapping water from a bowl. Various racks and shelving units were set up to contain leather items that resembled horse tack and folded Mexican blankets. There were also two runs visible from the front, both empty as all the dogs were organized for the trip. The ones that were already harnessed to pull freight were surprisingly patient as they waited.

Behind this outdoor structure, a long trailer with aluminum skin sat up on blocks. A squat man with a five o'clock shadow banged the door open to greet us. He had no front teeth and greasy hair, but he was inviting. As soon as he said my name out loud, I recognized the voice. Al.

He shook James's hand warmly and pulled me off balance for an unexpected hug. "Ah, Lauren, Pamela speaks of you like a daughter, so to me, you are a niece." He led us into the trailer and, all business, pulled out a weatherproof map. "This," he began as he pointed to our current location, "is your starting place. It's where we are…start, here, today. You, Lauren, will ride with Genout, and Mr. Superman here rides with Pappa today, here. Now, no worry love birds, only for the first day 'til you get the hangs of it. Then you two on one. Father and son on heavy one. Okay, so you go here." Al traced his finger up the coastline on the map. "By dog and then at this, uh, hall?"

James looked to where Al had pointed. "Pass," he offered, "a narrow pass."

"Yes, well, there you take your things and forty kilos of goods to canoes. The rest will be split equally on your sled and Pappa's. He can transfer about sixty kilos of goods over both sleds. Then Pappa will hook a double sled and line up all dogs to pull the bulk of the weight through the pass, the narrow one. You two go with the small load and Genout to the canoe. Then, you reunite at this point." His finger traveled up the coast toward Pamela's remote community. It was easy to see there were mountain ranges barely inland of the coastline. "Sleep in traditional igloo and separate dogs back to double file for each sled, balance out the goods and BAM!" He clapped his hands.

I jumped in my seat.

"Time for best part of trip, for you and dogs. You go over large, flat area before getting up to Pamela's village. It's a field, like glass, dogs love! They can go straight and fast with all weight balanced. You will like it best too."

This ended his summary of our trip.

As I caught my breath, I looked over to James wondering if he felt as daunted as I did after seeing this detailed map in person. Greenland was right above us and there was no turning back now.

"Where will we stay before we arrive at the igloo?" James asked.

"At this juncture." Al glanced my way for recognition of using such an impressive word.

I rewarded him with a smile.

"My sister house, she has good guest room for tourists. After you eat and sleep with sister, it will be canoe time." He tapped the location of her house on the paper with a decisive flick and then pointed to the end location for the canoe portion. "Right there is the igloo we have kept good for many years. Sleeping furs and fire will keep you warm for the night. Next day you make it quickly to Pamela's, you will remember—smooth as glass." After trailing his finger off the map in a fast, straight line, he sat back on his squeaky chair and interlaced his hands languidly behind his neck. "It's good, right?" The gap where his teeth should have been was framed by a relaxed smile.

The first part of the trip was rocky and awkward as I tried not to press any part of my body against this thirteen-year-old boy while he guided our sled at insane speeds.

After not even an hour of me attempting to keep an appropriate distance between us, he implored, "Miss, please, you must move with me. It's better for the dogs."

At the first rest stop, we anchored the sleds and fed the dogs. Pappa's lead, Silas, caught my attention so I extended my cupped hand to introduce myself properly. Silas was predominantly German shepherd, and at least an eighth wolf, according to Genout. He was more mature than the other dogs and calmed me merely with his presence. Silas periodically checked in with Pappa, even if it was just a look his way. Silas appeared to be constantly taking the temperature of the group while he let me scratch the soft fur behind his ears. When he looked back at me after his assessment, I could have sworn he understood my thoughts at that very moment.

The time to harness the dogs back up to their towlines came. Genout directed me to secure Silas at the head of the lead tug line. I hooked his metal fastener and silently thanked him for keeping my secrets.

James and Pappa switched places so James could drive.

Genout asked, "Maybe you drive next?"

"On the smooth part, I think."

"Okay, miss."

Several hours later, we came up on the edge of Al's sister's land. Smoke was rising from the chimney of her modest brick house. When we were close enough to breathe in the smell of campfire, Genout shouted, "Gee over!"

The dogs veered away from the small road leading to her house and onto a snowy incline that came up to the rear.

"Easy! Easy! Whooooaaa!"

The dogs stopped perfectly by the single-room barn behind her house.

Genout helped me out of the sled and directed me to go inside as James pulled his pack into the spot right next to ours.

Al's sister had hung a dry sweat suit on the bathroom door with a pair of fur-lined moccasins on the floor under it. I slipped into all that fabric gratefully, then sat in front of the fire while she gathered up my outer gear to hang in the kitchen. Sister pressed a steaming hot mug of licorice root tea into my hands right before the three guys entered.

They were carrying on an animated conversation interspersed with Genout's boyish laugh. James, Pappa, and Genout had secured both sleds and released the dogs into the pen in the same amount of time it took me to make it to the couch.

Once James removed his outer layers, he found me on the couch and kissed my forehead. It was scratchy from the beginning stubble on his chin.

"I'm sorry I didn't help you guys anchor everything down," I attempted. The truth was I could barely move. My muscles were going to be on fire tomorrow.

"You shouldn't have to do that." He caressed my cheek before tucking a lock of my hair behind my ear.

If circumstances were different, I could easily fall in love with him.

Dinner consisted of roasted, braised caribou topped with a peppery gravy whisked up from pan drippings and flour. Genout pushed the smallest portion of raw muk-tuk toward me. "Some need to eat it with bread, like butter."

I chewed and chewed, feeling my jaw ache from the fishy rubbery fat, but I ate the whole portion with gratitude. Then, at the first appropriate moment I could excuse myself to bed, I did so. I didn't bother to turn on the light in the guest room before crawling into the bed.

Downstairs, Pappa and James lounged in front of the fire drinking rye whiskey. The back door slammed shut as Genout went out to check on the dogs.

I had just dozed off when I heard James raise his voice downstairs. His tone was sharp, so I crept to the top of the stairs and listened.

"He will not sleep out there with the dogs, it's freezing!" James was adamant.

"Ah, sir, but he was not expected," Sister explained. "Pappa sleeps on couch by fire, no room for boy. It's okay, there are warm spots and dogs make for good sleeping partners."

"No!"

"It's okay," Genout interjected, "I have slept like that before. It's not so bad, really."

"You will sleep on the floor in our room."

Sister started to protest, but James overtook the conversation. "He will have a blanket and go on our floor." This was not a request. James was the alpha of this group and Sister knew she needed to back down.

Something fast and furious in Inuit followed the thud of Genout coming up the stairs as I scurried back to the room to turn on the light for them.

James's expression was receding from red frustration to exhaustion as he made it to the room.

Genout ducked past James to take up the space on the floor to be at his hero's side. James stepped over the boy and climbed in bed next to me. He took the one pillow designated for him and handed it down to Genout.

"We all need this sleep," James declared and flipped off the light.

I tapped his shoulder so he would sit up a little. I maneuvered my own pillow under his head and nestled into his armpit.

chapter eleven

SEDNA SHADOWS

Genout was already harnessing up the dogs by the time James and I made our way downstairs.

Sister didn't say anything about Genout's foray into the house last night. She tapped a bottle of aspirin on the coffee mug she extended to me.

I held out my palm and nodded.

Pappa determined James was capable of driving without his assistance, so I arranged myself on James's sled. He looked like a kid who won the county fair prize at the prospect of our independence.

At James's sharp whistle, Silas looked back at me before leading us out and psychically said: *I will protect you.*

We started off behind Pappa until Genout looked back at me to give a signal. The packs slowed for the planned pass. I hopped off our moving sled to run up and get between both lines of dogs while James overtook Pappa. Unexpected aerobic activity blasted sharp cold pains into my lungs. My legs burned from the push I made.

Frosty wind rouged my cheeks as I laughed from the rush of adrenaline that shot through me. I was alive running amidst these packs of dogs as their keeper. Moving in the center of these creatures on foot at such a fast pace instilled a fundamental confidence inside me that kept my eyes focused on both sets of dogs. During the pass, the two pack lines had to run parallel to each other. If one dog from either line snapped at another, then my job was to surprise the aggressor with a stiff smack on the backside. I was empowered for that moment, and as James started to take the lead, I sped up to hustle onto his moving sled.

James hollered, "Lauri, honey! That was perfect."

I landed on my seat next to James and whipped around to see Pappa and Genout shrinking in the distance. Grinning widely, I waved to them.

Pappa only nodded since both his hands were on the reins, but Genout shook his fists over his head in victory and let out a howl.

In contrast to yesterday, I easily relaxed into James while he drove. The wind ripped loudly around us and the biting cold air would gust shards of freezing daggers on any exposed skin as we sped along. Every nerve ending in my body was awakened and my throat grew hoarse from shouting "Look!" so many times.

When we backed off the speed, James laughed at my excitement. "Lauren, you are worse than a dog that can't mind its own business."

Once we reached the canoe depot located in the northern region of Cumberland Sound, I moved out of the way to watch James show off his new skills—anchoring the sled and setting up ground stakes.

Pappa and Genout emerged in the distance on the path we had just sailed down.

I put my gloved hand on a huge boulder to steady myself since my legs were still jelly from the ride. After a moment, an overwhelming desire to touch the rock with my bare hand came over me, so I yanked the glove off with my teeth. The boulder had a freezing flat surface with ridges beneath the smoothness that could only be detected through the sensitive nerves of the fingertips. I traced those ridges and came to a still point so my hand could settle on top of the massive formation.

I experienced a whole body sensation best described as shrinking. My height reduced down like I was evaporating into steam and the transformation caused my wavelengths to align with the ones emitting from this boulder.

James remained in my peripheral vision, playing on the ground with Silas as happiness abounded from the boulder into me, then *through* me and out to the pack. The vibrational speed of pure, undiluted joy expanded out beyond Pappa and Genout. It looped us all together and then traveled back into me, grounding this shared emotion. It was such a profound connection and brought with it the entire essence of Nunavut.

"Lauri, come here." James snatched me off my feet and swung me around in a bear hug that caused Silas to leap up in excitement.

For the first time in years, the frozen cracks on my cheeks that were created to hold up fake smiles on my face broke. I laughed so hard that the sunshine trapped deep inside me erupted and shattered my false mask.

We helped Pappa and Genout divide the supplies and set everything up for the next leg of the trip.

Pappa took both sleds and roped them together, one in front of the other. He would drive from the front one, making the one in back a trailer. All the dogs worked together in an odd configuration called a "fan hitch" so they could pull both sleds, Pappa, and the bulk of the supplies. Silas remained in the lead position.

"This is the best way to spread the weight evenly over all the dogs, in case he needs to cross ice," Genout explained. "We will reunite with them at the igloo."

James finished heaving the parcels into his canoe and upon Pappa's approval, we shoved off the shallow shoreline. James in one, Genout and me in the other.

Genout steered our canoe and quietly reminded me to keep it slow and steady as I paddled. "We don't want to ripple out too far...Sedna."

Sedna was the only response he gave when I asked him why it mattered. As soon as he spoke the name, he would shush me.

The overarching snow-covered mountains on our left stood strong like gods as we glided over the quiet water. They contrasted the flat, white ice beds bobbing up and down in the water to our right. The three of us kept to our own thoughts during this subdued leg of the trip. There was no wind or crashing waves, just the quiet lapping of our paddles sliding in sync through the water. The water rolled over the paddles with each pull; a mini universe in itself, rising and falling.

Upon landing, Genout rushed to get us comfortably established in the igloo after we turned the canoes over as shields for the supplies. He instructed James to start a fire in the igloo while he inspected the area outside.

I stuck my head out the door to ask Genout for the flint and his face popped up displaying the most stressful of expressions.

"Shh," he whispered in an exaggerated tone. Then in an apologetic demeanor, Genout came close and quietly insisted, "Silence, miss, please. It is our way here."

He seemed to be praying outside the igloo so I went back inside.

James shot me a knowing look. "He still believes in some old wives' tales," James said in an off-handed manner over his shoulder while searching for the matches in his pack. "He told me not to tell you, but there's an old myth about some terrible ocean woman who lives deep in the sea. She was mortal, then her father supposedly cut her fingers off and drowned her, trying to protect himself from a spell or something."

I scooted closer to him.

The flame caught and James tossed me a wink and stashed the matches before continuing with the story. "So, she didn't really die and now she controls the other creatures, uh, spirits rather, who are associated with the ocean, land, and wind."

The fire grew and he blew on it before he stood up and spread his hands out to commence his performance. James leaned heavily into his accent as he continued, "Sedna, the one down there, also talks to the seals and if a tribe has mistreated one of its members, she will call the seals away from the shore so there will be nothing to hunt. She brings about blizzards that ferociously descend upon hunting parties, taking away all their visibility in order to blind them in a storm of white."

Without breaking character, he captured my hand and inched me over to the ice bed. My heart skipped a beat as the front of his body closed in, causing me to take a few steps back until I reached the edge of the bed. I sat down, watching him back away with a flirty smile.

"You just love an audience."

"Shh! Quiet now, wench!"

I clapped my hand over my mouth to suppress a laugh.

"Where was I? Ah, yes, Sedna, she is also the one who provides blessings and practical items to the tribe. The joints from her horrible dismembered fingers create blubber and whale skins—something you and I might take for granted, but are considered to be indispensable staples for the Inuit tribes up here. She is a paradox. The indigenous folks' biggest desire is to stay on her good side or she'll steal the souls of men to keep for herself, and then curse sickness on the tribe." His eyes momentarily looked up as if to recall the next part of the myth.

I reached down to unlace my boot when I heard dogs barking. *Something's wrong! Something's wrong!* That's what I heard them say.

"Stay here!" James commanded, zooming out the entryway at full speed.

I watched from the door as James hauled ass out into the dusky grey wilderness to intersect four loose dogs tearing toward us with their bridles twisted and frayed over their backs. James made it to Genout, who was panting at that point, and they took off on foot into the ashy expanse.

I ran up to meet the dogs, and by some small miracle, they came right to me—jumping, excited, and unsure what to do without their master. I fumbled with their harnesses to get them into some sense of order and led them inside the igloo.

Exhausted, they all snuggled down by the fire and promptly fell into a group slumber.

The sky darkened to an even more ominous shade of slate as time stretched on. Standing still as I waited, I shifted my weight from one foot to the other in a steady rhythm, now paranoid about causing too much noise.

Ripples.

It wasn't until several hours later that the familiar sound of a sled cropped up in the distance. Genout was bringing Pappa in on one with James right behind them driving the other. The incoming dogs must have been spent, for there were only five dogs split between the two sleds. Silas was not in his spot at the lead of either.

James came to a stop and rushed over. "He's hurt. Pappa lost control. I think it wasn't balanced properly and he drifted off, crashing into the side of a tree. There was a rollover. His leg, Lauren, it's broken."

Genout stumbled over his own feet coming to us, the little boy in him was creeping out. James steadied him by firmly gripping his shoulder.

"I need to take him down to the village at the base of the mountain. They can treat him and set his leg," Genout told us in shaky words that rushed out.

"Aren't we capable of finding something to set it here so we can rest and go with clearer heads?" I asked in disbelief that he would choose to go back out at this point.

"No, miss, no, there is too much temptation here for him to make a blood deal to fix it. There are things that can bring no more pain, but in end…" he trailed off. "In end, no…NO." Genout's mind was made up. "This is what Pappa needs. Please understand."

"Okay," I said, looking to James for guidance.

"Let me help you get him ready for the journey," James suggested.

"Yes," Genout choked out.

Pappa spoke some hushed Inuit and moaned as James secured him on the sled.

"Where's Silas?" I tried to wait until Pappa was out of earshot, but I couldn't hold the question in any longer.

A guilty look filled with hurt came over Genout. "He is dead, I think, I didn't see him when we got to Pappa.

But I know, I know he has been called away," Genout wiped the back of his sleeve across a tear that was streaming down his cheek.

An unspeakable anger welled up in the pit of my stomach. *This amazing dog to be called away? Dead? For what?* I didn't even know what that meant but it boiled my insides. *Why does this accursed shit always happen?* The anger turned to hot tears and I bit the insides of my cheeks to keep the looming sobs at bay.

Pappa and Genout left.

I waved mournfully as they went into the unseen while praying a silent blessing over them.

James brought me inside and peeled opened an MRE. We ate the meatloaf and green beans and a flood of tears spilled out of my eyes. I collapsed into his arms as we perched uncomfortably on the edge of the ice bed. There was a turning point in our embrace when we held each other in mutual care as we bawled over the loss of Silas. We couldn't find the words. The crying calmed and we finally slumped across the fur blankets, both of us too exhausted to change out of our travel clothes.

It must have been a couple hours later when I woke. Unable to determine the time, I shifted to look at the dogs. They hadn't budged an inch. I had to pee. I had to pee *now* or I might wet my pants. I wiggled out of James's arms. He didn't rouse. I had hoped he was sleeping lightly so I could wake him without feeling guilty. No luck there. I pussyfooted toward the door experiencing a brief moment of déjà-vu from sneaking out on him less than a week ago.

I decided two steps out from the entrance was plenty far.

My joints ached as my stiff fingers began to unhook my snow pants. I scanned the horizon and couldn't get my bearings. With my snow pants dropped, I slid my hands under the waistband of my tights and paused to let the bare skin of my hips warm my palms.

Something shifted a few meters in the distance. Or was it a kilometer? IT glided straight toward me and brought with it a horrible chemical smell of toxic waste.

I gasped, momentarily forgetting my urge to pee. This ghostly form was a human figure hovering close to the ground, and I mentally observed that IT was creating and controlling the breeze.

IT was a blacker than black shadow that whispered, "The Wind Incarnate," sending a chill down my spine.

If this were a scene from a movie, the special effects would show the breeze manipulating this opaque smoke figure so IT could shapeshift.

I feebly hoped IT was Genout, but it seemed to be wearing a hoodie and Genout didn't wear those. I tried to force my eyes to focus while remaining perfectly still.

Ripples.

My voice cracked as half of a hello came out.

As if IT finally *allowed* me to see IT, my vision cleared up. Two red eyes flashed like laser beams. IT wasn't hunting me, rather something right next to me.

Please, Genout, my brain emitted.

The outline of the hooded figure vanished into the mist, causing the toxic smell to burn my nostrils.

For a split second, the fog reflected against the white fur of a young Baffin Wolf less than a meter in front of me. The young white wolf was stalking on full alert.

Some divine knowledge inspired me to make a commotion and wake the dogs. I started to move, but awkwardly tripped as I yelped out a strange cry, completely ungraceful in appearance and sound. Instantly the dogs came leaping outside, all barking and growling as they shoved their way past me.

The wolf chased away the hooded figure that had come to torment me. None of the dogs pursued it. Instead, they jumped up on me, checking for the smell of an intruder to their pack. One wildly circled the igloo.

I peed my pants.

chapter twelve

THE ENDANGERED BAFFIN ISLAND WOLF

James harnessed up the last of the dogs a few short hours after the bizarre interaction in front of the igloo. Thank God he didn't draw out my humiliation from the whole thing. I was mortified enough when I took off my urine-soaked long johns and put on his brand new Nike running tights. "I'll buy you another pair. These will smell like pee," I mumbled when he came back inside the igloo.

"Then I shall sleep with them every night under my pillow."

"God, you're sick!" I quipped, thankful to have something to laugh at.

We made it to the clearing and James pulled over to give the dogs some extra food before launching onto the smooth, fast part. He unfolded the map and determined we had seventy kilometers to go—a straight line leading to Pamela's village, Pangnirtung.

"We'll use the GPS hooked to the rail here." He pointed to the front of the sled, where he had been mushing for the last few hours.

As I kicked the snow off the bottom of my boots on the railing, James stopped me and guided me around to the driver's side.

"No, Lauren, you take the lead. This is where you're going to drive us, fast and smooth."

His sincerity to truly take care of me on this trip was fascinating, as he barely knew me. Everything he did so far, looking after my comfort, serving as an uncle to Genout, always taking the heavier load, and even turning over his expensive pair of Nike tights solidified my first impression of him. He's authentic in his generosity. Now, after all that, he easily turned over the lead so I could drive the pack on the most rewarding part of the trip.

Someone inside of me would have normally refused and insisted, *No, you take it; I don't deserve it.* But I was departing from that person and took the lead with confidence.

He adjusted my stance by clasping his hands on my hips and steering them to aim forward in alignment with the dogs. James remained standing behind me with both legs and arms engulfing mine, so he could assist with the reins at the start. Once I got the hang of it, he backed off, allowing me to bring us into a speed that blazed us through the grand finale.

Not only were we elated, but the dogs were ecstatic and relished in their top speed. It was a light load combined with the space and freedom for them to swiftly fly over the ground up to thirty kilometers per hour…mush heaven.

Four hours later, we arrived to the dog sledding outpost on the outskirts of Pangnirtung. It was a bit of a scene when my wide turn into the staging area displayed my novice skills.

The main outfitter drove us to Pamela's house in a beat-up CJ-7 Jeep. He was a lively character with a round body, and was happy to have new faces to tell his old stories to.

"Pappa's not Genout's real dad. They ain't blood, you see. The boy was abandoned at the old mission church down in Iqaluit when he shoulda been still suckling his mother's teets. God's man there, a foreigner from Norway, had no success with converting us savages. He was afixin' to close up shop and try his luck south in the lower territories. The refined Canada, you see. Pappa's old wife wanted nothing to do with the boy. She is very superstitious, you see, and she named him as child of Sassuna Arnaa. She's called Sedna round these parts, you probably never heard the story."

James interjected, "The woman who had her fingers cut off by her father, now in the bottom of the sea?"

"Yes! Why you DO see!" he responded in elation. "Anyhoo, the old lady, she didn't want nothin' to do with the boy, claiming she had a vision of sorts, that the boy could transform into a Baffin Island Wolf. Now that's a rare type of wolf, considered endangered by those anthropologist people who brave the winters to get up here every few years. I think she just didn't want the responsibility of raising another child, you see, no one believes in all those silly omens anymore. Besides...." He flicked us a look in his rearview mirror. "Pappa's a stubborn one. He persisted and, truly, the boy turned out just fine. The way she thinks Sedna would waste her time calling up a land creature isn't how legend has it, anyway. Not if she thought he could transform into a sea lion or something. Well, then...." Distracted by the arrival at a tidy little cabin, he announced, "Now, here we are."

When Pamela came out her front door, I scrambled to her, almost crushing her with a huge hug.

We toted our burden of things inside where it became acutely obvious that I reeked of urine. "Do you have a bath or shower I could use?"

"I have something better. We are lucky to have natural hot springs up here. There's one on my neighbor's property, right over there." She pointed out her kitchen window that was framed with delicate lace curtains that looked as though they might disintegrate any moment. "All we need to do is go across that footbridge."

She produced a strong cinnamon wine that tasted like mulled apple cider and some stone wheat crackers, which we inhaled. James ate an entire block of cheese as well as two cans of mandarin oranges with proper manners, even though he was famished and required at least three thousand calories on a daily basis. We had been living off the bare minimum for a few days. Always the gentleman, he hid his hunger behind a kind expression.

We lined up behind her like baby ducks across the quaint footbridge. As we approached the gargling hole, an inescapable thick stench of sulfur greeted us. But after a few minutes, the smell was no longer noticeable.

James took everything off except his underwear to submerse into the spring. I stripped down, and Pamela entered wearing a nightgown.

She hushed me when I inquired about this cleansing ritual she had spoken of with such importance.

"Tomorrow," was her only response.

chapter thirteen

ANCESTRAL BLOODLINES

The following day, we took a leisurely stroll around the village. The slow pace may have seemed boring compared to the intensity of the past few days, but it was a welcome change. The night before was relaxing, and after a strong release of orgasms for the two of us, we flowed right into this calm walkabout.

Pamela's melodic voice entranced us with stories of the history behind the sparse, poorly built buildings. With reverence, she spoke of the "way of the dog" and how ancient hunting practices were still in place today. The blubber station was the last stop on our tour before we drove to an elder's cabin that overlooked a portion of the Pangnirtung Fjord.

There were ten other Inuit natives there, older women and gentlemen who were all associated with the local Tribal Council in some fashion. A buffet had been spread out showcasing local and imported food. The oddest thing from the south that they were obsessed with were Oreos. I hadn't thought about those cookies for years.

I assumed the main attraction at this gathering would be James; however, he was unknown to them.

After a late lunch, we set out on foot to a stone temple-like structure to take in the view of the fjord. The elders held back near the edge of the rocky cliffs while James and I bounded up and down the large boulders at the water's edge. The sky darkened to a grey-blue dusk and Pamela called us back up. Someone had started a fire and the council members were all sitting in a circle around it. Pamela sat me down between two weathered, ancient men and directed James to take a seat on the other side of the fire facing me. I winked at him, not understanding the seriousness of what was about to happen.

Once settled into my seat, a plastic cushion of sorts on the ground, a regal presence emanated from the two elders on either side of me. Instinctively, I sat up straighter.

James was evaluating the scene with casual interest when Pamela stood and spoke. "Now we have come before YOU and the skies above to ask a release in this woman." With this introduction, the Northern Lights grew in color and size above us.

She turned to James before she commanded, "You are to remain seated. No matter what you see." Before he could comment, her attention focused back up to the sky. "We cast the embedded curses from the St. Germain bloodlines to YOUR power! We humbly beg of YOU to make yourself known by removing the psychic bonds that continue to torture her. These psychic bonds brought about by the unholiest of unholy…the Djinn!"

Several of the elders spat at the word.

Djinn?

I've heard of them before, from Collin, but they were just part of those ghost stories he used to tell. Genies in a lamp? That was just folklore, like demons. Or the devil.

"Allow her to be freed from the evil Djinn blood curse so she may re-enter this realm no longer carrying the St. Germain curse. We are demanding her karmic contract with the red Djinn and their leader, Iblis, to be severed at this point. Now!" Pamela reeled on me and spewed, "This is much bigger than you."

My core shook from fear. Initially, I thought this ritual was going to be some aromatherapy or sage burning, perhaps with a light massage. Not in the slightest. This Inuit gathering had the same tone and formality of the military tribunal back in DC. I withered inside, fighting against my urge to slouch and hide.

The circle began chanting in a foreign language driven by the beat of a single drummer. The green talons of light swirled in the skies above us, casting a dizzying effect. There was definitely a connecting force from the Aurora Borealis to the fire created here on the ground, and Pamela seemed to be balancing the two.

The forceful presence and unyielding intent of the group was intimidating.

I closed my eyes and waited. Something was holding on tight in my chest, squeezing my heart as if I were having a heart attack. I reached for an internal touchstone and briefly thought, *Genout.* He had to have been there, the endangered wolf child who wanted to protect me from IT, the hooded figure known as Iblis.

This ritual was supposed to release my hold on Collin, but I wasn't ready to do that. Pamela's talk of his family's curses, or whatever these Djinn entities represented in all of it, shouldn't have anything to do with the longing I still felt for him.

A chapped hand clasped my elbow and the elder pushed me up. "Go there, to the left side of your ribcage. Go where you know how to find God," he spoke directly into my ears as the drumbeat was deafening.

I was desperate to breathe into that spot; a place I'd traveled to so easily many times before. The forceful squeezing inside my chest caused me to double over.

The elder didn't let me linger and yanked me back up.

My eyes were opened, but my sight tunneled into blackness as if I had stood up too fast. I concentrated on the elder's strong grip, hoping he would keep me tethered to this spot around the fire.

"You must combat it. You must release it. The shadow of your past life will not go easy, but we will clear a space in you to allow for a new beginning." The elder spoke with authority.

The comforting smell of the woodsy campfire was overpowered by that of a dangerous electrical fire giving off the horrid stench of ozone, as if someone poured battery acid onto it. To my horror, an even darker shade of blackness arose in my field of vision, carrying malice and evil events. As if IT knew what would tear me down the most, terrifying and disturbing images emerged in my line of sight. Indescribable things slipped into my brain as if they were really right there in front of me. Beautiful elephants with their kneecaps shot out were crashing to the ground with great thuds as hundreds of pointy hoods moved in quickly to feast on the agony of their lost memories. Blacker than black claws tore into the massive carcasses of these majestic creatures in order to knife their wrinkled flesh and rip it from them.

The uncontrollable urge to burn myself came over me. It was as if feeling the most extreme amount of pain possible might quench this tangible nightmare. Unexpectedly, I ducked. Hallucinations of burnt soccer balls covered in blood and dirt were flying at me.

The elder shifted quickly to keep hold of my elbow. "Ground yourself, girl!"

The hollow sound of the rhythm was faint, but I located it somewhere down there in the depth of dirt. I mentally clamped onto it by a thread, willing that string to grow thicker so it might prevent me from floating off into the depths of my mind.

Pamela was commanding something in Inuit, presumably ordering IT to go from me and evacuate her land. Her voice was vicious and furious—as it must be to exorcise this demon, or Djinn, called Iblis. Her shouting became a beacon to guide me out of the hallucination I was experiencing.

As my tunnel vision began to open and I saw her jump to her feet and fiercely kick up dirt, I wiggled to get out of the elder's grasp.

"Don't fight it," he instructed. "Calm down, find a breath. Find a lifeline. Tether home now. A fast, smooth line across the glass."

It sunk in and I bonded to him. My sight fully channeled into focus and Collin was sitting there instead of James. From across the fire, I could tell he was disappointed in me.

"Why?" I cried out to him. "Why did you leave me?"

125

The sound of my plea morbidly sliced through the mounting tension of the group and the elder let go of my elbow. I crashed down on my knees and my head must have flung forward because an intense wave of heat stung my face before my head was yanked back. A sob escaped me and the ritual was over. Was IT gone?

I remained crouched on my knees and buried my head in my hands, crying from the pain of Collin's memory; the memories of the life we had together before the attack. My sobs mellowed to a hiccup and I rubbed my eyes to look up.

James was staring at me with a look of terror, revulsion, disbelief.

Bye bye, handsome movie star.

The elder at my side offered me his hand.

"Thank you for your guidance," I said.

He smiled blankly.

Pamela giggled, her softness coming back. "He doesn't speak English, Lauren."

When she spoke a quick translation in Inuit, he chucked a brief noise back to her.

"He says you're welcome."

chapter fourteen

GOODBYE

Time caught up with us. James was two days overdue to leave for filming at the next location for *The Purpose*. They would be shooting Bronne de Luca's pilgrimage to a remote Ashram in northern India. The layers of warm clothing peeled off as we made it through the helicopter trip back to Iqaluit, and then first class to Quebec, continuing on to LAX. By the time we were somewhere over the Midwest, we could almost pass for normal people again, dressed down to fly comfortably in wrinkled yoga clothes from the ship.

At the start of our adventure, we agreed to not take any pictures. So while he slept, I studied his face, trying to memorize every aspect of it. A light beard coated his wind-burnt cheeks and chin as his eyelids twitched periodically.

After the touchdown in LAX, neither of us initiated any movement to deplane. We just stared forward in a zombie-like daze as the rest of the passengers trudged down the narrow aisle. Some of them did a double take when they walked by James, but no one said anything to us. Once the plane was empty, the flight attendants began to give us *the look*.

I nudged him. "Come on."

"Excuse me?" James called and waved to one of them. "Could you give us a moment, please? We just need a moment."

"Yes," she said with a smile indicating that she'd bend to whatever whim he had. The curtains snapped shut.

He turned in his seat and faced me. "Listen, I know you have unfinished business here, but you can always reach out to me if you ever need anything. This card has my personal number on it, and I want you to use it. Anything, Lauren."

I carefully folded the card and slipped it in my purse. "Go make a great movie. If I...." I corrected myself. "When I miss you, I can always go to the movies." Tears sprung up in my eyes. "Films, I mean, I'm sorry, you will always be my superhero, James."

We hugged without getting up.

I broke our hug to stand and he begrudgingly got up to go out first.

The script of lies we just acted out rewound and re-played in my head as I waited long enough for him to appear to have been traveling alone. I will call him—doubtful. He would be there if I ever needed anything—not a chance. I'm neatly folding this whole thing up into a tiny little card and slipping it deep into the same box I locked all my visions from the ritual in.

My car keys were still in the side pocket of my tote bag. It felt like a lifetime ago that I had tossed them in there, along with a long-term parking ticket.

The flight attendant opened the curtain and apolo-getically informed me, "We need to ready the plane."

TWO WEEKS LATER

chapter fifteen

FORMALITIES

Inuit parents tell their children stories of a woman with curling, green fingernails who resides off the ice banks under the depths of the freezing ocean. A sage mother warns her little ones that should a child wander too close to the edge, this terrible creature just might come up and snatch the child to keep for herself at the bottom of the ocean. I read this tidbit of Inuit mythology on a Nunavut tourism site called Our Land. It exemplified the universal lie we all tell ourselves; we have the belief of guaranteed safety while on the ground we inhabit, but we turn a blind eye to any evil forces creeping up under our paths. Those evil forces have insatiable cravings and want to take us down and keep us for themselves.

The other tab left open on my computer was Djinn Universe. Articles on how these Djinn beings were the original genies seemed to be the dark inspiration for the Disney movie, *Aladdin*. Even different colored ones existed. Back in the modern comfort of my condo, the idea that a supernatural being had anything to do with my husband's family, or me, seemed ludicrous. I read the website but stopped short of buying the book.

Wanting to look at things other than mythological women at the bottom of the ocean or genies who torment humans, I clicked through the last few photos on Al's website that showcased a tribute page for Silas. Al put up close to fifty images of Silas from when he was a puppy to three days before his disappearance. Those pictures stirred immense grief in me, but I couldn't help but look at them every day.

I shut down the computer; it was almost midnight on Thursday and tomorrow was going to be the day of reckoning. I would find out if my clearance could be reinstated. I was hoping Pamela really did exorcise my demons. If so, luck may be on my side. *But is going back to work luck? Or is it a curse?*

My former boss, Dani Bragg, also left El Paso shortly after my verdict. She weathered much of the blame for the Burak Yilmaz investigation. The company put her on professional leave until my trial was complete. She gave hours of testimony detailing my competencies as an investigator and was pressed to answer endless questions about my loyalty to the United States.

Once I was exonerated from charges of assisting in a homeland terrorist attack, she was transferred to southern California. Ever since, she continued to make it abundantly clear that I could come back to work for her whenever I was ready. Initially I dismissed this offer, but now I was seeking normalcy. And a salary. Completing cases and packing up the finished products to ship off to adjudication and the satisfying sealing of the FedEx Tyvek envelopes had a comforting rhythm about it. So did paying the bills.

When I finally called her, she answered on the second ring.

"It's so good to hear from you, Lauren, our long-lost investigator." She got right to business. "I imagine you're calling to come back."

"Yes." There was no beating around the bush with her.

Since a backlog of cases and a shortage of cleared investigators were the norm in LA, the process of getting my creds back would be expedited. It had been eighteen months since the attack, and on that very same day, my clearance was suspended. In theory, I was eligible to have my clearance reinstated, but I wasn't sure what that entailed now. At the very least, I would need to bring my resume up to date and disclose my recent trip to Canada.

"I'll send the forms over to you," Dani advised. "You have seventy-two hours to drug test and you'll get that email today, I think. You know how this goes, so I won't bore you with all the new-hire details. I look forward to working with you again, Lauren. You were always one of my go-tos in, uh…." We didn't say El Paso to each other. "Back there. Anyway, we can definitely use you over here." She hesitated, allowing the steady tap of her pen on the desk to fill the pause. "I know you're ready, but I still have to ask, are you ready? They'll need me to vouch for you, which I will, but I need to hear it from you."

"To be perfectly honest, Dani, I think coming back to work would be the best thing for me now. I'm ready to focus, and all the stuff in the past, well, it's in the past." The magic words to get me back on the hamster wheel again.

Sure enough, the reinstatement forms arrived with their endless questions. Security sent out guidance on referencing my trial on those forms. It wasn't necessary to hash it out all over again. Anything they could possibly want to know about my involvement with Yilmaz was documented in a 500-page deposition. Adjudication already had that document.

The rows of little boxes filling my computer screen blurred together, signaling me to pull out my reading glasses. Once I had them on, I hesitated at a follow-up question concerning my recent foreign travel.

Did you have any close or continuing contact with a foreign national with whom you have, or had, ties of affection, loyalty, obligation, or financial ties? No.

Since my response to that question was negative, the "ties to a foreign national" dropdown box didn't open for follow-up. I moved to the next section without giving it any further thought.

I disclosed my Lexapro and Xanax prescriptions from the time prior to the attack. Fortunately, I was not required to disclose details about our marriage counseling back then. Any counseling or medications as a result of the attack were also not required to be explained in detail because it fell under the PTSD category—Post Traumatic Stress Disorder—and no, the government does not want to open that can of worms. Besides, dealing with my PTSD by chanting and burning incense would revive all the rumors about me being a hippie.

Sunday night before the first day back on the job, I pulled my work clothes out from the back of my closet and spread them across the bed. The oversized white shirts, black skirts, and matching blazers laid out looked like wide, two-dimensional versions of my former self. Overwhelmed, I ran into the kitchen, grabbed a trash bag, and shoved all the clothes, still on hangers, in it. There had to be better choices in my closet that would, number one: fit, and number two: have more ease in their style. It came down to a pair of navy cargo pants, ballet flats, and a three-quarter-length sleeve cream-colored tunic.

I woke up before my alarm and went for a run on the beach. The salty moisture lingered on my face, reassuring me that I was connected to my new home. The gritty sand exfoliated my lips when I rubbed them together. Back inside, I slid into my unmade bed and vibrated myself to three, no four, orgasms with the safe fantasy of a braless Scarlett playing on a loop in my head. With every bit of nervous energy wrung out, I got dressed in my updated, albeit "Casual Friday," work clothes. This new look sealed my decision to never go back to the way I was when I fit into those bulky suits.

My vehicle was chosen for a random inspection at the guard gate, so I pulled over and popped my trunk. From several feet back, I watched as the guard thoroughly checked my car with a mirror under the carriage and then a flashlight for the interior. I knew better than to hover. There were numerous occasions I'd driven past an inspection area while people were losing their shit during a random search. It never ends well.

Once in the main entrance of Dani's building, I signed in on the visitor's log. Using my professional voice, I stated, "Lauren St. Germain for Dani Bragg.

She's expecting me." I didn't bother to look up at the guard as I wrote down the "in time" in military format.

The guard inspected her daily roster and then issued me a yellow visitor badge with ESCORT REQUIRED printed boldly in red across it.

The badge flapped over stupidly from the inner fold of my top. I didn't think about the lack of a lapel last night.

Dani greeted me with an awkward side hug and smirked at my badge. "Come on back, let's get you out of visitor status."

This was the first time we've seen each other since she limped out of the Special Committee Inquiry, where we had both been broken. We made no mention of it. Instead, she jumped right in to rattle on about how the updated OPM handbook would no longer be issued as a hard copy, only in an interactive format, which was already preinstalled on my new laptop.

"You can have your pick of locations to zone in on," she told me as we sat down in her impressive new office. "Obviously, we want to get back your OPM,[4] CBP,[5] and

[4] Office of Personnel Management
[5] Customs and Border Patrol

Holmes[6] creds. Our ICE[7] contact already denied you for any work with them, though. Where are you living?"

"Malibu, the southern tip."

"Well, that's awfully nice." She spun a list around on her desk. There were three even rows of cases printed on it, highlighted in green, yellow, and blue to designate their territories. "We can shoot you down to Inglewood and Hawthorne, those are blue and green. There's mostly contractors down there. Yellow is Thousand Oaks, hmm, that might be a better location for you. Oh, and I'll need you to work Port Hueneme."

"I really don't care. Where do you need the most help?"

She reached over and plucked the list from my hands. "If you're not opposed to traveling right away, I need someone who can go up to Modesto for CBP." She fetched another packet from her top drawer and slid it across the smooth, lemon waxed, oak desk with a flick of her wrist. "My team down here is on rotation, but only a few have CBP creds, so they're turning around to go back right after they come home." She looked at me with anticipation. She knew no one relocated here with me.

"Sure," I answered absently. "I don't mind moving around on detail for you."

---

[6] Code name for a classified contract
[7] Immigrations and Customs Enforcement

"I have your OPM creds here and can release them to you once we finish up today, but CPB will take a little longer. I'll assign you down near LAX for now, and by the time you clear that backlog, we'll have your CBP creds back."

"Then I would go up there, to Modesto?"

She gave me a curt nod. "Would six weeks be too long? I can authorize a flight home on one of the weekends."

"That should be fine. I don't have pets or anything." Once again, the magic words.

Dani commenced with a multitude of releases for me to sign. They would be turned over to an investigator much like myself so that he or she could take them to any person I've been involved with for the past ten years in order to obtain information about me.

Privacy Act of 1974. *Done.*

Proper handling of classified information paperwork. *Done.*

Briefing terms and specific requirements for my work computer. *Done.*

Future intent to disclose any adjudicating issues that may occur after this date. *Done.*

Foreign travel briefing. *Done.*

Polygraph. *Done.*

I could cite these papers inside and out as well as their utter lack of limitations. I've had to do it hundreds of times to anxious individuals being investigated for their clearances. Those people are referred to as "Subjects," and now I was one.

After a long first day of tedious and redundant questioning, I exited the building no longer a VISITOR. Be it Pamela's exorcism of my bad luck or Dani's understaffing issues, I once again held a Top Secret level clearance. My OPM creds and CAC card both retained the same washed-out photos taken five years ago in El Paso.

Later that evening, my VPN[8] was up and running to provide access to my assigned cases in my home office. The sun was setting outside, streaking the sky with vibrant pink, orange, and silvery shimmers outlining fat fluffy clouds. I glanced out my window briefly, and rather than getting lost in it as I've been doing for months now, I snapped the curtains shut. The blinking, green cursor glowed brighter on the screen in the darkened room.

The workload was an ambitious list. Dani must have remembered my old numbers in order to forecast this heavy of a workload. As I prioritized my week, I mused what it would have been like for the girl smiling with her

---

[8] Virtual Private Network

lips pressed together on those credentials if she knew she would have ended up here. It was time to move forward. I dropped my creds in my purse so I wasn't tempted to study my former self any further.

c h a p t e r s i x t e e n

STARTING OVER

June 15, 2009
Malibu, CA

After proving myself valuable, I was assigned that six-week TDY[9] up north a mere month after coming back to work as a federal background investigator. I schlepped all my stuff to Modesto, CA and enjoyed the simplicity of staying in an efficiency while focusing on work. Background investigations needed to be performed on the mass of new hires for CBP. It was imperative they had their security clearances before they graduated training. I closed all those cases in five weeks.

---

[9] Temporary Duty (working a location outside of home territory)

Upon returning to my empty condo daily, I'd pour all my lonely feelings into frantic exercise, when I wasn't hunched over my laptop, that is. Then, six weeks in, another sizable stack of cases was sent my way to keep me down near LAX for the next couple weeks working "contractor row." Federal contractors either needed initial security clearances or updates to their existing ones.

One case began to straggle behind. Daniel Martinez was an engineer employed by Aerospace who traveled frequently, and we'd been playing phone tag for the last two weeks trying to set up his interview. On Wednesday he called to reschedule, again.

"I'm sorry, but can we do this when I get back next week?" Mr. Martinez was polite, but I needed him to move our interview to the top of his priorities.

"I can come to you tomorrow. I need to close your case by Friday."

"Well," he stalled, "I have a meeting in the afternoon that I need to prep for in the morning. It's really not an ideal day."

"You could prep for it tonight," I suggested, my patience waning.

The next morning, feeling exceptionally good, I powered through my usual workout on the beach at the crack of dawn. My cheery mood could have been from the exercise endorphins or from closing so many cases recently, but whatever the reason, I'd take it. I was inspired to take a little extra time on my appearance with some makeup and a pair of black heels. Pulled together with a new pair of slim black pants and a grey fitted jacket, I lightly bounced out the door.

Today was my first visit to Aerospace Headquarters since I had come here TDY from El Paso four years ago. The guard recognized me.

"If you don't mind me asking, what are you doing out here? Aren't you from Fort Bliss?" he queried while waiting for my printable badge to appear on his screen.

"I wanted a fresh start."

"I'm kind of surprised they let you be an investigator again?" he half-asked before showing me the image of my Aerospace badge from his screen. "This you? Looks like you're still in our system."

"Can I get a new picture?"

"All right, go stand in front of that beige wall." He waved me over to get the shot. It took a few minutes for him to upload and print the badge before he sent me on my way. "Fresh starts and all, ma'am."

The interview with Mr. Martinez went smoothly. At the end, I reminded him that I still needed to speak to his boss.

"Eric Merski," Mr. Martinez said, "he's the project manager. He should be in his office now. I'm sorry, I forgot to let him know you were coming today. He's usually pretty busy, but he might be able to do it."

"Just walk me over to his office and we can ask him. It won't take more than ten minutes." There was no way I was driving all the way back down here tomorrow to interview his boss.

Mr. Merski's assistant wasn't at her desk and Mr. Martinez hesitated.

"I'll knock on the door for you. Don't worry, you can blame me," I said when he blanched.

Mr. Martinez scurried up next to me as a voice called out, "What? Come in!"

Mr. Martinez poked his head in the door. "The investigator lady is here and needs to talk to you."

From inside the office I heard, "This for your clearance, Dan?" Then the tone turned amused. "I'm going to tell her all your secrets, those crazy trips to Mexico. You better dust off that resume, amigo!"

I shouldered past Mr. Martinez to step into the office. "Hi," I said, catching Mr. Merski off guard. "It'll be quick, I promise." These bosses knew they had to grant interviews for their subordinates or it would hold up the clearance process. They just made such a big deal about having their precious time wasted. Like it's so much more important than mine.

"I didn't realize you were standing out there waiting." Mr. Merski's eyes dilated as he looked me up and down. "Come in, have a seat." He was all charm now.

I turned to Mr. Martinez. "If I need anything further from you, I'll call you, but I think we got everything today." I shook Mr. Martinez's hand with a polite but firm dismissal. "Close the door on your way out."

I had no qualms about making this request in someone else's domain, as it was a requirement for all interviews. Instantly noting Mr. Merski's surprising youth and attractive face, I fumbled my notebook open. As I pulled out my creds, I felt my face flush from the gaze of his clear, blue eyes.

"Lauren," I introduced myself as I flipped over my creds. "Special Investigator retained by OPM."

He didn't bother to look at my identification. "Eric."

We sat down at the meeting table in the alcove of his office. I've always liked conducting interviews in offices containing a second table for group meetings. There was something about the power of the person inhabiting the office that bled over into my psyche.

I filled up the odd moment of silence with the Privacy Act of 1974 before pushing forward through all the questions. The script of the questions let my brain relax, since I could spit them out in my sleep. Without thinking, I tilted my head to one side and twirled a lock of hair, as he responded to the misuse of information technology question. His answer was a brief no, but I was transfixed and didn't write the "N" down on my paper right away. I stumbled over the next question, realizing the pace had gone off track for the interview.

"Have we met before?" Eric asked when the interview concluded. "You look very familiar to me."

"I don't think so." A few drips of sweat streaked down my ribs from under my boobs.

"I've met all the investigators who come through here and I would have remembered you."

"The last time I was here was four years ago, to Aerospace anyway, uh, that was on TDY. I live here now, but most of my cases by the airport are over at Northrup Grumman."

"Where did you move from? If you don't mind me asking."

"Oh, no, not at all, I moved here from El Paso."

Like most people, his face scrunched up a little at that answer. "Military?"

"No."

There was a knock on the office door and a look of resignation flashed across his face. "It was nice to meet you, Lauren."

"You, too."

He stood up and I followed suit to leave, slowing my gait to allow him to open the door for me. On cue, he did, but a female cut between us and dropped a legal pad and Diet Coke down on the conference table.

"The budgets, Eric…" she groaned.

"I'll be back in a minute, I have to escort Investigator, uh, Lauren here, back down to the guard desk."

I didn't correct him; he knew my badge said "No Escort Required." Once at the elevator, I pushed the down arrow and turned to face him. "I can go from here. I don't need an escort."

"I know, but I figured since you were new to the area, you haven't tried The Fish Market."

"I have not."

"How about tomorrow then?"

"Where is it?"

"You're the investigator, you figure that out," he flirted.

"So you like holding out on information?" I gave it right back.

The elevator door opened and I stepped halfway in to keep the door from closing.

"What time should I show up at this unknown location?"

"Seven."

"See you there." I stepped all the way in and pushed the button for ground level. He stood there watching me disappear between the silver curtains. Perfect timing, it must have been my extra mojo today.

The silky material of my white shirt clinging to my sweaty midriff was proof enough that I was more than a little excited at the prospect of commanding some flirty attention, a date even, from such a good-looking, confident man. He did seem like a bit of a player; after all, who asks a woman out like that? Tempting as it was to stop right outside the entrance doors and pull up The Fish Market on my phone, I didn't. I felt unreasonably paranoid he'd see me out his window. Nothing but the buzz of some swirling bees and the hum of the panning security cameras escorted me to my car. Before pulling out of the parking lot, I blasted the A/C directly onto my chest and checked my phone for directions to The Fish Market.

chapter seventeen

SUSTAINABLE DATES

The Fish Market is an established, old-school kind of place that serves fresh-caught, never farmed seafood. Their real claim to fame lies in their anchovy-infused Bloody Marys. Their website highlighted a wrap-around deck overlooking the ocean for a romantic view of the sunset.

It's been so many years since I've been in the dating game that I didn't know how much effort to put into getting ready for it. This was one of the times I wished I could call my sister-in-law for advice. She married recently, but I wasn't invited. When she was single, she used to entertain Collin and me with stories about all her colorful dates, no doubt a result of her exuberant confidence. I wanted to drop her a congratulatory note, but it might not be a welcome gesture. I sighed and made a mental note to focus on making some girlfriends.

Thursday, a.k.a Date Day, was an extremely annoying day. Traffic was especially slow, causing me to be late for two interviews. My first person didn't care since I came to her office. But, my second one was a complete prick about it. My clickety clack heels beat out a fast rhythm across the marble floor in the reception area of Northrup's west campus as I tried not to approach my Source in a breathless sprint.

His head was bent over his phone as I slowed to a moderate hustle a few feet from him. It was obvious he was trying to act like he didn't hear my clamor across the lobby. I pulled myself back from collapsing on the couch next to him and apologized right off the bat. He gripped onto my tardiness as a springboard to complain about the security clearance process in general.

I neutrally nodded and broke into his dissertation with, "Just another question please. I know we already went over the 2014 security violation, but do you happen to recall the year of the other one? Or, are you still referencing him bringing his cell phone into the SCIF[10]?" This Source ended up blabbing away for a little over a half an hour.

---

[10] Sensitive Compartmental Information Facility

Once disentangled from a rant that resulted in little pertinent information, it was time to go home and get ready for my date.

Deciding what to wear was a challenge. Again, longing for a girlfriend, I wanted guidance on how to look effortless. Everything was either too formfitting or too baggy. I finally settled on a pair of dark wash boot-cut jeans. They were the most current style with a few seemingly unintended scrapes resulting in white threads breaking up the deep indigo. I cut the tags off a soft, white T-shirt that skimmed my narrow waist and pulled on an oversized cardigan in hopes that we would sit outside.

Eric was waiting outside the entrance. Before I could get in a "Hi," he opened the door for me and said, "I knew you would come."

Our table was situated in the corner of the outside deck, setting the stage for our date with a picturesque sunset view. After the waitress left us with menus, Eric leaned over the table and confided, "I should disclose that I wanted to ask you out the moment you walked into my office. The best restraint I could manage was forcing myself to wait 'til the end of the interview."

"Well, that's a first," I said in a friendly tone, "at least that I know of."

We started with a couple Bloody Marys and ordered a smorgasbord of food to share. Our conversation was easy, flirtatious, and remained on the surface. There was plenty of opportunity to study his looks. He had a broad, German face and thick, blond hair that was borderline shaggy, but neat enough to be professional. His blue eyes were clear and piercing. They read as cold or amused, but not warm, even when he was being friendly. He was tall enough for me to wear heels and appeared to work out regularly. His arms had thick, large biceps, which pushed into his sleeves when they involuntarily flexed. When they relaxed back, there was a minuscule gap between his arm and shirt sleeve.

As he told me about his job, I caught myself comparing him to James. Both were classically handsome with obvious traits of European ancestry. Darker in appearance than Eric, James had olive-toned skin topped with dark hair. Eric's face was round and direct, whereas James had a long face and deep, hazel eyes that studied the inside of the person upon whom his gaze fell.

Eric started talking about the Padres, while I wondered about his hair. Was it soft? I imagined how it might feel to run my fingers through it, pulling it. I guessed his chest was bare, waxed? Perhaps.... He seemed into his appearance.

The alcohol hit my bloodstream, allowing a loose head tilt followed by an absent fingering of my earrings.

There was finally a lull in the conversation and I sat back, feeling a little stuffed, but so relaxed that I slid my feet out from my shoes under the table.

Eric placed his napkin over his plate. "Coffee?"

"No."

He set a long unbroken gaze upon me before switching gears. "I was trying to figure out why you looked so familiar and it wasn't 'til after you left that I got it. You're married to that contractor from the Fort Bliss IED Attack." He paused just long enough for me to nod slightly. "I remember that story. That was true heroism he displayed. But you were involved as well, weren't you at the scene when the explosion happened?"

"Yes."

"What happened there? If you don't mind me asking."

My feet slipped back into my shoes as I sat up straight. "It basically went down how they reported it. I did Burak Yilmaz's background investigation for his TS, you know, Top Secret clearance, a few months prior to the attack. The investigation I turned in fell short of OPM's standards. In other words, I missed critical information that may have indicated he was the leader of a sleeper cell. I didn't go after the right Sources who could have exposed him as a double agent. In the end, I was the official scapegoat."

Eric sat back deciphering what I told him, trying to calculate which parts of my response were prepared statement content. "What about the morning of the attack? They said you had second thoughts and went to warn your husband."

"Collin just left his CAC card at home and I dropped it off. When the IED blew, I felt this rattling in my ribcage before I was knocked off my feet. At first, I thought my jaw was dislocated, like if I had been punched, but it was just the impact slamming me down to the ground. My right eardrum burst, and I was hit with a smattering of nails and shrapnel—it embedded into the left side of my torso, right through my clothes. I certainly have the scars to prove it. I was literally knocked out of my shoes, which was good, because one of them landed three feet away from me, completely incinerated." I paused and pulled the silver elephant charm out from under my neckline. "I haven't taken this off since that day. Ganesh, he's my lucky charm. Anyway, it's a nasty business, those IEDs. Really nasty and dirty. It was actually Angel who pulled me away, not Collin; the news reporters always got that part of the story wrong."

A seagull swooped down on the beach in front of our table.

"Collin, my husband."

The flapping of the seagull's wings as it flew away kept Eric from responding.

"They took me to Beaumont, the VA hospital, for surgery. A lot of skin grafting, but eventually I healed and 'survived.' In the movies they always show people going through these massive explosions and then they just continue on, saving the world, rescuing the girl, like it was nothing. Truth be told, you really can't hear anything for days."

We both looked toward the ocean.

"He lost a leg," I finally confessed with regret.

The words came out so easily…had I really said them out loud? Cutting-edge prosthetics used for soldiers after IED-related injuries had been highly improved; however, the physical therapy during recovery was grueling and slow. It's the type of scenario that breaks apart families…marriages…bank accounts.

People salivate for the gory details of the metallic blood simmering into the storyline of dramatic events. They're never interested in the rehabilitation, the severed relationships, or the embarrassing trips to the supermarket afterward. The sensationalism of the national tragedy resulting in one patriotic hero and one scorned adulteress was fodder for the tabloids.

Blinking back to Eric's face, I was relieved he wasn't wearing the sappy, sympathetic look I had grown to despise. Nor did he look away, not knowing what to say.

Something about his willingness to listen without pity put me at ease.

My hand slid up my neck and I pulled my fingers back slowly to rest on my collarbone with just enough sensuality to rouse his interest.

The desire to ask for more erupted on his face. Consciously or not, he extinguished it and took the bait of my exposed neck. His craving for the details had been momentarily tempered with a whiff of fleshy sex being rubbed delicately by perfectly manicured fingertips.

"I'm sorry, this isn't really great first date stuff." I gave him a weak smile.

His eyes narrowed as they penetrated the edge of my neck. It was so punctuated it sent a pulse shooting down between my legs.

But then he responded in the most rehearsed way possible. "Is that what this is then? A date?"

Thankfully, the server came over to drop the check.

Eric picked it up without looking at it and set a pile of cash under it…very smooth.

He kept an arm around my waist as he guided me to my car in the poorly lit parking lot. I leaned back against my car with anticipation as he closed in to kiss my cheek. He didn't break contact with my face as he moved his mouth from my cheek to my lips. His lips were baby smooth.

I parted mine in an invitation just as he abruptly pulled away.

As I recovered from my moment of embarrassment, he offered up, "I have tickets for the Dodgers game Sunday. Why don't you come with me?"

Sunday? My brain had to calculate what I had going on. "I have brunch plans with my friends that day."

"I could meet you there and we can go to the game together."

NO instantly flashed in my head. Tyler and Thom would eat Eric alive; he'd never come back. "It's a girl thing." Basically true.

He clasped the top of my shoulder with his hand and inched in as he pulled me forward. "All right, when do you want to go?"

"Dinner on Saturday," I chirped. I instantly regretted it when his grip released in an *oh shit, she wants to be serious* movement.

Like a pro, he rearranged his face. "Sure, how about eight at Old Mill?"

"Sounds like a plan." At that point, the desperation fence was diminishing under me. It was time to go.

"Goodnight," he declared and waited until I put on my seatbelt before closing the door.

"Um, goodnight," I stammered. He threw me off kilter and I glanced in my rearview mirror before pulling out of the parking lot just in time to catch him checking his phone while he sauntered over to his truck.

chapter eighteen

DRUNK DIAL

Prepaying online for an early Sunday advanced hot vinyasa flow class kept my eating and drinking in check during the Saturday night date with Eric. After the torturous class, I showered at the studio and donned my most fashionable post-yoga garb.

Tyler chose the trendiest of trendy garden restaurants for Sunday brunch near Boy's Town. It was always busy, especially at eleven on a Sunday morning when most of the patrons hadn't been home from the night before.

Tyler, Thom, and another friend, Aimee, had been waiting in the lobby almost forty-five minutes when I waltzed in.

Openly annoyed, Thom greeted me with, "If you would have been on time, you could have been waiting like the rest of us instead of strutting in all breezy, your highness."

"I was at yoga—hot—be happy I took the time to shower," I snapped in a playful manner, immune to his bitchiness.

Aimee knew Thom before he even met Tyler, so they huddled away on one side of the booth, Tyler and me at the other. Once the mimosas were topped off, we settled into the latest PuraYoga gossip.

Midway through brunch, Tyler asked, "Where were you last night?"

"I had dinner at Old Mill."

"I know, but with whom?"

"Wait, what do you mean, you know?" My fork stopped halfway to my mouth.

Tyler pulled up Facebook on his phone and showed me a picture of a couple taking a selfie at the bar right in front of the table Eric and I were at last night.

I pulled Tyler's hand up to get a better look and fawned, "Ooo, I look pretty good."

Tyler maximized the image and the scrutiny began. "You looked okay."

"Why couldn't you just ask me if I had a date last night instead of being all stealth and pulling it up on Facebook?"

"Why were you so late this morning?"

"Yoga!"

We both erupted in a fit of laughter.

"No, for real," I insisted as I wiped my eyes. "But, yes, I was on a date last night that ended promptly at midnight with my panties intact. One of my Subject's bosses asked me out to dinner last week. This was our second date."

"Really?" Tyler leaned in. "Well, this seems promising. What's he like?"

"He's…." I had to give this some thought; it was Tyler I was dealing with here. "He's a little cocky and very cute, even though it's in a Hitler Youth kind of way. He has the perfect surfer blond hair and he's in great shape, CrossFit, I'm sure."

Tyler rolled his eyes.

I ignored it. "He knew who I was and wasn't afraid to be seen in public with me. That says something, doesn't it?"

Tyler opened his mouth to comment when Thom shoved his phone in front of Tyler's face. "Oh my God!" Thom was breathless. "Look! It's our boy with Elle Benning. They are so hot together."

It was an *OK Magazine* picture of James Bayer and Elle Benning captioned, "The Reigning Queen of the Big Screen and the Sexiest Superman!"

I faked a cough to cover the stab in my heart. "Most of those stories are just unfounded rumors," I unconvincingly snubbed. It was unreasonable for me to think he wouldn't be off dating or fucking other women. Of course he wouldn't be carrying a secret torch for me with the intent of celibacy until we magically met again. *Still....*

"Let me see that." Tyler maximized the image with his long, graceful fingers. James's deep, hazel eyes penetrated the camera over his shoulder while he curled his arm protectively around Elle.

"Matt alluded to him being involved with a big name. I don't remember how he put it, but there definitely was someone even before the ship," Thom informed us.

Internally, I was trying to pull my shit together and I must not have been doing a good job because Tyler joked, "What's wrong, Lauren? Little jealous, are we?"

Thank God Thom turned to get the waiter's attention instead of witnessing the pleading look I shot Tyler.

Sensing something was wrong, Tyler locked the screen and placed the phone face down on the table. "That reminds me," Tyler began, "our contract was extended to take on a few more days to work with the extras on set for *The Purpose*. They need to capture the final yoga studio shots for the film and apparently, our presence was deemed crucial. Can you work it?"

"When?"

"In about six weeks. I'm hammering out the addendum tonight. I was thinking I could subcontract you in the same way as before since they all liked working with you so much."

Thom pretended not to eavesdrop while keeping his face toward Aimee.

"Sure." It was absolutely not thought out on my part and definitely an emotionally-based decision. "I have some personal days that rolled over from before."

Another round of mimosas arrived and we carried on, gushing at Thom's graphic details surrounding the unraveling of their yogic lifestyles at the club last night.

Tyler and I lightly touched on the subject of Eric again. For some reason I had not yet placed, I kept my descriptions of Eric broad and generic. Tyler seemed pleased that I was dating (something he has been trying to get me to do for the past six months). "Quit carrying the torch, Lauren," he had insisted, but he was still sniffing around for what bothered me about that picture of James and Elle. Even though I really wanted to confide in Tyler, I didn't give in. I was too scared to risk exposure.

By the time I got in the car, I had two texts from Eric.

Eric: *Still wish u ditched ur friends & came w/me, u would look cute in a ball cap ;-)*
6/07/2009, 12:01 p.m.

Eric: *Not a stalker☺ but why no text back☹*
06/07/2009, 1:20 p.m.

I was stumped on how to respond. Our date went really well last night and I didn't want to mess it up with a misinterpreted text.

Lauren: *Phone was off during brunch, just seeing this now* (delete)

I tried again.

Lauren: *We all keep our phones turned over in the corner of the table and whoever looks at theirs first has to pick up the tab* (delete)

That seemed like an even worse response.

Lauren: *I was at brunch, done now…what r u up to?* (delete)

Even though it was better than the others, it still didn't sit right with me.

By the time I got home, it was already three o'clock, so I just called him instead. He sounded a few drinks deep.

"You don't call, you don't write...." He tried to come off as if he were kidding by speaking in a rapid-fire Groucho Marx voice. I could imagine him tapping a cigar on the other end but there was an unmistakable sliver of resentment in his tone.

"I just got home." It took an effort not to sound defensive.

"You don't text...." He tried to keep up the joke.

"I thought I'd just call you back. How was the game?"

He backed off and rambled about the game, losing his train of thought a few times before he got to the point and suggested I come meet him for a drink.

"I can't, I have a report due tomorrow that I haven't even started. Sorry, I would if I could." It all came out so fast that I was certain he'd be able to tell it was bullshit.

"Come on...." Eric was still trying to keep it light, but it was drilling. "Fuck that report, can't you get an extension or something? I was really hoping to see you today, doll." It reeked of booty call.

"How about lunch this week?"

"Lunch?" he groaned. "Okay, lunch, what day?"

"Hold on a sec, I need to look at my calendar." I scrolled through the upcoming week. "I'll be over your way on Tuesday. Are you free?"

"Yeah, how 'bout some sushi? Noon?"

"Where should I meet you?"

"There's an Iron Chef over there on Hacienda, do you know it?"

"I can find it." I didn't want to be too abrupt and stalled with a question. "So, who won the game?"

He laughed with the assumption that I wouldn't even know who was playing before he answered, "Good, hon, good. There was this really weird janitor there, total raghead, uh sorry, Muslim, who thought he might fuck with me, though."

"Really? That's kind of odd," I replied as I walked over to my bedroom window to watch the sun make its way down to the horizon.

"He was standing way too close when I was taking a piss and I told him to back off. He had this blank look on his face, so of course I took a moment to really check him out on my way back to my seat. You never know, these kinds could have a suicide vest on in a crowded stadium...." Eric trailed off, not as dismissive about the whole incident as he was initially. "I guess you do know, sorry, I probably shouldn't have brought it up."

"It's okay." I couldn't help it; I could only picture Yilmaz's face wearing that janitor uniform. "Did you report it?"

"Naw, he was skinny as a rail. No way he had a weapon or a vest. I did see him again, though, in the parking lot looking all stoned or something. He wasn't

close enough to touch my truck, but I had this, this,"
Eric struggled for the right word. "This *feeling,* this prem-
onition, that he was gonna mess with my truck. God, I
sound like one of those New Ager's!"

He laughed it off, but a chill went down my spine.

"I'm sure it was nothing." My voice cracked as I said
it. Swirling green lights of the Aurora Borealis popped
into my mind. "Did he look like he had red eyes?"

"Yeah, Lauren, like fucking laser beams shooting out
of them. What kind of question is that? He was just
stoned or retarded maybe. You're funny, hon."

"Hmm," I hummed and joined in on his amusement
with a slight chuckle. "Well, you never know, Eric, there
could be demons following us all. Right now, mine is in
the form of this report. I really have to get on it. See you
Tuesday then?"

"Text me later, send me a pic." His tone went mischievous.

"Okay, later, bye."

My own buzz was waning into a headache, so I
opened a bottle of wine and made popcorn. As I twisted
the corkscrew, my eyes closed, desperately seeking an
image of James that I had put on lockdown somewhere
in the depths of my memory. The only image that appeared was the one that had slapped me earlier in the
day. I brought the whole bottle and the oversized bowl
of popcorn to the living room. The remote was slippery

in my hands, but I still managed to find *Alien Abduction: Forbidden Secrets* on Netflix.

By 9:00 p.m., I was tanked and could fast forward to every scene with James like a pro. The urge to connect with him came over me like an addict craves heroin and his card called softly from the bottom of my drawer. After a brief, and probably very annoying, conversation with a Verizon rep, I obtained international service.

The ring was foreign and clipped before going straight to voicemail. His smooth British accent flowed into my ear. "This is James, leave a message and I'll call you back. Enjoy the day."

"Hi, it's me, Lauren, I was just thinking of you. I hope you're well. I would love to hear you, from you. Okay, bye." I dropped my phone on the floor and fell into a fitful wine sleep. I woke with a start at three in the morning, profusely sweating and tightly wound with anxiety. I shouldn't have called him. I didn't know if Matt checks his messages, or worse, if Elle did. My greatest fear was that he checks his own messages and would delete it without a second thought. I pulled a Xanax out, broke it in half, and left the other half on my nightstand.

The bottle of wine and popcorn charged a hefty price. No jumping out of bed to make coffee and work out. In fact, no movement for the first twenty minutes after waking until the urgency to pee won. The second half of my Xanax went down with a sip of water. Then there was the phone; an assault of beeping notification messages hammered regret into my already pounding head.

They screeched, "Hi, Lauren! You have an international calling plan! Bienvenida!"

I switched the volume to silent. The recollection of my night stirred in just the right amount of shame and humiliation with my headache to banish me deep under my covers for another hour.

As with any hangover, it eventually passed. By late afternoon, I was typing up reports and making calls to set up my week. Five o'clock came and I wondered about Eric, who was probably leaving work, his own hangover gone too.

I snapped a cute selfie with my shoulder exposed so he wouldn't know if I had a top on or not and texted it to him.

chapter nineteen

DRESS SHOPPING

Six Weeks Later

Eric and I fell into a routine formed around our work schedules, consisting of lunch in the beginning of the week and dinner or happy hour on Thursdays. We spent most weekends together and even went to see fireworks on the Fourth. After a week of getting to know each other better, then a week of me on my period, we moved past second base and had sex. The first time was after several cocktails and when it was over, I figured the next time would be better.

At the end of summer, Eric was included in a formal senior staff event to take place in Santa Barbara, so he asked me to go with him and make a weekend of it. I thought it would be the perfect opportunity to focus on each other without distractions, and maybe establish a more gratifying physical connection. If we just slowed down from our busy schedules, away in a romantic spot for a few days, I felt confident we could get to that place of *(like the ship)* bliss with each other. Maybe I could even get him to go to a yoga class at the resort.

"I'm curious why you haven't brought your man around again?" Tyler broached lightly while we were flipping through a clearance rack at Nordstrom's.

I pulled out a short little black dress with a scoop neck and cap sleeves to hold up for Tyler's inspection.

He barely looked up. "No, you are not in mourning and you're not in your forties, put it back."

"That party wasn't his scene. He had fun and all, but he's more into the sports bars. We'll come around again. I don't think he's ready to hit up the gay bars, though."

"Collin adjusted."

"And that turned out so well?"

We stared each other down for a couple of seconds over the crowded rack.

Tyler conceded. "Sorry, hon, sometimes his name just slips out. You guys were together for so long. All I'm saying is I want to get to know Eric better, especially if you get serious. I don't know, Lauren, there's no one looking out for you here like Collin did when you lived in El Paso. I kind of feel like I should, you know," he said with a smirk, "batter up to the plate."

"Thanks, D," I said in sincerity. "He's just into his friends and likes going to places he knows. He's a creature of habit. I didn't realize how much I liked that about him until I just said that, actually." I pulled out a cream dress.

Tyler shook his head.

"Why don't the four of us go out to dinner when we get back from Santa Barbara?"

"No, we're good, better than usual really, and we want to go out with you guys as a couple. But not 'til after shooting. We'll be due on set every day at 5:45 a.m. Thom wants to take the reins that week. I think it's best, don't you?"

"He did such a great job on the ship and everyone loves working with him. I think it's a great idea."

Tyler pulled out a soft mermaid dress that had a shimmery gold overlay. There it was: my new dress to go out with my new man.

Later that week, Tyler messengered over my contract to work on set for the final takes of *The Purpose*. My title was finally decided upon—Yoga Aesthetic Consultant. I was expected to be on set down in LA for five days during the beginning of September. A lot of fancy verbiage about my responsibilities was written into it, but basically the job was to babysit extras. Lastly, Thom emailed me a list of all the potential sequences and poses they might use for the sweeping class shots. There were 106 bullet points in his email.

chapter twenty

WEEKEND GETAWAY TO
SANTA BARBARA

I still hadn't told Eric about the following week's filming…yet. I was hanging onto the "yet" part as a bullshit
lie to myself. I rehearsed about a half-dozen scenarios I
could use to avoid him all next week. He knew I went on
a cruise to Canada recently; the specifics were murky and
since he didn't ask for any details, I didn't offer.

Lately, we slept over at his place most nights so he
could beat rush hour. My condo was a little too disor-
ganized for him. The last time he stayed over after a
booze-filled evening, he was late to work the next day. I
sensed there was something else about my space that
made him uncomfortable. Last night, I stayed in my
condo alone. As I waited for him to pick me up, I un-
loaded the dishwasher.

Eric's good looks were sun-kissed by windblown hair as he strolled into the kitchen, bringing the sunlight in behind him. Usually he wore some form of a suit, but not today. A fitted, broken-in denim shirt hugged his muscular chest and was left untucked. The pearl snaps were undone almost halfway down to show off his smooth, buff chest. He must have bought a stylish new pair of Oakley's as well, because I'd never seen him in mirrored aviators before today.

I was starting to look forward to our weekend getaway even more. My exaggerated hip swing brought me over to greet him and I curled my body around his.

He reached around to pull my bottom close into his pelvis. "Well, hello to you too," he growled in my ear.

He released me to finish the dishes and sat down on the bar stool so he could keep me company without being in the way. He pushed a stack of mail to the side. Eric always liked a clear surface in front of him.

"How's your day been?" I asked.

"Same old, I was able to get out of there before Dan could track me down with the financials for next quarter. I can get to that shit Monday." There was a shuffling of papers that ended with the unmistakable sound of a thick piece of paper being pulled from an envelope. "What's this?" he asked while inspecting the large, gold-sealed invitation.

I resisted the urge to snatch it out of his hands. "It's for a Wounded Warrior fundraiser back at Fort Bliss. I'm not going."

"It would help raise money for wounded soldiers. Why wouldn't you go?" He paused for a breath and his agenda surfaced. "We could go together."

"Even if I went, it would be really inappropriate for me to bring a date." I shut the empty dishwasher.

He changed his approach and came around the counter to take me in his arms. "Listen, doll, I wouldn't let anyone there get near you, and why would they? You were exonerated and they invited you." He pulled my head into his shoulder; the forced comfort was so transparent on him. "What do you say? At least think about it?"

"I'll think about it."

I flipped off the kitchen light with a huff that went unnoticed, as he was engrossed with the calendar on his phone.

The hotel and grounds for Eric's work event were spectacular. It was an over-the-top weekend for the upper tier of management and executives at Aerospace. Throngs of wealthy men and their spouses flocked from the West Coast to indulge in a decadent soirée on the company's dime. Eric had been pining to attend this annual event for the past four years. He led the top performing team in his region. As we checked in at the lobby with giant, gilded mirrors overlooking the crowd, Eric waved to his colleagues. His confidence excelled as that small seed of insecurity buried inside him seemingly vanished.

Our west-facing room had a top-of-the-line king bed made up with creamy ivory linens and a remote view of the ocean from the balcony. I stretched my arms high over my head and inhaled deeply. The soapy scent of blooming hydrangeas shifted my focus away from our exchange back at the condo and toward the carnal desires that sprang up from standing outside barefoot. I drew the sheer curtains for privacy and allowed one of the see-through panels to slither over my skin as I reentered the room.

While Eric was washing up, I opened the bottle of champagne and peeled my clothes off. The warm cotton sliding on my skin as I sprawled across the bed initiated a growing wetness between my legs.

"Well aren't you a sight?" came from the bathroom door.

I crooked my right pointer finger and motioned for him to come over. I got onto my knees, spread wide, at the foot of the bed. I briskly pulled him toward me and kissed him with an open mouth. I ripped apart the rest of the snaps on his shirt and ran my hands up over his pecs and shoulders. My busy mouth trailed along his neck, further down the middle of his expansive chest, and landed at the top of his flat belly.

Like a praying mantis, I unfolded my legs and dropped down onto the floor in front of him. With a seductive look up, I unbuttoned his jeans.

It began with a flick from the tip of my tongue on the head of his cock. Then I traced my tongue down the underside and back up the shaft before finally taking his whole length in my mouth. I bobbed my head up and down, applying suction here and there. I ensured I satisfied his visual desires by fully arching my back so he had the view of my long, loose hair hanging halfway down my back. My round ass poked out from under me. His panting was so primal; I moaned in desire from the sound of it.

In no time, he was bucking in sync with my head dips and his hands grasped my hair. I brought him to the edge and felt the vein on the underside of his cock pump and then release cum right into my mouth. I sucked as hard as I could to increase his orgasm, then swallowed quickly and neatly.

"Fucking-A!" he exclaimed and collapsed onto the bed, lying back with his arms spread. "You give the best head, Jesus."

I downed my glass of champagne.

"That was incredible. I've never been able to come just from head," he confessed as we relaxed on the bed, sipping the glistening golden bubbles afterwards. His hand draped lazily on my cheek and he caressed it with tenderness. "You really are beautiful," he told me not only with his mouth, but also with his eyes.

Could I fall in love with him?

"I wanted to make sure you could fully concentrate tonight. It's a big night for you."

He set his glass down and rolled over to kiss me carefully on the lips, making a point to keep his mouth sealed tightly. His lips finally parted as he nibbled on my neck and licked down to the area between my breasts. He lingered, taking one, then the other nipple in his mouth while his hand tweaked the other.

I held my breath in anticipation that he was about to return the favor, but he pulled away and said, "You're the best," with a friendly pat on my thigh.

He glanced past my shoulder to check the time. "I'm going to get in the shower."

I flopped back down on the bed and groaned in frustration. I wished I had brought my vibrator; batteries are never squeamish.

That night, I primped with extra care. This caused him to make a little bit of a show, worrying that we might not make it on time. "We're fine, babe," I tempered him. "All we have to do is take the elevator downstairs." Calling him babe won me an approving smile as he sifted through his toiletries bag.

He held out his hand so I could help him with his cufflinks. Two brushed-silver Superman S's appeared in my palm.

"Those are a limited edition style from the DC comics, the original Superman, and I have number sixteen out of the one hundred made," he boasted.

"I didn't know you were such a big Superman fan."

"The comics, yeah, the original ones. Even the movies they made in the '80s, but not those remake bullshit ones. Especially the one coming out with that British guy…he's such a fag."

At a loss for words, I fastened the cufflinks and abruptly took a step back. "How do I look?"

"Like I don't want to let you out of my sight all night."

A spectacular reflection glittered in the full-length mirror encapsulating our glamourous presence. My hair was pulled up away from my face in a soft French twist. The mermaid dress Tyler chose was constructed of the softest gold material that pleated in all the right places to give my silhouette a cinched waist. It had an elegant sweetheart neckline, no sleeves, but a sheer gold overlay, which draped from the bottoms of my shoulders. A minimal amount of cleavage was revealed. I accessorized conservatively with nude strappy sandals and diamond stud earrings.

Eric stepped up behind me to admire our reflection together as a couple. "See how stunning you look." He caught my earlobe between his teeth as his arms circled my waist. "We should go to these things more often."

The event downstairs was both grand in scale and refined in taste; no detail was left to chance. A tuxedo-clad horn section made it seem as if the whole room was transported back in time by a century. Round, greying men with their conservative wives were joined by a smattering of Indian men and their brightly dressed women.

I didn't offer any information about myself as we worked the room. Everyone in that world knew exactly who I was without an introduction.

Eric and I were assigned to sit at a ten-top round table with his boss, some other lateral directors, and their wives. There was a single woman who was an executive team lead designated to sit next to me. The chair on her other side was empty.

During dinner, Eric frequently laid his hand over mine when he spoke, and I caught the ladies stealing glimpses of my left hand. When the last of the plates were cleared, I excused myself to powder my nose. One of the wives joined me and we leisurely took our time to stretch our legs.

I hadn't made it back to my seat, but could see that everyone at our table was intently listening to Eric. The lady executive was settled in my seat next to him. She leaned in as he spoke, giving him an obvious view of her cleavage.

"...And when the shrapnel hit her, it knocked her out of her shoes! Literally. The blast knocked one of her pumps off and it landed a few feet away from her. She saw what had happened...."

I noisily pulled out an empty chair, causing the lady executive to awkwardly get out of mine, and return to her seat.

He immediately stood up to pull my chair.

All eyes darted sideways.

"Doll," he started in a pleading, low voice, and then continued with more volume. "I hope you don't mind, Lauren, I was just giving them some inside details about the Fort Bliss IED Attack. It's still on everyone's hearts and in their prayers. No one wanted to be rude, of course, and ask you about it."

I sank down and let him help scoot me in.

"It's okay, it's probably for the best since my mascara is not waterproof tonight."

Relief flooded into Eric's face and the table was once more at ease. A collective lean-in occurred.

I pulled Eric out of the hole. "The details of what happened after I was knocked unconscious in the field were briefed to me about forty-eight hours from when I awoke, post-surgery, that is, in the hospital. I don't recall regaining consciousness while still in the field, even though there were a few accounts indicating I screamed out. It's estimated that eighty-four troops would have been killed if the bombs exploded when they were supposed to. Fortunately, the EOD techs, Explosive Ordinance guys, were able to control the rest of the explosions after Angel Rodriguez-Torres called 911. Only one *live* IED was triggered." I sat back on the conclusion of this prepared statement and then capped it off with the almighty, "Thank God." Even though Ganesh gets the thanks in my head.

I've recited this exact phrase so many times before into microphones in front of hundreds of faces and flashing cameras. These words were cauterized into the DNA of my scar tissue. I used to choke up when I would say this, but now I could get through the speech calmly and even ignore the pitiful nods. I had a harder time getting past the other thing I saw, the wanting of more. More details, more tragic conclusions, more Hollywood, and I was not about to pour out the dramatic insider story that Eric was so eager to impress upon his colleagues. I shut that shit down right then and there.

It was late when Eric and I took a silent elevator ride back up to the room. I was tired, irritable, and dying to take off my strappy sandals as well as the gown.

"I didn't mean to put you in an uncomfortable spot. They all recognized you and were curious. It was easier for me to explain it."

"It's not the passing of information that bothers me, but the charge of excitement in everyone's eyes that makes me feel like I'm some kind of side show." I left out that it was *his* excitement that grated on me the most. I sat down heavily in the chair to take off my shoes. "It's okay, it's a tough situation for us both." I stood up flat-footed. "Can you please unzip me?"

He did so without saying anything.

I slipped out of my gown and dropped it over the back of the chair. I rose up on my tiptoes to give him a kiss on the lips and whispered, "I'm really tired. It was such a great night. Now let's get some rest so we can have a good day tomorrow."

He conceded and we washed up separately in the bathroom.

chapter twenty-one

EXTRA FANCY SKYPE FOR FANCY PEOPLE

For the rest of the weekend in Santa Barbara, I drifted along on autopilot as the fiery fighter in me had been drenched by Eric's cold, sea-blue stare. My own mother existed in this state of purgatory for decades with her boyfriend; this dulled Vicodin way of navigating each other was the key to longevity.

Then to my surprise and wanton delight, we consummated Sunday morning with hot, connected sex, and I got ninety percent of the way to an orgasm. The fighter in me reared up and insisted that patience and more work would make it happen.

Afterward, we lounged on the deck with coffee and I saw us from the outside; reclined next to each other together while engrossed in our own separate worlds.

The stray chirp of a bird punctuated the easy silence. I wanted this scene to matter. A simpatico existence with him should fulfill me. I lazily looked over and mused that if we made it a priority to spend all Sunday mornings like this we could….

I lost my train of thought when Eric started aggressively swiping through his phone.

"Everything okay?" I asked.

"Yeah," he answered distractedly. "It's just really inconvenient."

"What?"

"I just found out, it's so last minute, but I was chosen, *finally chosen,* to head the setup in New Zealand after we get back. It's a twenty-one-day mission. I'm so sorry, doll, I didn't want to tell you while we were having such a good time." His eyes looked up from his screen in hopes that I wasn't going to give him a hard time.

"Oh, that is soon. It's okay, but that reminds me, I might be going TDY this month for CBP up near the bay area. I was waiting 'til it was solid before I bothered you with it."

He took this piece of information better than I expected, although it could have been due to the timing. Over the past two months, I had come to realize he liked to be in control of everything. He knew, in theory anyway, travel was required for my job, but he had yet to deal with the reality of it. He appeared surprisingly indifferent.

We were in an unspoken truce of not complaining to the other about our mutual short-notice travel plans the whole way home. Still, I wondered exactly when he knew he was going to New Zealand. Bosses don't usually spring an overseas mission on anyone with only two days to get ready.

As we continued the drive down the coast, cloud cover rolled in causing a mist to expand over the ocean. My mind drifted back to those Superman cuffs, rather to Superman himself, my Superman. He never called back and as sappy as it sounded, what we had was magical. I tried to ignore the flashes of hot anger when I thought about Eric's cuffs. Those slices of possessive rage caused me to go into insanely tight Muhla Bandha locks so I wouldn't slip up and lash out at Eric on the drive home.

I turned my head to take in Eric as he drove; even his profile exuded an air of entitlement. James was mine and I didn't want him tainted through any association to Eric. Or his cufflinks.

He caught me staring and winked. "Don't worry, doll, those three weeks will go by fast."

Real life is not magical. Magic was the stuff for movies and action heroes.

Eric didn't leave right away after he carried my bags up. He pulled a device from his pocket and said, "Let's set this up on your laptop. It's a WTG that creates an encryption code so you can access Centrix from normal Wi-Fi to call internationally."

So he did know about this trip before today.

Once it was installed and tested, he determined it was good to go. "Now we can easily Skype while I'm down in New Zealand, but you need to create an account."

I was too tired to come up with a catchy username, so I keyed in LaurenMadelineUS, and with that, an international profile over the secure Centrix network was automatically created for me.

"This isn't just for feds or active duty," he explained as he showed me the directory and how to search for other users. "It can be used by contractors, retired military, or civilians that need heightened security during communications." He found his username, BEricContracts333US, and saved it as my first favorite contact in the auto dialer. "You should see if any of your Bliss friends are on here. Anyone going out of the country for TDY now is required to use one of these. It has a much faster and safer connection than anything else out there. You'll be happy I got this for you. These puppies are pricey."

I thanked him and kissed him goodnight.

chapter twenty-two

NAILED

The following week was a mad rush of daily yoga classes—the long, hard, hot ones. It was also a painstakingly irritating week of case kickback after case kickback. Eric left Monday, the morning after he dropped me off. After arriving in Auckland a day or so later, he organized his quarters and called me over the Centrix network from his laptop.

Thursday night of the first week he was gone, my hair was up in a messy bun with my reading glasses pushed up over my head while I transcribed a medical release. I wore a white tank top with pajama bottoms, as we were quite comfortable with each other.

Eric complained about a battery charging deficiency. I interjected the appropriate responses to let him know

I was listening. With all his focus on work, there was no mention of the Wounded Warrior thing, and I thought we were in a good spot.

"I have to go." Eric got up off his bed. "We start an hour earlier tomorrow and I still need to get over to chow."

"Okay, see you later." I air-kissed the camera and went to pee. Then, while I was in the kitchen topping off my tea, I heard the familiar beeping noise of him calling me back.

I sat down with a thud, causing my chair to roll back a foot, so I bent over to click the mouse without looking and the screen lit up. There was an unusually long lapse before the image came through. During that pause, I glanced up to see the incoming username. It wasn't Eric's.

"Lauren? Lauren? Are you there?"

The ease, the accent, his tone, oh God.

Within a second, James and I were staring at each other. I was so shocked that I didn't even check the image of my own face in the lower corner to make sure I looked okay. I blinked and smiled almost to the point of a nervous laugh as I feasted my eyes squarely on his handsome face.

"There you are!" He grinned. "Oh my God, Lauren! I've missed your face, girl."

"James," my voice said underwater. "How did you get this number?"

"I've been looking for you on this for a while. I assumed you would have some clever Sanskrit or yoga-y username. That resulted in some very, uh, *interesting* calls. Anyway, you finally showed up in a search yesterday. Just Lauren Madeline, where was your imagination?" He winked. "How are you? Where are you?"

"I'm good, wow, I can't believe I'm talking to you! I'm home in Malibu. I was just up late working on a report."

"Ohh…." He put it together. "You went back to work then?" There was a twinge of disappointment in his voice.

"Yes." This hung in the air for a moment.

He didn't press the topic and began telling me about his adventures in India. We chatted away for an hour and quickly settled back into the comfortable space of communicating as if no time had passed.

We were so loose and cozy I wanted to pick up my laptop and squeeze it hard into my chest. As it turned out, he was scheduled to be in LA for the same shoot I was working next week. When we ran out of things to catch up on, he finally moved to the meat.

"Lauren, I was hoping to see you this weekend before shooting starts. I don't, um, I don't know if that's okay. It's been so long and you didn't ring." He looked hopeful.

"I'm going to be home this weekend," I started off, enunciating each word to figure out what came next. Immature, emotional daggers hit me, though, and I broke off, "I left a message on your phone. At least, I think it was your phone. It went right to voicemail."

"I didn't get it." He looked down at the device in his hand. "That's odd, I had really crap service when we were filming in the mountains, but I was still able to get all my messages when we came back down. There wasn't ever anything from you."

"It must have been a fluke." My defensiveness strengthened. "Listen, I don't know how to say this, but we both know it's different down here, especially in LA. There are so many eyes. Also, I'm under a lot of scrutiny at my job and, and...." *Oh God*, I stopped short of telling him about Eric. I couldn't bear the thought of James thinking of me as someone else's woman. In retaliation, my mind drummed up the image of him and Elle on the *OK Magazine* website. "And I know you're probably involved with someone else...I expected that, but I can't be one of those others. I'm sorry, James."

Feeling too ashamed by my deceitfulness to meet his eyes, I stared down at my shaky hands trying to clasp them into stillness.

"Well...okay then, Lauren, I guess I'll just see you on set. Um, I had better go. It was nice to see you."

He disconnected as the "good" came out of my mouth but before the "bye" choked out in a whimper.

Shattered.

For the first time since Silas went missing, I sobbed myself to sleep.

Friday's early morning yoga class was a nightmare. My eyes were puffy, my hair unkempt, and my balance was off. I stumbled out of almost every standing pose. When I slinked out before savasana, I was followed by unanimous, unsympathetic looks reserved for the beginner who dares to venture into an advanced class.

All my life, I've known guys like James, completely present and emotionally available when they're right in front of you. But elsewhere—and they always go elsewhere—they become ghosts who haunt the next delicious woman that lands in front of them. There's no keeping one of these types around for the day-to-day stuff, especially a movie star.

Then there was the fame aspect. In El Paso, paparazzi camped out in my cul-de-sac, causing bitter resentment in my neighborhood. The connection to Collin's family, the only real family I had, was lost since they ate up everything *Fox News* spit out. During that time, onlookers leered everywhere. The lack of personal space or privacy at every shop, restaurant, and grocery store forced me to do everything on post.

And then, there were the trolls on the internet. I didn't have a manager or even a knowledgeable friend who could tell me to quit reading about myself on the web. I started to believe the horrible things those faceless demons wrote, even to the point of questioning the reality of my own marriage before the IED attack. I drowned in those posts. Finally, I ran away and vowed to start over with a life-altering move to California.

If I were spotted even once with James Bayer, the cycle would start up all over again; of this I was certain. He said he understood that about me. He had to recall all those conversations we had in Canada.

My rational mind implored that I leave it alone. James would be gone in a week, never to be heard from again. But once more, my hand clutched the phone and my heart directed it to dial. It rang without end before rolling over to voicemail.

"James," I started to say and then stopped. "I wish our conversation had ended differently. I...I...." The tears mounted and my throat choked up. "If you're still interested in getting together this weekend, please call me." I hung up quickly and my head dropped into my hands to cry it out.

In my dream that night, the reverberation of a faint rapping noise came from behind a weathered, Spanish-style wooden door. Collin was trapped under a propane tank behind it. Cement prohibited me from running across that expansive warzone to get him.

I tried to fly by engaging my psoas muscles and sent my breath deep into my abdomen. It exhausted my core, spending all my energy and going nowhere. A terrifying panic set in with the realization that I may not be able to save Collin from being crushed.

The confusion caused my brain to search for another way out and my subconscious kept repeating—*you're dreaming!* So I tried with all my might to yell, knock, or cry at Collin to wake me up. No sound came out even though I was screaming so hard it hurt my hair follicles.

"No! Baby, No!"

Knock, knock. The sound echoed and the louder it got the less time he had to keep his leg.

"Collin! Wake me up, I'm having a nightmare!"

Knock, knock…KNOCK, KNOCK.

I shot up. Once more in my bed, I gasped at being released from the chokehold in my dream. In the split second after waking up, I was convinced that Collin might really be just outside my door. The door to my condo.

Standing on the other side of the peephole was James, not Collin. The pounding only ceased when I opened the door and pulled him inside. He reeled back on his heels when I reached in front of him to close the door. He was drunk.

"What are you doing? My neighbors...."

"What are *you* doing?" he spat right back. "Leaving me that message after all, but telling me you don't want to see me? What kind of mind fuck are you playing?" The volume of his voice and the expression on his face told me there was no rational discussion to be had at this time.

"Come inside."

"Are you alone?" he barked as he stumbled behind me.

"Yes."

In the living room, he wouldn't sit down, so I perched on the armrest and pressed my lips together in a nervous habit.

He started in on me with a rant that he must have gone over in his head the whole way up here: "I don't hear from you for months after Canada, months, Lauren. Then when I look you up on Centrix, you act like nothing happened...you know, like nothing transpired...between us and that it's perfectly acceptable you haven't called. Then, fuck, *then* you leave me this...this message!" He flung his phone onto the floor. "What is it now, you poor thing? You're crying your eyes out and want to see me? Seriously, what the fuck?"

He came up for air and sized me up sitting on the armrest. "What the fuck?" He repeated in a more defeated tone and then regained his momentum. "I've had enough with hanger-ons like you. You really had me going the whole trip you know, like you were some authentic person. Someone who saw me, really sees me for...." He lost his train of thought. "But you dropped off as soon as I had to get off that plane. Poof! You were gone and couldn't even be bothered to see me when I made the effort. I made the effort, you know."

I had to derail him with something before this turned violent. Quickly.

"James, I'm so sorry, it's not like that. Talking to you last night was the best thing that's happened to me since you left. Oh God, I...I didn't think you were interested beyond that week, and I thought we parted in a good way. Like with an understanding that you were going to go on, to do your movies, be super successful, and we...we both would have this special memory from up there, from Canada, like with Silas. Seriously, James, I never meant to offend you." All my disjointed thoughts overcame my ability to form proper sentences.

"I witnessed your Linda Blair head spin up there and still told you to call me. But you just don't get it, do you?" He slumped down onto the couch. It seemed like the jetlag, alcohol, and drive here in the middle of the night caught up with him at last.

198

"And anyway, I assumed you were dating Elle."

He looked up sharply at that, and then…guilt.

"It's okay," I slid off the armrest into the spot next to him. "I didn't want you to feel like I expected anything. Really, it's okay." I tentatively put my hand on his arm, which melted him somewhat. "Let me get you a blanket and pillows."

Along with the bedding, I fetched a tall glass of water and Tylenol from the kitchen.

When I returned to the living room, he had dozed off, still sitting up and looking rather uncomfortable.

I knelt down in front of him and loosened the laces on his shoes. I wiggled them carefully until they slid off his feet. He also had on a jacket, so I guided his arms out of the sleeves and put it aside. "Come on, James," I said tenderly, "lie down." I guided him into a reclining position on the couch.

He lifted his head long enough for me to place a pillow under it. Once he was all snug, he repositioned himself on his side facing the back of the couch. Finally, his breathing became deeper. I placed the water and Tylenol on the end table and shut off the lights.

James Bayer was passed out drunk on my couch.

My underestimation of his true feelings had been revealed by the alcohol. Even though I longed for him, self-preservation had caused me to protect myself from being exposed to the hurt that would eventually drop like a nuclear bomb. My dismissal for anything after Canada was justified by this, but now it seemed to have been sparked by cynicism.

What if I had hurt him? Is my self-esteem so low that I denied myself the possibility that I could be desirable to him in a real relationship? I should have meditated more about this.

I woke up Saturday morning with the distinct feeling that I had overslept. Then the notion that James might have left caused me to fly out of bed and rush into the living room. Holding my breath, I tiptoed over. I quietly sat down and placed my hand on his chest.

He was lying on his back staring up at the ceiling, his pants and shirt in a pile on the floor. The water glass was empty. Without saying anything or breaking his stare, he placed both his hands over mine.

"Would you like to come lie down in my bed?"

The effort it required for him to just shift his head my way silently screamed of a raging hangover.

"If you like, I can make you a nice, warm bath," I offered. "It'll help."

He nodded.

I drifted off to my bathroom where I dumped several handfuls of Epsom salts and a tiny bit of lavender essential oil under the running water. When I returned to the living room, he was gone.

He was standing in the kitchen holding the Tylenol, refilling his water glass.

"I have something a little stronger." I pulled a Hydrocodone out of the prescription from after my last surgery. "I'll make you a piece of toast. You don't want to take that on an empty stomach."

He placed both hands on the counter and leaned over enough for his washboard abs to flex with more definition. He let out a long exhale as he dipped his head between his shoulders.

The timer ticked down to a ping and I spread some butter on the toast. I took a quick bite before handing it to him.

He smiled at this, just as I had hoped. He took a couple reluctant bites before setting the plate on the counter. Once he washed down the pill with some water, I took his hand and led him to the bath.

"Lauren," he began, "I—"

"Don't, just get in the bath, try to relax. I'll bring you some coffee? Or tea? In a bit."

"Tea with sugar."

"Okay." I played it off lightly. "This was all a ploy to see you naked."

Another weak smile.

Once he was set up in the bath with the door closed, I checked the attempted call list on my personal computer. Eric had tried me twice. I sent him a visual text message over the server.

Lauren: *Fell asleep early last night ☹ will try u later when u get back from site. Heading out to yoga and maybe beach.* 03 SEPT 2009, 08:14 a.m. PST

I shut down my computer, as if cutting the power was an extra layer of protection from exposing my houseguest, and then fixed a cup of tea for James. I gently tapped on the bathroom door a split second before entering. I set the mug down on the ledge and sank down on the footstool to face him. "Do you need your phone for anything?"

"No, today's an off day, at least for now. Matt knew I was out late last night and I don't have anything 'til tomorrow. I can check in with him later."

"Do you feel better?"

"Yes, thanks. Sorry to put you in this position. I was a bit out of my mind last night."

"I know, you're fine. I'm sorry I gave you the impression I don't care. It's not that." I shook my head and we locked eyes. "At all."

He lifted his hand out of the bath and laid it on my leg. Water ran down the inside of my calf. He sat up taller. His hand slid up my inner thigh to my waist in order to untangle the loose bow holding my robe together.

"Come in," he requested.

He held my hand for balance while I lifted my inside leg over so I could straddle him. It was a tight fit and water sloshed up over the sides of the tub before settling back down again. I wrapped my arms around his neck and he grasped my pelvic bones with both hands. With the desire of wanting to do this for months now, I pressed my mouth against his and openly kissed him, softly at first, but as it went on, our tongues became intertwined and our breathing deepened to a desperate panting.

He rocked my pelvis in and out, causing the floor of my vagina and clit to grind on his lap in a calculated way. His cock grew hard and pressed against my lower belly. He guided it inside me with no hesitation.

We simultaneously rose and fell in our private reunion.

"Get up," he said.

I shakily stepped out of the tub as he got to his feet and engulfed me in a way that caused me to back up against the counter next to the sink. When I felt the cold laminate, I brushed all the products to one side just in time for him to lift me up on top of it.

His thumbs came down to my inner thighs and he expertly massaged the creases where they met the base of my pussy, causing my legs to open even wider. I leaned back against the vanity mirror, giving him the whole view of my spread legs, flat belly, and round breasts with dark, damp hair brushing over them. He indulged in a long look.

"Oh God, Lauren," he half-sighed and half-moaned in a wistful way.

He rose up on his toes to fully insert his dick into me. He fucked me like this. I mean *fucked* me. He thrust into me with the sole purpose of consuming me. The sting of his hard ride would leave a mark on me, claiming my body for his own. The soreness would continue for the rest of the day as a physical memory of this moment. His fingers gripped my upper arms tightly as he bucked harder and faster.

My whole body quivered and at the height of my orgasm, he also came with force. I felt the energy of his pleasure and frustration all wrapped together and directed toward me from his explosive orgasm. I took it all. In this communion, I sacrificed my need to maintain complete control over my emotions.

Once we both relinquished ourselves, he pulled out of me and leaned against me with his head nestled into my shoulder.

"I needed that," he finally said.

"Me too."

"I'm hungry and I want you to go out to breakfast with me." He left no room for argument as he stepped back into the tub to release the drain and turn on the shower.

I closed the door to the private commode and peed, taking a moment to evaluate. Even though I would love to go out to breakfast with him, the chance of a run-in with a fan or worse, a photographer, paralyzed me from doing so. All the same, my desire to stay in his presence overrode my fear and I returned to the shower just in time to see him open the curtain.

"I wish I had a change of clothes."

"I have some men's cologne you can spritz on yours to freshen them," I offered, thinking of Collin's bottle tucked in my nightstand.

We were so compatible in my small condo as we got dressed. James acted right at home without being intrusive or nosy and I didn't have the desire to micromanage his movements in my space.

"Should we take separate cars?" I asked while locking the front door behind us.

He sighed as we approached his rental car parked diagonally in the space by mine. The reality of the day was coming to him through texts and alerts—what his schedule would be for the rest of the weekend. "I suppose so."

Both of us kept our sunglasses on at breakfast…a meal that became more awkward by the minute.

"I'm dating someone and I don't know how to do this," I confessed. The statement came seemingly out of nowhere even though it had been occupying my thoughts for the past thirty minutes.

He exhaled in relief. "I thought that might be the case. I'm involved as well, even though I think of you often."

"I missed you more often than just the one time I called. My guard was down that night because I was watching your movie on Netflix and had to hear your voice. I also may have had a little too much wine."

He chuckled.

"When you left me on the plane, I told myself it was good while it lasted, but I never expected anything from you because I knew, I know, it's not possible."

"I didn't leave you on the plane. That's an unfair statement." His defenses shot up.

"I'm sorry, I shouldn't have said it like that."

We were silent for a minute, both seething at our own miscalculations. It felt like an hour playing in slow motion.

"We will be working together next week," I tentatively started the conversation back up. "Where do we go from here?" Fear of rejection and appearing clingy stopped me from saying more.

"Fuck, Lauren, why can't we try?"

"Because I'm afraid of being made out to be a fool." As the words vomited out, I was horrified to hear them. There it was, my ego taking into account first and foremost how I will be perceived.

"For someone who's all for zen oneness, that's pretty hypocritical," he snapped. "Maybe no one else will tell you this because you were married to the guy who's the pinnacle of this country's patriotism, but you're living in the past. The bitterness of whatever *really* happened there has stunted you, the real you. Now you're using sex as a way to keep me both drawn in and pushed away all at the same time. I want something more than just the sex part. I want what we had in Canada, on the sleds. That was real, at least on my part."

"You're not being fair," I almost shouted.

The adult couple from the family sitting one table over jerked their heads around.

He was holding his presence with me and I knew I would be an idiot to let him go. "You're right, James." There was no hiding the truth. "I want to be with you all the time, and I try not to think about it because it hurts so much to miss you. I know what we had was special, but I'm scared that my ordinary life won't be enough for you. I fantasized about trying, sure, but I had no idea you might want me as well. That trip, it was real…for me, too. We can try, I mean if you still want to." Tears welled up in my eyes; letting him in still felt like a violation to Collin.

James's anger disappeared as quickly as it came and he scooped up my limp hand across the table. "I don't think you have an ordinary life. You're anything but ordinary. I've had plenty of time to think about you, the possibility of us, and I'm not scared. But I have to tell you, this isn't some game for me."

My other hand dropped down on his with a bit of a slap because I was so out of sorts. "Okay."

"Okay."

chapter twenty-three

LIGHTS, CAMERA, IMPLOSION

"Where have you been?" Eric asked first thing, interrupting me as I said hello over the network.

"I went to yoga and have just been around all day."

The next snap didn't come, instead there were silent accusations that came through the screen loud and clear.

"So why are you calling me on a Saturday night? I figured you would be out, doing something,"

"Well," I dawdled, "I need to talk to you, Eric."

"What?"

My nervousness turned to conviction. "It's hard for me to tell you this, so I'm just gonna level with you. Someone I used to see came back into my life and I think we're going to, um, going to try to make it work, I think."

"What are you saying? There's someone else?" He leaned into the camera and the movement was so quick that his image distorted. His head transformed into a point, like he was wearing a hood. "What the fuck are you saying here?" As quickly as the hood appeared, it turned into a red flame and vanished.

It's just the distortion on the screen, Lauren, calm down.

"Before you and I met, there was someone else, but our timing was off and we didn't want to do a long-distance relationship. Anyway, he, well, he came back and wants to try and make it work." I paused. "So do I."

"Have you seen him since I've been gone?"

"Yes."

"Did you fuck him?"

I didn't answer, which is the same thing as saying yes. The words could not form in my mouth to say what happened between James and me.

"Who is he?"

"I'd rather not say."

"You'd rather not say? You'd rather not say? That's rich, why?"

"He's, um, he's well-known, kind of—"

"That Brit? That James Bayer guy?"

My head snapped up in shock that Eric came up with James's name. I never mentioned James in front of him. I instantly feared that Eric had been home the whole time and was spying on me.

CATCH A FALLING STAR

"You're a fucking slut, you know that? Your faggot friends told me all about the rice queen boat. I knew you had it in you to be a slut, but a groupie too? That's the icing on the cake. He's not even an American…have you reported that? Do you know what kind of shitstorm you're gonna have for this? And work will only be the start of it! They're gonna crucify you all over again and you know what, sweetheart? This time I'll be with them. Fucking whore."

I leaned over and clicked the little telephone icon. My hands shook even harder as I typed in the command to block his calls. Adrenaline pumped through me as the feeling of isolation kicked into full drive. I finally took a whole Xanax and lay on top of my bedspread. The pill began to do its magic and I texted Tyler.

James had a talk show appearance tonight and publicity events all day tomorrow, so we wouldn't see each other until Monday morning on set. We hadn't really talked about his relationship with Elle. James knew I was going to end it with Eric, but that was the conclusion of the conversation about our other relationships. He was running late by the time that topic had come up over breakfast yesterday.

The following morning, Tyler and I met at this hipster breakfast joint halfway between our houses. He was wearing a white short-sleeved button-down and a red bow tie. His ash hair was slicked back in an old-fashioned style and he wore light grey skinny pants. Dapper was the only word that came to mind as I saw him approach. As I shrank into the booth at the back of the restaurant, I noticed that he had a spring in his step. He looked so fresh.

"Why are we all the way back here?" Then he took a seat and really focused on me. "What's wrong? You look terrible."

"Tyler, I'm in over my head here. I don't even know where to start. I broke up with Eric last night."

"Well, that's no surprise, but why exactly?"

"Well, I want to tell you but it really has to be between us for now, at least."

Tyler rolled his eyes. "Of course."

"James and I had a thing and I thought it was over but he came back and it's not." The words rapidly ran together as I spoke them with no strategy—rather symbolic of the events that actually took place.

Tyler's eyes widened. "What? Wait…." He put it together. "James? James Bayer, James?"

I nodded slightly.

"Jesus, when? Wait, how? You barely saw him on the ship."

"We slept together on the last night and then he came on the dogsled trip with me."

Tyler's face reflected a mirror of every emotion one unabashed gay man could have in less than ten seconds. "Start from the beginning."

"I didn't think he really noticed me during the training. But on the last night, we were talking and he invited me up to his state room to soak in his saltwater hot tub and watch the Aurora Borealis, instead of going down to the party. So I did and well, I mean hot tub…Aurora Borealis, you know."

The wheels were turning for Tyler. "So you didn't go to bed that night?" He chuckled. "Well actually you did, but…."

"Oh, and he talked to me one day at lunch."

"He talked to everyone at lunch, but what about the day after you hooked up? How did you end up going on that dogsledding trip *with him?* I thought you were going with some Eskimo Shaman to find your inner soul?"

Tyler, who can be hilariously cruel at someone else's expense, was all business when I disclosed how everything went down. When I got to the part about what occurred this past weekend, he had already finished his eggs. Mine sat cold on my plate. He glanced at them and motioned for the waiter.

"Can you please heat this up for her? I need her to have something to put in her mouth while I bandage up this scandal."

"Finish those," Tyler insisted when they came back. "And keep them down. This isn't college anymore. I'm not pulling your finger out of your throat."

"Why would you bring that up?"

"Remember, I was the one who saw you at the end of your days in El Paso. Trauma ignites our demons. Anyway, you look like you haven't been eating, and haggard won't get you anywhere. Now, I'm going to ask you a few questions and you need to be honest. This is between us, okay? I need to know exactly what we are getting into this week."

I was crestfallen.

"Now, Lauren, don't look like that. I always knew you would end up with some perfect and delicious man once you got out of your funk, but James Bayer, myyyy, that takes the cake, dear. It's going to be fine. Let's just figure out how you're going to handle this without falling into pieces."

Thank God he was on my side.

"Now, when you were at breakfast yesterday, did anyone see you?" With this question, Tyler pulled out his phone and keyed in *James Bayer dating photos recent*.

"Just the people in the café. No one seemed to recognize him."

"But, you had your first fight in public."

"It wasn't like that, I mean…." I stammered and then thought about it for a second. "I don't think they knew who he was."

Tyler scrolled through his phone. "There's nothing here, about you, anyway, which is good, I think. The first thing you should do is go home and unblock Eric. You need to know if Mr. Psycho is trying to get a hold of you."

"Did you tell him about the training on the ship?"

"We were talking about it at the party, yes." He squinted his eyes. "There wouldn't have been any connection to you. Shit, neither of us had a clue this was going on. Thom never put you and James together even by the smallest margin. So, yes, Eric knew you were on the ship and that the star interest was James."

Tyler looked at his phone one more time before he set it down. "How did you guys leave it for this week?"

"We didn't."

Tyler rapped his fingers on the table. "Do you have any thoughts?"

"I was going to act like we did on the ship before, professional and polite," I weakly offered. I hadn't really thought about that part, the "work" part. I wasn't even sure when he was leaving California, where he was staying, or anything. The conversation from yesterday was quickly slipping into fantasy.

"He really is dating Elle," Tyler informed me with resignation. "You need to know that. And you need to be prepared for her to visit him on set. And you need to be prepared for him to like it."

"I know." I sighed in full realization of the mess I had waded into, led by my heart to a guy who was slippery. Not to mention the mess I created with the guy who would have given me a steady relationship.

We sat there with our separate thoughts for a moment. Tyler broke the silence. "Go home and get some rest. I think you have the right idea—go in tomorrow all professional and polite. Just keep your shit together and eat regular, nothing extreme. Either way."

We left and went our separate ways. I didn't go straight home, but instead walked along the water at the beach. I wished for the simplicity of Collin.

Tyler: *Work on your scorpion pose. Get it right, no bs*
09/13/2009, 7:50 p.m.

***

James: *G'morning...u better b up n on ur way* ☺
09/14/2009, 3:51 a.m.

I snapped a pic of my smoothie and bag.
Lauren: *Leaving now*
09/14/2009, 3:52 a.m.

The set was surprisingly calm when I checked in with the props master who smiled and gave me a hug. "Lauren, so happy to see you. Listen, we need the mats set up and the altar behind where James will be tweaked. Can you do a few variations and snap pictures on your phone for each setup? I can look at them later."

Before I saw him, I heard James being greeted by the director's assistant near the camera area. My heart pounded in my chest, so I quickly bent down to adjust a mat and pretended to scan the set for anomalies in order to catch a glimpse of him. Apparently, he had already been to hair and makeup since he was in yoga clothes and his hair was waved back off his face. He told me the other day they were considering a wide headband to pull back his hair; I was relieved to see that didn't happen. The hairs on the back of my neck bristled as I sensed both James and the assistant director were focused on me. Instinctively, I turned and James waved me over.

As I came into earshot, I heard him say, "Well, let's just ask her."

"Good morning," I greeted them politely.

"It seems we have an issue with the ability of some of our extras' yogic capabilities—" James started.

"Can you hold a scorpion pose for long periods of time?" the assistant director finished.

"Yes. Wait, how long do you mean?"

"We need a student in the shot who can do scorpion, and Thom says you have the pose. Do you want to be in the shot?" James asked.

"I could do that. Do I have to say anything?"

"No, I have some dialogue and will need to make some adjustments on you in front of the class, but the important thing is you need to hold it, for say, two minutes at the most. We'll have a few takes." Then he shot me a sneaky smile. "Are you comfortable with me touching you in order to make the adjustments? It's a requirement for the scene, but completely professional."

Thom and the director came over. There was no sign of Tyler. Thom gave me a quick nod of acknowledgment as they joined our huddle.

The director spoke to his assistant. "We need to at least get a couple screenshots of her before I commit to this. I could get a call out for a card carrier who can do this pose today and we could shoot it at the end of the week instead." The director looked me up and down, sizing every part of my body and evaluating my features.

"Take a look at her on the screen," Thom said, defending me. "She's done this a million times in front of huge workshops and classes."

This was an exaggeration, but I kept my mouth shut.

"She's thin enough and she moves like a dancer." Thom was laying it on thick now.

"Get James's stand in. No, Thom, you get in there and do the test shots with her." The director turned to me and said, "Lauren, they all seem to think you would work as a student who successfully gets into scorpion in a studio shot. Let's take a look." He strode off while we all stood there staring at each other.

The assistant director jumped in and took charge of the conversation. "Okay, so essentially the shot has our yoga teacher, Mr. Bayer here, using you to demonstrate the pose. Getting into and out of it, and so on. The class will be watching you with their oos and ahhs, then you go back to your mat. He will then continue with the class and you can follow along 'til the end of the shot, got it? You've done this before, like that, right?"

"For Thom's classes before and some workshops, yeah, I can do it."

"Get her in the right clothes!" the assistant director called to no one in particular.

A woman about two feet away jumped to take my arm. "I'll go work this out and make sure we're approved for it with Diane," she told James.

I felt more at ease as I followed the woman, who I soon found out was named Susy, to wardrobe where there was a huge cache of every size and style of Lululemon garb. I resisted the urge to start thumbing through it, but my eye wandered.

"Do you have on underwear?" she asked with no preamble.

"A thong."

"Perfect, let's see if what you have on works. If not, I have some. Go ahead, you can just change here." She thrust a coral bra and grey capris at me.

Modesty wasn't an attribute in the costume department. She eyed my entire body before honing in on the scarring all over my ribs. "Well you certainly have a dancer's body," she conceded with relief, "but those scars—what are they from?"

"An explosion."

"Okay, okay," she laughed, "stand up straight and let me take a look here." She took a step back and twirled her right pointer finger around.

"I like this," she decided, "but I think black, actually, I have a better idea. Let's do this." She produced a black halter top that looked more like a bathing suit and a pair of galaxy print booty shorts worn for hot yoga. They barely contained my ass. She carried a loose hoodie over her arm. "Come on."

Once in hair and makeup, Susy instructed the female makeup artist to even out my face for a non-made-up look with luminous skin and a low ponytail. Susy paused at that and asked me, "How would you wear your hair for this?'

CATCH A FALLING STAR

"For inversions, I usually go with braids or pigtails on either side, but most of the time I just pull my hair up in a top knot. Then when the instructor gets into inversions, I can pull my hair down and leave it. It isn't very neat, but that's what I usually do."

Susy and the makeup artist looked at each other, it was more information than they anticipated. "I'll go find out," Susy decided. "Start on her face and cover up any visible scars." With that, she turned on her heel and headed out the door.

The makeup artist was softer in her demeanor than Susy. Her name was Nina and her thick hair was a medley of faded color experimentation fringing her dark brown eyes. About fifteen minutes later, Nina was done with my face and privy to my childhood.

"He says loose, low pigtails," Susy directed Nina. "He also loves the booty shorts. Did I call that or what?" They both laughed and then Susy turned her attention to me. "You wear this over your top." She held up the hoodie. "When Mr. Bayer calls you up for the demonstration, he will instruct you to remove it before you go into the pose. Make it a little sexy when you unzip it and hand it to him."

Really? I thought in disbelief.

"But don't give it too much hope," Susy said with a knowing look. "From what I hear, he's already taken."

Nina looked at her inquisitively and my heart skipped a beat.

Susy mouthed, "*Elle Benning.*"

Susy looked back to me. "They're going to run through it a couple times with Thom to mark it. He'll teach James on the adjustments, you know, how a yoga teacher would make corrections on your body in class."

Thom will be teaching James how to handle my body?

"Do you have any questions?" Susy asked somewhat irritated. I'd already put together that giving me direction was not part of her job.

"I need to warm up. Thom will know that." I matched her confidence but left out the irritated tone.

She gave me a brief smile. "Of course. They need you in five."

Nina removed the paper cover-up from my neck. "Go on," she encouraged. "You're going to be amazing." Then she went back to plucking her bold eyebrows in the mirror.

With trepidation, I followed the bright lights back to the set and entered from behind a cameraman.

Thom turned to me. "You okay with this?" he asked, dropping his bigger-than-life persona for an instant.

"Yeah, I know what to do." I wondered if Thom knew how many levels there were to his question. "Where's Tyler?"

"He's taking care of some things down at the La Jolla location. He'll be in tomorrow. Give me that hoodie and start on some sun salutations. Get warm so we can jump right into this whenever the director is ready."

Wanting to make him proud, I shot Thom a quick look of sassy confidence as I stepped onto a mat. "I got this, your highness."

Rounding out each sun salutation, my body built heat from the core and my spine lubricated in limberness. I synced into the sacred Ujjayi breath and added some warriors and floating handstands into the sequence. Once ready, I pressed my forearms to the ground and with all the grace of an expert aerialist, my heels tipped up over my head into the inversion. Strong and steady on my forearms, I curled my back and lifted my head up so I could connect the balls of my feet into the smoothed hair atop the crown of my head.

Muscle memory doesn't let these beautiful asanas go. All eyes in the room were now a witness to my travel back in time.

As if on cue, Thom stepped to my side and put his forearm on the bottoms of my feet. "Push," he told me, demonstrating the cue to James. I catapulted energy down through the bottoms of my feet and pushed into his forearm, creating an even deeper C shape.

Without being instructed, I performed the next cue and extended through my chest to raise my sternum up and away from the ground.

"Good," Thom said and removed his arm. "You have about two inches."

I held my inhalation to absorb the prana and scanned my body to locate the space I could use to cover the last couple inches. I had to go past the tips of my toes and connect the entire bottom area of both feet to my head. With a strong exhale, my elbows drove into the ground and my shoulders popped up out of their slightly dropped position.

One inch.

Then I vertically expanded my cervical spine as if my neck was being elongated.

One more inch.

After we went through this a few more times, with James doing the cues on his marks along with his dialogue, there was a short break.

The director actually started to make eye contact with me by lunch.

At the end of the day, my back was a raging fire. We were all sitting on chairs waiting for the director to announce he had the take and release us for the day. My scene with James wrapped by 1:00 p.m., but arranging and rearranging yoga mats still needed to be done.

Thom got up from the chair next to me to call Tyler, walking far away from the director. We could sneak a sly text here and there on set, but if the director heard any cell phone related noise, all hell would break loose.

Even though he'd been circling the chair for at least fifteen minutes, James acted completely casual when he stole Thom's seat. "You're doing great," he leaned over the armrest toward me.

"Thanks, but, where can I get some Advil?"

He pointed to an onsite medic across the room. "I'll get it for you, hold on."

He returned with the Advil and a fresh bottle of water. "What are you doing after this?"

I shrugged indecisively. "I don't know, going home?"

"It's an early day tomorrow and you live a ways. Why don't you come back to my hotel and spend the night? It's just a few minutes, and Susy will give you a change of clothes. Obviously, no need for pajamas." He winked.

"There's nothing waiting for me at home. Sure."

James was summoned to do one more run-through and Thom returned to his chair.

"You can stay," Thom told me, "just don't get in the way."

"I won't."

He stalled for a moment like he had something more he wanted to say.

"Thanks for giving me this opportunity," I started him off. "I really hope you're satisfied with how it all turned out."

"I wouldn't have suggested it if I thought you couldn't do it, obviously. But, do you know what you're doing *here*, Lauren?" Thom glanced James's way.

"I think so."

"Be careful."

I shifted in my seat, trying not to think of myself as a groupie.

The week of shooting went on without a hitch until the last day. Every night I went back to the hotel with James and every morning we came to set together. By Wednesday, we gave up all pretenses by driving back and forth in the same car. No one remarked on our seemingly newfound relationship. In fact, everyone went out of their way to not make eye contact with either of us when we arrived on set. Hookups were part of the deal when shooting.

Near the end of the day Friday, there was a flutter of commotion as Elle graced the soundstage with her personal assistant and hairstylist. Excitement shot across the room as the dramatic confrontation anticipated by the crew loomed.

As I went through some finishing poses with Scarlett, eyes bore down on me and hands snuck into pockets ready to draw out cell phones.

I glimpsed over my shoulder to be shot down as Elle hugged James and kept her tanned arms locked around him. All of his attention was directed on her.

My flesh was peeling off my body in such extreme heat that I wanted to jump in freezing cold water.

Scarlett gracefully came out of her pose and looked up to me for approval.

"Beautiful," I praised, even though I was distracted. The next thing I said had already been predicted by every single person on that set. "I need to go to the ladies' room, excuse me for a moment."

With the bathroom door firmly locked, I dropped my head in my hands. "Fuck," I muttered as tears sprang into my eyes. More than five minutes in here would confirm everything everyone assumed anyway. I splashed cold water on my face and adjusted my top so it was even. I even flushed the toilet and washed my hands for anyone who might be outside the door. With a few deep breaths, I checked my emotions and returned to set. One more take and then I would be released from this hell.

James and Elle peered into a monitor watching a playback over the director's shoulders. She had her arm around his waist and her other hand resting on his stom-

ach flashing little flints of silver my way from the brace-
lets gracing her wrists. It seemed to be a warning signal.
Back off.

James absently stroked her hand while purposefully
avoiding eye contact; not just with me, but with every
other spectator to our affair.

Elle noticed something on the screen and pointed it
out to the director. She moved ahead of James so she
was standing shoulder to shoulder with the director discussing the footage. The director nodded steadily and
took her direction with reverence; even he swooned in
her presence. Fucking traitor.

"We got it," the director announced so everyone
could hear. "It's a wrap, thank you very much. You're all
dismissed."

There was a general murmur around the room and
people started to disperse for the wrap party. James
shook hands with some of the crewmembers, thanking
them for all their hard work. She scrolled through her
phone. I slowly rolled up a mat and Nina rushed over to
help me finish cleaning up the set.

"Come to the party with me," she pled. "Let me do
your makeup. I've been dying to glam you out." She
caught wind of my face and instantly moved in closer.
"Okay," she soothed, "why don't we slip over to makeup
and close the door while we get ready. No one will even
notice."

How many times has a woman erupted in tears behind the closed door of hair and makeup? Add one more to that list.

Once my crying slowed to a few erratic gasps, Nina sat me down and said, "Let's put some cold compresses on those eyes, it'll take the puffy out. They'd love to see your tearstained face, but we won't let 'em. Want to talk about it?"

I leaned back so she could place the cold discs on my closed eyes. "I'm sure you can figure it out."

I heard her rummaging through boxes of every type of beauty product imaginable. "Yeah, unfortunately it happens to the best of us."

"With him?" By this point nothing would surprise me.

"No," she chuckled, "mine wasn't a Brit."

"What happened?"

"Pretty much the same thing. He was so enigmatic and engaging. He singled me out and started to bring me coffee in the morning. The feeling of those first few days before anything really happened was just…." She paused. "It was like being a teenager again." She laughed bitterly. "But, I gave in, of course, and when it was a wrap, there was no big movie star to be found." She flipped the discs over on my eyes and pressed them briefly. "At least James let you spend the night with him. I mean he had no qualms about letting you guys be out in the open. When Rob was finished with me, he'd walk me out the back of his trailer and duck away before anyone could see us."

My jaw dropped and I pulled the discs off. "Rob? Rob…!"

She purred.

I flopped back into the chair. "Oh my God, what was he like?"

"Amazing. Hot. Fantastic lover. But completely self-centered and egotistical as all hell. James is a nice guy, not like most of the male leads out there. Everyone was surprised he was cheating on Elle. He never really struck me as that guy." She tilted my face up and began applying some kind of foundation or moisturizer or base…I couldn't even guess what it was, actually.

I absorbed this information with a new view of this whole situation. I was the other woman. I was the groupie. James is a nice guy. Déjà-fucking-vu, how did I end up here again?

"Does everyone think I'm a total slut?"

She gave a short bluster of a laugh. "No one cares, hon. It happens all the time. And anyway, it's good gossip to keep the crew amused while we're stuck here." She switched products. "Close your eyes."

I pondered whether to tell her it all started on the ship. I wanted all of them to know he wasn't taken when I met him. *At least, I thought he wasn't.*

An hour or so later we were both dressed up in her clothes—short, trendy dresses with high heels that pinched my feet.

I wanted to pick up my car first, but she refused to drive me to it.

"If you go there, you will go in," Nina insisted as we pulled up to a large sports bar that was packed with good-looking, go-getter types, along with our group.

I wanted to enjoy myself. More importantly, I wanted to give off the impression I was enjoying myself immensely. However, this desire was rooted in bitterness and the cocktail I tried to suck down tasted rancid because of it. Even though I was getting plenty of male attention, I hated every one of those guys who looked me up and down as if I were a mere commodity—a hole with two legs around it.

I pulled Nina aside. "I need to go. Can you please drive me to my car?"

"If you go there, you'll sleep with him again."

"He's with her!"

She released my arm and shrugged in a *suit yourself* way. "Call a cab."

The cab dropped me off behind my car at our hotel. *Their hotel.*

Nina's impossibly high heels were balanced in one hand, while the other was tugging down on the short skirt. I set the shoes on the top of the car and fished around in my purse for the keys.

"Hey." James startled me from behind.

I jumped and the contents scattered. "What are you doing here?"

"It's over, Elle and me. She doesn't want to do a statement about it, but it should make it through the pipeline into all the outlets soon enough." He looked me over. "Cute dress."

The frigid wall came up again, and I crouched down to gather up my things.

James made no movement to assist me. "So what is it now, Lauren? Pissed that Elle came to the set?"

I hated him for his flippancy. I stood up and yanked the hem down again. "I would've liked a warning at least."

"I had a feeling she was coming, but I didn't want to tell you in case she didn't. There's no reason for you to be so upset with me." He spoke as if it were no big deal.

"But you left without saying a word!" I knew I was grasping now, but couldn't stop. "Everyone knew. It was so humiliating!"

"What was I supposed to do?" he demanded, dropping the casualness with growing irritation. "Break it off with her in front of everyone? Ban her from the set? I dealt with it as it should have been dealt with—in private, face-to-face. I wasn't about to call her to end things."

232

This underhanded—and hopefully unintentional— blow reminded me once again that James was a better person than me. Just like Collin.

Calm yourself, Lauren. This will play out with the best possible ending; somehow it already has. The bad luck is gone—just need to make it to the finish line.

James remained still. Didn't even take one step toward me. He came after me once; he wasn't going to do it a second time. He needed me to go to him, to stop pushing away, and cover the ground between us. He stood there, facing me, but not in a position of pleading.

I walked over the pavement in my bare feet to embrace him.

chapter twenty-four

BOYFRIEND/GIRLFRIEND

Nina: *Make it home okay? Text me when you do, ttus xxoo*
09/19/2009, 3:46 a.m.
Lauren: *Everything is fine, will touch base later*
09/19/2009, 10:01 a.m.

James's phone rang. He was in such a deep slumber that he didn't answer it until the fourth ring. When he did, he said quietly, "Yes?" From James's end of the conversation, I gathered his breakup with Elle was already all over the internet.

"I am, though," he said and turned to face me. "She's right here."

It was Matt's voice that rose on the other end.

James interrupted him. "We're getting up for breakfast now. You can figure out how you want to play this. You worry too much, man. It'll be fine."

It sounded so swoony, having a movie star boyfriend. The honeymoon aspect of last night when we returned to the room was blocking out the horrible reality of what lie outside, though. Maybe following James's lead would result in everything being fine. Easy breezy.

"I have a bungalow rented for the next thirty days in Brentwood. After that, my itinerary takes me to Toronto for shooting, maybe six weeks there," he called from the half-open bathroom door as the toilet flushed.

"Brentwood is a bit of a drive from Malibu," I noted as I peeked in to see him haphazardly wiping his hands on a crumpled towel.

He squeezed toothpaste on his toothbrush and left the cap next to the faucet. "Yes, well, I have a couple of things lined up this week, but then after that, it's a bit of time off for me. I don't have to stay there, you know, I could come up closer to you. It might be hard to find something last minute, though." He started brushing his teeth.

"I would like to spend as much time as I can with you, of course, but I have to go back to work this week." Not sure of what any other options might be, I took the plunge. "You could stay with me."

He spat, rinsed, and then wiped his chin with that same towel. God, he even made brushing his teeth look sexy. "That would be great." He was quick to answer and gave me a pearly white smile in the mirror. He'd baited me right into that.

We parted ways Saturday afternoon with a potential dinner date during the week. It was a solid plan that he would come to my place on Saturday and stay for three weeks.

Driving home, my thoughts turned to Eric. I still had some unresolved guilt, and I debated if I should call him to make nice. I chickened out and texted Nina instead.

She arrived with two bottles of wine and made herself at home sprawled out across my bed while I unpacked.

"So," she said as she pushed herself up to pour more wine, "he's coming here to stay with you for three weeks? And you're not worried how it looks?" There was a twinge of disappointment, or jealousy, hidden behind her encouraging tone.

"I don't think it looks that bad."

She studied me as I pulled a black yoga top from my bag. "Did you take that from the set?" She playfully snatched it out of my hands.

I grabbed it back. "I fucking earned that top!"

We giggled uncontrollably.

"Let's go out," I suggested. I was restless to get out of my condo; it was still tainted with memories of Eric.

She raided my closet and determined that sexier options were needed if I were to be out and about with James Bayer.

The first bottle of wine was empty and we were almost out the door when the computer rang. Nina paused, but I headed toward the door. "I'll check it later," I told her.

"Who was that?"

"Who?"

"The phone, the computer, whatever it was…who was trying to call you?"

I sighed and tilted my head back. "The guy I broke up with to be with James."

"I'm guessing that didn't end well."

"You think?" I joked sarcastically. "Seriously, I'm pretty sure he fucking hates me. I broke up with him the day after James came back. Over Centrix, it's like Skype. It was messy."

"What does he look like?"

Once in the car, I unlocked my phone to pull up some pictures.

She swiped through my pictures from Santa Barbara. "He's really cute."

"I know. I'm not particularly proud of how things went down."

She moved past the pictures of Eric. "Any on here of you and James?"

"Give me that!" I reached for the phone and she held it away from me for a moment, causing me to swerve.

"Fine, fine," she conceded as she tossed the phone in my purse. "Care if I smoke?"

"No." I glanced at her. "Let me have one."

My regimen of waking up early every day caught up to me as midnight rolled around. We were at a party and one of Nina's friends had Ecstasy.

"C'mon," she urged. "We can split it. Half a tab isn't going to kill you. When's the last time you really let your hair down?"

In a moment of impulsiveness, I took half of the pill and washed it down with champagne. The effects came on quickly and, in no time, we were dancing from room to room. We made our own party while the majority of guests checked their phones looking for somewhere better to be. For me, this was perfect, rolling and flirting with handsome guys.

Nina kept her arm around my shoulders in a way that let her hand rest comfortably on my breast, keeping the men intent on us. We were playful in our sexuality, not all the way kissing or making out, but in a way that let everyone think we would once the bedroom door shut.

We stayed until 5:00 a.m., in love with each other—
in the way that one falls in love with a turtle on X. With
my pupils big as saucers, I drove us back to my condo.
Nina spent the night and we slept side by side in my bed
like sisters.

Sunday afternoon, the drugs and alcohol wore off
and I was antsy for Nina to leave my space. She tried to
cajole me to go out for a late lunch, but I declined and
she finally left.

I sent Dani a few emails first thing Monday morning,
but didn't hear back from her all day. Or the next.

The sense that something was wrong took over my
thoughts. I couldn't put my finger on it. It could have
been the Ecstasy leaving my system, or the guilt I carried
about Eric. Whatever it was, I tried to ignore it.

My work computer was locked Wednesday morning.
Just as I picked up my phone to call the OPM IT support
desk, Dani called me.

"Lauren, you need to bring your laptop and credentials down to the office," she coldly informed me.

"What's going on?" I asked, immediately fearful of a
random drug test.

"There will be an SO[11] to meet you at the gate and
escort you back to a conference room where you'll meet

---

[11] Security Officer

with me and two of my bosses. Lauren, this is serious and I don't think there's anything I can do to help you this time," she said, starting to soften.

"What, Dani? What is it?"

"You'll find out when you get here. I can't tell you. Just come down immediately."

A text came in from James confirming dinner for Thursday night. I just responded "yes," not wanting to bother him with this.

When I arrived at the guard gate, I had to leave my car outside the compound and be escorted to Dani's building in a golf cart.

From there, I was led into an intimidating conference room where Dani, a female SO, and two men were waiting.

The two men were Internal Affairs Agents for OPM, more commonly called "IA"—the same department that submitted damning evidence during my trial.

After inspecting everyone's creds, a formality to which we all subscribed, I sat on the opposite side of the table with my head up and spine straight. The SO sat at the head of the table as if she were going to mediate.

"Do you know why you are here?" the first IA agent asked me.

"No," I responded and motioned to Dani. "She only told me to gather my things and come to the office immediately."

My heart raced in anticipation of a medic appearing with chain of command paperwork in order to obtain a drug test. I knew that I should tell them it would be positive for Ecstasy before I peed in the cup; disclosure is always best.

The same IA agent said, "Falsification of your reinstatement documents can lead to fines and imprisonment, as you well know. We need details regarding your close, ahem, rather intimate relationship with James Bayer."

Did you have any close or continuing contact with foreign nationals with whom you have, or have had, ties of affection, loyalty, obligation, or shared financial interests?

I was shell-shocked and needed them to tell me exactly what they knew, or thought they knew. My lips pressed together.

The same IA agent sighed in irritation. "Are you really going to make me do this? Do you even understand the ramifications of this?"

I didn't budge, so he made it official. "Over the course of the investigation, information was developed indicating you started and are continuing a close relationship with a foreign national, James Bayer, and that he has also had access to your home office."

"Who told you that?" It was the most rookie question and I couldn't believe I slipped. *Tighten up, Lauren.*

The IA agent smiled wolfishly. "It was information developed over the course of your investigation."

Damnit, he used the exact phrase I would have used.

"Was this information obtained through a record or a Source?" If it came from a record, like a police report, he had to disclose it. But if a *person* told him this information, the agent could keep the identity of that person a secret.

The IA agent probably knew I would ask that. "A protected Source."

"Was this information developed over the course of my background investigation to reinstate my clearance?" I wanted clarification about exactly which investigation we were discussing. It seemed unlikely that I would have been able to get my CBP or Holmes creds in hand without my background investigation completed, adjudicated, and closed. And I had both. OPM might have reissued my creds even if my case was not yet closed, so long as it was projected to be adjudicated favorably. Not CBP or Holmes, though.

"I'm asking the questions now," the IA agent responded.

My brain fog from the past two days lifted as I pulled my guard up. This wasn't the first time in which judgmental, middle-aged men saw me as a girl. Not just a girl, but a hussy liberal bitch.

"When did you first meet James Bayer?"

"When I was in Canada, on the cruise."

"How many times have you seen him in person since then?"

"I saw him daily for the training week on the cruise, daily for the week after that when we traveled in Canada, then there was a break of in-person contact until approximately two weeks ago. He came to my house on a Saturday night and spent the night. We've had daily contact last week down in LA."

The second IA agent was taking notes and the first continued with the questioning. "Phone, email, in person, or all three?"

He went on, in the same order of mandatory questions required to ask any Subject who had a foreign contact. At least this was familiar territory, even though I anticipated that the other shoe was going to drop. "I'll save you the questioning," I began, pushing my regret of lying to Dani aside and honing in on the IA agents. "I don't know his birthday or place of birth. I assume he is a British citizen and saw his passport once, confirming that. His job title is 'actor.' I don't know how to clarify his work address. I don't know his home address. He has no ties to terrorist groups or foreign governments. I don't have any further contact with foreign nationals due to my association with James. There is nothing about my contact with James that could leave me open to blackmail and we have no shared financial interests. My friends Tyler and Nina are aware of my relationship with him." I sat back, waiting for a rebuttal.

"Thank you for showing us that you can resolve a foreign contact issue thoroughly," IA Agent One said sarcastically.

This unprofessionalism warranted a disgusted look from Dani, but I let it roll off me. "So what's this about?" I prodded. "You want to take away my clearance?"

"We already did that."

They wanted me to be broken, to beg for another chance at my job. They wanted me to tell them every slutty thing I ever did with James and throw myself on their mercy. I read this situation like a book.

I picked up my bag that had all my work-related things neatly organized within it and opened it up on the table. "Three sets of creds," I said as I pointed to the flap holding them. "One CAC card, one grey IC[12] badge, one laptop, cord, air card, and," I opened up the outside pocket containing a stack of files, "all case material I have printed so far." I stood up. "You can either send someone to get my printer or email me the address to ship it. I assume we are done."

"We are not done," IA Agent One sneered.

---

[12] Intelligence Community Badge–allows access to multiple national sites so an Investigator does not need to acquire ID for each individual site.

Still standing, I opened my hands. "Then what? What do you need to know? You aren't a criminal investigator, and if my clearance was reinstated while OPM had knowledge of my relationship with a foreign national, they messed up. Why are you coming to me with this now?"

"Lauren," Dani warned, but I cut her off.

"I want them to tell me."

"It was brought to our attention that you're involved with a foreign national and when we reopened your reinstatement papers, there was no disclosure of your British *friend*." IA Agent One was fuming. "You'll never work again. And you have disgraced your country, yet once more, young lady."

I bit the inside of my cheeks to keep from hauling off on this guy. All the rage that welled up inside me was really covering up the deep part that believed him.

I turned to the SO. "Now, I think we're done here," I heard myself say in a thick voice from becoming so dizzy. "Will you escort me to my car?"

I gave Dani one last look while following the SO out, knowing that this would probably destroy her career.

Her eyes were hardened.

chapter twenty-five

AS IF THINGS COULDN'T GET ANY WORSE

Now unemployed, I would need to sell my condo and possibly relocate to a more affordable neighborhood closer to PuraYoga. It was the same idealistic plan James and I discussed in Canada.

A stake of regret pierced me as I imagined packing up that cozy beach condo. It was my own place, my safe place. But I couldn't afford to live there without a decent salary.

Unless James....

I didn't know how I was going to tell him I'd just lost my job.

My phone was flooded with texts by the time I got home. I flopped down on the couch and put on my reading glasses to go through them.

James: *Can't wait to see u tomorrow night, let me send a car for you so we can drive back to your place together. 6 ok?*
09/22/2009, 1:23 p.m.
Nina: *One last night to party b4 u r a kept woman...drinks tonite? Shiloh's? Won't take no for an answer*
09/22/2009, 1:44 p.m.
Nina: *Take a break from work & text me back*
09/22/2009, 1:50 p.m.
Tyler*: Whassup? Come to yoga tonite, miss u*
09/22/2009, 2:00 p.m.

The next eighteen texts were a mix of pictures and memes all sent from an unknown number. There were naked pictures of me getting out of the shower, lying in the sun on the deck outside the hotel room in Santa Barbara, even sleeping in my own bed. Then, several memes that had been created during the height of the military tribunal at the time of my trial regarding Yilmaz. These images were photoshopped to make it look like I was sucking his dick while holding a bomb detonator. Others portrayed Yilmaz and a variety of traditionally dressed Muslim men doing various sexual perversions on me at once. Those were the tamer ones.

The final text carried a message. It came in as I was wearing a path down in the carpet.

Unknown number: *You raghead fucking whore, this isn't over*
09/22/2009, 2:14 p.m.

Panic set in, the inescapable kind that choked me. I brought up Centrix on my laptop. My hands shook so violently that I had to enter my password four times before getting it right.

I knew they would be horrible, but I had to see them. The first of the 100+ video messages from him were just a few seconds in length. He used the foulest language I've ever heard to describe my cunt, including, of course, the word cunt.

Closer to the end, they became more disturbing as he jacked off in full view, sometimes squirting his cum right into the camera. In the last one, he laid his Superman cuffs on a workbench and used a sledgehammer to destroy them. After he had ejaculated on them, naturally.

This isn't over rang in my head.

Eric knew my car, my workout schedule, coffee place, code to the gate. I removed the SIM card from my phone and headed to the nearest Verizon store.

Lauren: *D, its L, new # save me a spot in class tonite*
09/22/2009, 5:44 p.m.

chapter twenty-six

PAPARAZZI

The following day James came to pick me up from Tyler's. The driver opened the door to the SUV and inside sat James, completely relaxed with a drink in hand. Maybe it was vodka on ice; there was a lime on top.

"What's going on?" His gaze stopped on my shoulders.

"It's Eric, he went to my, he contacted someone at my work and told them about you. I lost my job yesterday," I stuttered out. "And that's not the worst of it." I broke off and looked toward the driver.

"Can you give us some privacy, please?" James requested.

The driver closed the divider without commenting.

"Lauri, honey, take a breath. What happened?"

"James, I don't even know how to tell you." But I had to. "He sent me these." I handed over my phone. It was a very low point to see James look at that filth degrading me as we drove along the peaceful road.

"Those aren't new images," I said as he got to the memes.

His face grew more disgusted with each swipe.

"They were put up by trolls when I was on trial. I don't know where they originated. He must have dug pretty deep to get to those."

When we were in Canada, I told James about the horrible press during my trial and he had appeared to be well-versed in my case, but I doubted that he'd ever been exposed to those images before today.

"The first ones." He cleared his throat. "The first ones aren't old, are they?"

"No. I didn't know he took those."

James downed the rest of his drink and reached in the minibar to pour himself another Grey Goose. "Want one?" he asked.

I nodded and he silently made me a drink.

"How long ago were those pictures taken, Lauren?" he asked quietly.

"About a month before you and I spoke that first time on Centrix. He was gone to New Zealand when you came to my house that night. For the record, I broke up with him a day or two after we, uh, after that Saturday morning. It was over the Centrix network while he was still there. He didn't take it well. At all. I haven't seen him since then, but…." I stopped mid-sentence. The video messages were worse.

"But, what?"

My forehead smacked into my hand as I heaved over. My elbow dug into the top of my thigh, and I pushed it, that bony elbow, down hard trying to make it hurt because I was crawling out of my skin. "He left me, like, a hundred video messages over the past week or so, ever since I broke it off with him. They're disturbing."

By this point we were crawling on the highway on our way to some hip restaurant where we would be forced to exit the vehicle into a multitude of camera flashes.

"Tyler knows," James concluded. "Why didn't you call me? You should have called me first." He glared out the window for a moment. Then he jerked his head back, as if the first part of the conversation finally sunk in. "You lost your job? Tell me everything from the beginning."

I told him what happened over the past forty-eight hours.

"So, you're saying he went to the authorities and told them about us, and this caused you to lose your position—clearance—because I'm a Brit? That seems a little excessive, do they know I've been in the States for ten years?"

"I don't think they ever wanted me to come back."

We pulled up to the restaurant. "Are you sure you want to get out here?"

The shadowy images of all the photographers jockeying around the back door trying to get the first shot were blurred from the heavy window tint. "Will you hold my hand when we walk in?" I asked in a small voice.

He cupped my face with both hands. "I will hold all of you," he assured me and kissed me squarely on the lips. "It's us now and I'm not going to let anyone run you out of your own home."

A flurry of movement occurred as James confidently stepped out, took my hand, squeezed it, and helped me out.

I nervously glanced over my shoulder as we walked into the restaurant.

chapter twenty-seven

STEPFORD WIFE?

"After the break, we will tell you who the new Super-man, a.k.a up-and-coming star, James Bayer, is romantically linked to. A definite twist from his previous connections, including most recent ex-girlfriend, Elle Benning." Guiliana Rancic left her viewers hanging through commercials and promos for *Keeping Up with the Kardashians* before they could get a glimpse of him and me walking into Boar, holding hands.

Guiliana Rancic came back on the screen.

"This is the type of story that gives every ordinary woman out there hope that no matter how scandalous your past may be, there's always a chance that Super-man will court you. Lauren St. Germain, notoriously known for being a suspect in the 2008 IED Attack on

Fort Bliss, was seen arriving at Boar holding hands with James Bayer as they walked in for dinner. Sources say they have been romantically involved since he began training for his upcoming role as a Philly-based yogi, Bronne de Luca, in the biopic The Purpose. *She was one of a three-person team from an exclusive yoga training company, DesignaYoga, who helped transform the now muscular Superman into the lean and limber de Luca. We will keep you posted on this "supercouple" and take a deeper look at DesignaYoga in an upcoming segment. Stay tuned—and namaste, Ms. St. Germain."*

There I was on the screen, looking over my shoulder like we were any normal couple heading in for dinner. Perhaps we could have been that couple in another life. But for this one, it was going to be a life sentence of constant surveillance and opinion.

James spent a good amount of time over the past week making himself comfortable in my condo. It was touching to see him on the phone or reading a script in my office. We ran on the beach together early in the morning and found our common place without sex as I started my cycle at the same time he arrived.

The contact from Eric ceased, on my end anyway. I completely disabled Centrix on my computer and reported abuse to my account. Still, these measures didn't prevent me from jumping at the slightest unknown movement. James regarded my behavior without commenting on it.

Also not discussed was the countdown of the weeks, soon turning to days, before James's departure for Toronto.

Eric was a threat.

I had no plans for my next career move.

My finances were murky.

Security in many aspects of my life had slipped away.

"Lauren," James said from the doorway. "Are you hungry?"

"Yes, did you see us on *E! News*?"

"Of course. Matt's finally coming around to all this. It's good press, the connection to my physical transformation. Not only that, but now he thinks having a 'normal person' girlfriend raises my popularity."

"I'm heading down to LA tomorrow," he reminded me. "Do you want to come? I have a pre-production meeting and some other stuff to attend. Most of the shots with the other actors for *Clan* are complete, so they're just basically catching me up to speed for my entrance into the film. You can hang out in the café or go shopping, or maybe even see Tyler."

I pounded out some chicken breast. "Yeah, maybe I can meet up with him for lunch. Can I have the driver?"

"Of course." He stood on the other side of the counter where Eric had seen the Wounded Warrior invite.

"When you told me what happened while we were in Canada, I didn't fully understand the magnitude of it all. The trial, the press.... I want you to know Matt's been researching you."

He was visibly uncomfortable with this discussion.

"There's so much stuff," James concluded. "I had no idea."

"Is he researching Collin, too?"

"Probably."

I nodded. I wasn't surprised.

"Now for Eric, I think you need to take everything to the police, maybe even the FBI."

"You're right."

James took a deep breath before he went on. "And I hate the idea of leaving you here while I'm gone, which is why," he exhaled, "which is why I thought you could go with me while I'm filming."

He said it so evenly that I wasn't sure I heard him correctly. "You want me to go on location with you? Where would I stay? What would I do?"

"You would stay with me, in my trailer. It's quite large and comfortable. You don't have to do anything, but I suspect you can keep yourself busy, maybe a little sightseeing or yoga classes." James began chopping a cucumber. "It's not just because of Eric, I want you with me. Plenty of leads bring their wives or their whole families, for that matter. I know the shit hit the fan for you here, there's no need to stay and wade in it. Just come with me, no pretense, Lauren, really."

"James, after Canada I thought the best way for me to move on was to recreate my life with Collin, minus Collin, of course. But now, I don't know, it's like I'm starting to think maybe I'm not that person anymore. Or maybe I never was and now I'm back to being myself before I knew him. Either way, I need you to level with me. Are you sure it's okay for me to just go with you? I feel like I would have no purpose."

"Look," he said as he set the cutting board aside. "I don't pretend to understand what happened with you and him. We all have complications. I don't expect you to forget him, but I want you to create room for me. I want you to want to come with me. You can trust me to have a great care for your heart."

Even as my throat tightened, I smiled. He said that exact same thing to the alien. Borrowed lines or not, James was speaking real words of love from one person to another. Not the way a girl hopes her new beau will say "I love you," but it was clearly expressed with intention.

"I'd go anywhere with you."

He came around the counter and gathered me up so I could weep into his shoulder.

"Your shirt is all wet," I finally said.

He pulled it off. As he went to the laundry room, he called over his shoulder, "Yep, just another ploy to see me naked!"

Instead of calling Tyler, I called Nina to see if she wanted to go to LA tomorrow for some shopping and lunch while James went to meetings.

"Well, aren't we becoming quite the Stepford wife," she joked. "Of course, I would love to. Can you guys pick me up on the way in? I wouldn't dream of missing a day of celebrity living."

"Um, sure." I should have asked James first, but I automatically agreed instead. "I'll text you the time before I go to bed tonight."

"Wear something smart," she directed, "and panties."

Clan of Justice has Mr. James Bayer cast as Superman. In the movie *(film!)*, he joins forces with three other superheroes on a mission to save Earth from an alien threat. Superman comes in at the end of the film to help the others in the final battle.

There had been endless meetings and phone calls over the past week, but this last one was the most important. The ride down to LA with Nina and James was uncomfortable.

He pecked me on the cheek before getting out at the studio. "I'll see you all back here around three, maybe four. The driver will collect you in time to get me."

Out of his sight, Nina rolled her eyes at me.

"Things seem to be going in your favor," she observed once we were alone in the back seat.

"I don't know if favor is the right word, but yes, things are going better than I expected." I wondered how much I should tell her about Eric. "There's been some pretty bad drama from Eric, the ex. I don't know if it's going to continue or if he just went on some kind of bender."

"Does James know?"

"Yes, he knows. He thinks I should take everything to the police, but I'm hesitant because if Eric's over it, I don't want to start contact back up. I blocked his number."

"Then how will you know whether or not he's trying to contact you? Did you respond to any of his texts?"

"No, I know better. There's more." I looked at the driver. "Can you take us to the place at the corner, One Eggless Wonder?"

"Yes," he responded and raised the privacy glass.

Sitting back in the seat, I went on, "Someone, I think Eric, reported my relationship with James to my work." My use of the word relationship caused an air of distaste to come over her. Also, she didn't understand why James would even matter at my work. So I explained, "He's not a US citizen and I'm supposed to report any contact I have with foreign nationals. But, I didn't and they found out, so they fired me." I paused. "And took away my clearance." I paused again. "And barred me from working for the government ever again."

"Shit, what are you going to do?"

"Well, I'm gonna go up to Toronto with James while he films *Clan*. He brought it up yesterday and, given all the circumstances going on here, it seems best."

"What about your condo? Can you break your lease?"

"I own it."

There wasn't time to continue the conversation as we pulled up to the restaurant.

Nina checked her makeup in the reflection of her window, trying to be inconspicuous, but there were no cameras waiting for us.

We spent a long breakfast talking, mostly about her rollercoaster life. On the street, there were three photographers snapping pictures and bombarding me with questions.

"Where's James? How long has the relationship been going on? Did Elle know the whole time? Any marriage plans?" All in rapid-fire succession.

We kept walking as I repeated, "No comment," while Nina nudged me to say more.

Irritated with my tightlipped responses, the photographers became more aggressive with their questions, unloading them like a machine gun magazine.

"Is he the first man you've been with since Collin? Is it true you were fired from being an investigator? How would Collin feel if he knew you were dating a movie star, a British citizen, no less?"

We ducked into the first storefront we saw and the shop girls hardly looked up. They were seasoned paparazzi shields.

"Privacy?" one of them asked Nina without getting off her stool by the register.

"What did she say?" I asked Nina, who appeared to understand.

"No, it's okay," she directed to the shop girl before turning back to me. "They have curtains they can pull over the windows to keep them from getting shots in here."

"Oh." LA was a whole different ball game from El Paso.

We stayed in the boutique while Nina tried on three different outfits; none of them worked.

I felt obligated to buy something. I selected a pair of earrings. They were almost a hundred dollars.

Nina brushed off my purchase with a sigh. "That's all you're getting?"

Hiding out in the next few shops became suffocating. For me, anyway. We were sitting in two deep, velvet couches outside some fitting rooms. Nina's feet were propped up on a maroon and gold Moroccan pouf as she texted someone. I was pawing a throw pillow.

Nina cocked an eyebrow at my hand's mechanized kneading and slipped her phone back in her purse. "So, how long are you guys going to be in Toronto?"

"A month. We leave this weekend. I haven't even started packing."

"That seems like a good amount of time for a cooling-down period with Eric. Are you worried he might do something to your house?"

"Not really, there's an overzealous HOA and 24-hour security. Still, it might be best to have someone around. Would you be interested in housesitting while we are gone?"

"I could do that. Do you have a cat or something?"

"No, just a few plants that need watering and the mail."

"No problemo." She was all chipper to the idea. "I can even take you guys to the airport if you need me to. Well, you probably won't, but just in case. Are you flying in a private plane?"

James: *Will be done at 4…u ok?*
10/12/2009, 12:59 p.m.

"Let's head back," I said, bypassing an answer about the private plane we were taking up there.

The day turned out to be an awful lot of effort for a couple eggs and a pair of overpriced earrings. Toronto was becoming more and more appealing.

The rest of the week flew by. James was occupied with his personal trainer, who came up every morning to cast a grueling workout upon him down on the beach. Days before we left, Matt booked him to do an appearance on a late show. I tagged along and sat in the green room while he prepped. Before the show started, the assistant producer brought me over to the two audience seats reserved for guests.

"Is there someone else coming?" she asked politely while pulling the reserved signs off the chairs.

"No, it's just me, but can you leave that sign on," I told her. "I don't want to sit next to anyone."

I shivered from the air-conditioned studio and from the evident passion that radiated through him during that late show taping. I knew under all his charm and exceptional physique he doubted his ability to be taken seriously as a dramatic actor. To see him so sincerely proud of his work made my heart swell.

The press junket for *The Purpose* had to be put on hold as all of James's itineraries shifted to allow him to shoot in Toronto. We spent the following night staging all of our luggage, and in the process, I cleaned out the hall closet.

"You can put as much stuff in there as you want," I told James as we packed.

Matt called while we were packing to set up a last minute meeting for the following day. It was going to be a long day for James; he had to meet his trainer at 5:00 a.m. sharp.

"Aren't you worried about being overextended?" I asked when we took the trash out that night.

"If you hire the right manager, they can worry for you," he answered. "Can't you just go with the flow for the next six weeks? He's got it." He pulled me close and kept his arm around me as we took our time walking back up to my condo.

The next day, the countdown to leave for Toronto began. James took the driver and left to make his gym session before I woke up. He was going on to meet Matt one last time before we left the country. I ran last-minute errands and dropped the keys off with Nina. On my way home, Tyler called.

"I am beyond happy to hear you're going with him and finally living," Tyler was quick to exclaim. "I can stop by to pick up your mail once a week. I hope that's frequent enough, I don't get up there much."

"Oh, it's okay, D. Actually, Nina is going to come housesit while we're gone."

"Are you sure that's such a good idea? You barely know this girl."

"It'll be fine. She just needs to water my plants and get the mail." I came to Nina's defense, feeling protective of the one person who took me under her wing during the week of filming at the studio.

Tyler sighed. "All right, but I still think you should be a little more guarded. You haven't been around all these Hollywood types. They can be manipulative. They're a different breed—all takers."

Bypassing a lecture, I changed the subject. "I'll text you some pictures from Toronto. Can you believe it? I get to go back to Canada, my motherland!"

"You were probably a caribou in your past life," he said, and with that we hung up as I parked.

NOTICE OF VIOLATION

On Oct. 16, 2009 at 5:30 a.m., the trashcans belonging to LAUREN ST. GERMAIN in UNIT 215 were found overturned with trash dispersed throughout the complex. This is the first offense of this type and a fee of $250 has been assessed to the homeowner.

I groaned, $250, really? I hurried down to collect my trashcans and take a look around the collection site. Last night, I had tweaked them after James rolled them into their slots so they would be completely straight. The lids were secured when we walked back up.

Even when it was extraordinarily windy, trashcans never fell over in this complex. They were set up in a long line against a wall that blocked the wind.

Come to think of it, I've never seen a single trashcan tipped over on trash day, let alone two.

chapter twenty-eight

WELCOME TO HOLLYWOOD NORTH

There were multiple filming locations for *Clan of Justice* in the greater Toronto area along with the sound stage, where James spent hours suspended on a wire in front of an enormous green screen. The expansive size of the production made the yoga studio set from *The Purpose* seem like a college film project. I was expected and welcomed wherever James had to go, but stayed out of the way when he was working. He was right; there were plenty of significant others on location as well. Most of the time I went back and forth from watching all the bustle around me to reading or doing yoga.

James and I didn't talk a lot while he was working, and it didn't bother me at first. I found myself with a great deal of time on my hands, so much so that I picked up some research on a topic which had been of interest to me, since even before I met Collin: the preservation of elephants. I fed my brain with histories, anti-poaching laws, and inspirational stories of people who rehabilitated elephants. At dinner, I lectured James all about the horrors in Africa happening to these regal creatures, sometimes getting carried away with emotion. He appreciated the distraction.

Whenever an elephant family came across the skeleton of a dead elephant, they would cry; something about that stuck with me.

The days became longer and his attention diverted. As much as he liked it when we shared a meal alone in the trailer, his carnal needs were on top of my daily to-do list. There was no other escape from the stress he faced daily.

Most evenings, he'd pull me in close to his chest while he slowly pumped his whole length into me. Other nights, he'd rip at my panties, sit me up on the desk, and fuck me with his pants still around his ankles. It just depended on how the day went.

It was near the end of our thirty days and he'd been run ragged. I was practically living on cranberry juice. He shut down faster at night and said less during his breaks. It began to sting, but when I told Nina about it on the phone, she advised me not to take it personally.

"He's under an enormous amount of pressure with millions of dollars on the line," she warned. "A needy girlfriend on set will get him shunned, and you'll find yourself alone."

"You're right. Just talking to you about it makes me feel better. What about you? How's everything going back there?"

"Good, nothing ever changes." She snorted with laughter. "I've been going down to the beach by your house. I figured I could take advantage of that exclusive luxury since I'm all the way up here." Nina had a way of making digs about money. They were just so slight that if I were to call her out on it, she'd simply defend them as innocent statements.

"Have there been any more problems with the trashcans?" I asked, not offering any more commentary on the private beach across the street from my condo complex.

"No, I didn't put them out the first week because there wasn't anything in them. Since then, nope, no problems at all."

I could tell she was smiling when she said this and it put my mind at ease.

At the start of our last four days in Toronto, the three other leads arrived and it was a complete spectacle. The battle to save Earth was upon us. It was time to shoot the scene where the four men would save civilization.

I chose to go souvenir shopping for Tyler and Nina, so I let James know I was taking a driver while he filmed the final metropolis scenes in the middle of downtown Toronto. James was surrounded by at least a half-dozen individuals primping everything from his hair to his codpiece. Included in the group was a local reporter interviewing him about the rigging procedures.

When I stopped a few feet behind the swarm and caught his eye to wave goodbye, James put his hand up to the reporter and summoned me over. "You going to find some souvenirs today?" he asked, as if he wasn't bombarded with a million other pressing things.

"Yeah, I thought I'd take my time over in the arts district. Do you want me to look for anything?"

"No." He brushed some hair away from my face and kissed me on the cheek, his fingertips lingered by my ear. "We'll have more time together next week in New York."

"It's okay," I said brightly. "Be safe on those jumps."

"Is that Lauren St. Germain? Are you in an exclusive relationship with her?" the reporter asked.

I paused just in time to hear him say, "Yes, now back to the rigging system."

My heart flew. I knew we were publically seeing each other, but to hear him say it on record with no contingencies felt amazing.

Always trying to blend in, I wore an oversized oatmeal sweater, dark wash jeans, and boots on my shopping excursion. I poked in and out of the galleries with no recognition while seeking gifts for Tyler and Nina. The perfect ones were found in a modern art gallery.

I handed the clerk my credit card.

"It declined." She handed it back.

"Can you try it again?"

It declined twice more and no text or email arrived from Chase prompting me to authorize the purchase.

I stepped outside and called the number on the back of the card. "I didn't call to report I was traveling to Canada. I should be here for three more days. Will you make a note of it on my account? I'm trying to make a purchase."

"Ms. St. Germain, your card has exceeded its limit. If you like, we can request a credit line increase." The customer service agent's foreign voice exuded politeness.

"What? There's no way the current balance is anywhere near its limit!" My stomach dropped. "I need to check my account online and call you right back, is that okay? In the meantime, can you suspend all activity on my account?"

"Yes, Ms. St. Germain. Would you be interested in taking a short survey to help improve our customer service?"

L E A H   D O W N I N G

I hung up without answering while my mind raced, unable to catch up with the information I had just received. But there it was, on the screen of my iPhone—three balance transfer checks in the amounts of $19,000, $10,000, and $24,000. All had been cashed last week. Along with their one-time fees, my account balance was $55,484, definitely over limit. Not wanting to reconcile this on the sidewalk, I waved the driver over.

Instead of returning to the shooting location, he took me to our trailer because I wanted to get on my laptop alone. I shut the door and inexplicably did a quick check to make sure no one was in there. I brought up the Chase website and there they were.

One check was made payable to American Express, one to a Franklin Capital car loan, and the last was made payable to Judy Wheeler. That name was familiar and it took a moment for me to put it together. She was Eric's assistant—oh my God, these were his creditors. He didn't even try to hide the fact that he stole from me.

My mind shot back to the week before leaving for Toronto, when I had emptied my shredder into a recycle bag. The next day, I received the balance transfer checks and went to shred them, but threw them in the trash instead since it was going out that night.

My brain knew what to do, for I had given the same advice to numerous soldiers when their wives or baby mama's had power of attorney during deployments. So many of those guys, after spending a year in Afghanistan, came back to crappy furniture and unpaid debt on their cards from dinners at Chili's. I used to hide my judgmental opinion of their lackadaisical care for their credit, and here I was, dealing with the aftermath of stupidly throwing my stuff in a trashcan for anyone to snatch up.

Still, the checks weren't my biggest concern—it was that Eric had dumped my trash everywhere while I was home. The personally invasive nature of his actions instilled a primal fear deep inside me.

I immediately called Nina. "Have you seen anything out of the ordinary since you've been at my house?" I asked tersely.

"No, nothing, why?"

I told her about the balance transfer checks and she became oddly quiet.

"Hmm…." She was stalling. "Well, I saw his truck parked in that small lot for the beach when I walked down there."

"When? How did you know it was his?"

"You told me to keep an eye out for it, Lauren, Jesus! It was about two weeks ago, maybe a little more."

"Was he in it? Why didn't you tell me!"

"Now calm down, I didn't want you to get all upset. He wasn't in it when I went over to the beach to walk, but when I got back, he was down at the beach, like at the bottom of the stairs where you wash your feet. Anyway, he left after I went up to him."

I reigned in my emotions. "Did you talk to him?"

"Only for a few minutes. I didn't know if he was looking for you."

"I can't believe you didn't tell me this, Nina. He cashed $50,000 worth of checks from my credit card, and now you're fucking telling me he was there over two weeks ago?"

"He's not interested in you anymore, so you can relax about it. You have James and I'm sure Eric will leave you alone when you get back. I don't know what to tell you about the money. Are you sure it was him?"

Call waiting beeped. It was James. "I have to go, Nina, but we're not done here. You should leave my place and lock it up. I'll get the key back from you when I get home. No, actually, leave it at the office when you go."

"I just bought groceries," she snapped.

"Take them with you."

I switched to answer James's call, but he'd already hung up.

I tried Nina again, but she didn't answer.

I called James and it went straight to voicemail.

"Damnit!" I yelled and smacked my hands down on the table causing them instantly to sting and redden.

The phone rang again. It was James. I didn't want to drag him into this right now and shouldn't have answered.

"What's wrong?" he demanded hearing my frantic voice.

I muted him for a second and took a deep breath.

"Lauren!" he almost shouted into the phone. "Lauren, are you okay?"

"Yes, sorry, I just dropped my phone and thought I broke it there for a moment. But it's fine."

His tone relaxed. "Where are you? We're going to wrap up in a couple hours. Are you almost done shopping?"

"Yeah, I didn't really find anything, though. How about if I head your way and stay there until you guys finish? We could ride back to the trailer together. How is everything going?"

"It's fantastic! Everyone is really on point today. Yes, come back here when you're done, sweetheart."

Everything was going so amazing and so awful at the same time. Something was brewing back in Malibu. I tried to not think about what it would mean for us when we returned.

chapter twenty-nine

STATUS UPDATE

I kept the credit card issue and Nina's interaction with Eric to myself for the rest of our time in Toronto. It was important to be cautious in how much was revealed to James at that point; his focus needed to be on the film.

With my tail between my legs, I called Tyler to ask him to check on my condo. Tyler reported back that she wasn't there, but her things were. On top of that, he saw dog shit on my patio, several pieces, and an empty water bowl.

Meanwhile, I left Nina voicemails. The only response was a scant text back: *Working now, can't talk…everything is fine ☺.*

Clan of Justice wrapped on time and there was a huge party to follow. We moved from the trailers to the penthouse suite at the hotel, where the party was being held.

There was a giant tub in the en suite area there, so I took advantage of finally being able to soak in a bath for the first time in weeks. James was being pulled in so many different directions that I was surprised when he entered the bathroom in a robe.

"Do you want me to add some more hot water?" I asked as he disrobed.

His body was in the most buff, muscular condition I'd ever seen it. No longer appearing to be a lean yogi, the solidness of his muscles put off an overly masculine vibe and really complemented his erection.

He stuck his hand in the tub. "No," he answered and sat naked on the edge. Even in the low bathroom light, bruises and scrapes up and down his torso remained visible. There was a two-inch gash on his forearm that had barely started to scab.

"You accomplished what seems to be the impossible to me, babe. I am so impressed and incredibly proud of you." I stroked his ego as I stroked his thigh; sincerity in both.

"It's good, isn't it? Really good, I'm so proud of my work here. It's different than *The Purpose,* that took so much inward digging, but this was like an explosion, shooting out in all directions. I think this is really it for me. I'm on this incredible roll of success with traction, thanks to *Clan,* and this is only the start, Lauren. The question is, are you ready to be catapulted onto the A-list with me?"

He was eager, half-joking, and thrilled. But underneath the manic act was a serious desire to be acknowledged as a bonafide action hero, capable of carrying a franchise. It was almost seeping out of him.

"Oh, James, it's better than good. You're Superman on so many levels. There's no doubt in anyone's mind, you're a force."

This comment was rewarded with a wide smile and he sank into the bath with me. I moved on top of his lap to kiss him passionately, arousing his unceasing desire for physical contact. I dropped back against his bent legs for support and began to make circles on my nipples with my fingertips. My hand traveled south as I leaned back harder against his thighs so I could hoist my hips halfway out of the water. This gave him a close view of my own fingers manipulating my clit. I pushed two fingers inside myself and moaned, coming to a quick orgasm.

He stood and pulled me up by my arm, apparently ready to take over. Water went everywhere in a fierce wave up as we stepped out of the bath and he pushed me back against the wall. He didn't hold back any strength as he kissed a path down my belly and sank to his knees. His hands were tightly clamped around my pelvic bones while he intermittingly sucked and licked my pussy.

I looked down at the top of his bobbing head and curled my fingers in his hair. It was with the next exhale that I fully sank into the possessive and intense pleasure he was creating.

James ran a hand up over my ribs to push my upper body against the wall. With my legs parted wide, he cupped the other hand under me, between my legs, to support and push every bit of me even more into his mouth and face.

I was consumed as one arm and hand trapped my upper body and the other hand, along with his mouth, controlled my whole pelvic area. He had me on complete lockdown. I released all control and let him rock me so forcefully that he lifted me up to my toes with each motion. I came so hard I saw stars, literally. My sight went black for a moment and returned in small spots of white. That orgasm started in the arches of my feet before bellowing up through every nerve ending in my body.

He stopped working me with his tongue and pressed it hard against my pussy lips; it kept me under his power. Not one muscle on him relaxed as I slumped toward him, a total release as he kept me propped up. We were just so perfect together, like this, in a private, locked universe where no one could get in.

He took his time to stand up as his lips were busy making a trail up my belly, tenderly kissing the groves of my scars, and finally making a pass over each nipple before he covered my mouth with his.

My hand to God, I'll never forget the way he kisses me.

"Come to bed with me," he breathed into my ear.

Once there, he beckoned me to his lap so we could make love sitting up, facing each other.

I inched him back so he could lean against the headboard and let me do all the work. I braced myself on my knees and used my quads to ride him slowly and deliberately. He moaned and thrusted as much as he could in this position, but I controlled the speed and depth. I finally gave him the ending he needed by speeding up my rhythm and bottoming out at the base of his shaft. My cervix felt a twinge of pain with him so deep inside me, but it was overruled by my own orgasm.

We came together in what felt like an orgasm suspended in time. The sensation radiated away slowly. My face was buried on his shoulder as his arms kept me close to him.

"I love you," he said. He shifted his shoulder so I had to look up at him. "You know that, don't you?" He searched for an expression on my face.

My hands cupped his face. "I love you, too, James, very much."

Downstairs, the wrap party for *Clan of Justice* was a real Hollywood blast, with a huge spread of amazing food, a top-shelf bar, and a DJ from Las Vegas. I let my hair down and gave everyone a chance to see the side of me that was carefree and wild. We did shots and I ended up dancing on a table at the peak of the night, letting my lacy black bra peek out from my dress. That night, I was the girlfriend they all wanted him to have—a fun, sexy, party girl who put on a show.

When the dance floor thinned and the crowd broke into small groups, James and I found a nook in the hotel that had a comfortable leather couch facing a fireplace. We cozied up on it before retiring to our room. I slipped my shoes off and extended my legs out in front of me. He pulled out his phone to scroll through Facebook and Twitter. I yawned and lazily looked over his shoulder to see his screen, which was on his official Facebook page.

He snapped a blurry picture of me.

I laughed. "It's a good thing those fans only want pictures with you, not *by* you."

"Come here, let me get a good one of us." He put his arm around me and held his phone out.

"Text that to me," I said. I watched him send it off and then he shared it on his Facebook page, tagging me in it as his girlfriend.

"I don't care what Matt says," James declared as he turned the screen my way. It was on his official Facebook page. James Bayer was officially "in a relationship."

The next day, we were snuggled up on a plane to New York City, fully reclined in first class. He snored lightly and I fell asleep with my head on his shoulder.

I wonder where we'll end up after New York?

That was the last thought that went through my head.

chapter thirty

NEW YORK

We made it through a week-long race to every interview, appearance, and lunch imaginable in a full-blown press junket. *The Daily Show with Jon Stewart* was James's final appearance on Friday night before we would hop on a redeye to LAX.

Matt was coming to the taping tonight and it would be their first meeting since we arrived back in the US. They greeted each other and Matt gave me a friendly kiss on the cheek, neither excited nor disappointed to see me. James followed an assistant producer out to the set while Matt and I turned our attention to the screen in our room. We were alone watching James discuss next week's premiere of *The Purpose*. James also fell graciously into Jon's jabs about him being so good looking.

"I need to talk to you. Matt, do you mind?" I asked as I moved seats to be next to him.

He gave me a look that told me he wasn't interested in anything "the current fuck of his client" had to say.

"Is everything going okay with you two?"

"Yes, but I need some advice. It's a different matter, something…" I thought for a moment, "…something I don't want to bother James with."

Matt turned the volume down on the TV. "What is it?"

"I know you know about my ex, Eric, and the texts he sent me."

"And the video messages where he came all over the screen, yes, I know about all that."

"Well, since we've been gone, he's been casing my condo and stole some balance transfer checks from my trash, which he cashed, to the tune of about $50,000. I don't know what to do, honestly. I'm worried." I looked to Matt for any sign of compassion, but he remained blank.

"Is it money you need? I'm not his accountant, nor would I expect his accountant to discuss any of James's finances with you. I'm sure you know he would tell James immediately if you went to him for anything."

"It's not the money, Matt. James wanted me to go to the police about the messages, but I didn't because, well, because I thought Eric was just on a bender or something. James doesn't know about the checks."

Matt put his hand up. "Lauren, I'm sure this is all very upsetting to you, but I can't advise you. I work for James, not you. I solve his problems, not yours. So decide what you want to do and do it, but I'm not here to get you out of any messes you might have with ex-boyfriends...or husbands." He checked himself at seeing the hurt expression on my face. "Call the police. Get a restraining order in place. You'll be fine, and you were right to keep it from James while he was shooting." He paused. "You were right to come to me with it. Sorry, I didn't mean to come off so abrupt."

"I didn't mean to be presumptuous, I just don't want James to be affected by this."

"I think you need to tell him and go to the police. Guys like that don't just stop harassing their exes." Matt seemed to be debating whether or not to keep talking. "Don't let this turn into a scandal. You're barely out of the woods with public opinion, and I don't want all that backlash transferring over to him. Being in Hollywood gives you a longer leash of what the public will put up with, but as far as the flyover states are concerned, you're still Al-Qaeda friendly...enemy of the state kind of shit."

There was no need to respond, he was right.

Matt turned the volume back up so we could hear James and Jon during the final moments of the interview.

Shortly after we saw James exit the stage to a roar of applause on our TV screen, we heard him coming down the hall with some other people, Jon Stewart among them.

"Jon, this is Lauren St. Germain. Honey, come here and meet Jon." James was all smiles as they bustled into the room.

Seeing Jon Stewart reminded me so much of Collin. We used to watch *The Daily Show* religiously.

"Nice to meet you." Jon shook my hand. "You know, I would love to interview you, maybe it could be on the anniversary of the attack?"

I was surprised by his bluntness. "I don't know, maybe."

"Who represents you? We'll set something up."

Matt stepped in. "Your people can contact me directly. I represent her for the time being."

Jon and most of his people went back on set to finish taping while James, Matt, an assistant producer, and I all relaxed in the green room.

"Let's have a drink," James said to no one in particular, but the assistant producer jumped to open a bottle of Grey Goose.

Matt snapped a sharp look my way as if to warn me that my current demeanor was anything but fun and easy going.

I quickly rearranged my face.

When the New York junket was over and we were flying to LAX, I knew I had procrastinated long enough and needed to tell James.

"Why didn't you tell me about this sooner?" he bit off in a hushed tone.

"I didn't want to distract you during filming, I wasn't going to keep it from you." At that statement, I cast my eyes down and James sat back in his seat with a long sigh.

I was rigid in my seat, not sure if he was going to have any part of this or if he would go back to being the kind and loving James.

"Excuse me," he finally said. It was a long time before he came back with a flight attendant in tow carrying glasses of ice and four tiny bottles of vodka.

James had his drink before resuming the conversation. "You need to go to the police. I will go with you, but it has to be your decision."

I took a sip of vodka and offered him the rest of my drink. He took it and relief washed over me; it seemed as though he wasn't going to punish me with coldness.

"And more importantly, I won't do this." He pointed back and forth between him and me. "Not if I can't trust you. I want to trust you, but you're making it really difficult for me to do that right now. Are you going to tell me if he makes any type of contact with you, no matter how small or insignificant?"

I nodded with wide eyes.

"Say it."

"Yes," I croaked, then cleared my throat. "James, I will tell you if anything happens. Right away. I won't wait."

The flight attendant came back with fresh cups of ice and four more vodkas. She smiled at him. "Would you mind if I took a picture?"

"If you like, I can take your picture together," I told her.

Easy breezy.

chapter thirty-one

AFTER NEW YORK

There was another red and white notice stuck on my door. I shoved it into my purse before James could see it.

No one was there except a black Lab puppy. The puppy started barking as soon as the door opened and it began jumping up on us, excited to play.

The mess of scratches on the inside of the front door caught my eye. The corner of the carpet that met the kitchen tile was shredded up as well.

James closed the door and whistled as he surveyed the apartment. "Where's Nina?"

"I don't know," I answered and immediately texted her as I walked into the bedroom.

Her things were still all over; products littered the counter of the bathroom, clumps of hair were swirled on the shower tile, and her laundry remained piled up in the corner. The bed was made, but the rest of the room was cluttered with her clothes and shoes. Some of the shoes were partially chewed up, presumably by the puppy.

The deck off the bedroom still had all the dog poop that Tyler mentioned, as well as the water bowl. The slider leading out there was smudged with shin height slobber and nose prints. When I opened the door, the stench of sunbaked dog feces breezed right into the bedroom. I slammed the door and called her.

"You need to come here to collect all your things and the dog now. I'm going to keep trying you until you answer."

I couldn't get a sense of how long it had been since she was last here. There was some mail piled in the kitchen and dried dog pee on the tile.

"Is there a leash or something so I can take him for a walk?" James hollered at me from the other room. The constant barking was creating mounting tension.

We found a leash between a couple couch cushions.

"A bag?" he said irritably.

"What?"

"To clean up after him if he takes a shit."

I got him a plastic grocery bag and he took the dog out for a walk.

3ᴿᴰ NOTICE FOR INFRACTION OF RULES
CONCERNING PETS

LAUREN ST. GERMAIN

All animals must be properly and legally registered before they can be approved by the board for residency. You have not put the proper application in to have a pet in this residence. Legal action has been taken in the form of a lein against your property for $6,000. You are summoned to appear before the board at the next general meeting: NOV. 11, 2009 AT 6:15 p.m. failure to do so will result in the lein turning into a judgment.

Not knowing what else I could do, I cleaned up all the dog poop and hosed down the deck. By that point, James returned, and the dog curled up on my couch to doze.

"Any luck?" he asked.

I shook my head.

"Well, I'm going to unpack and shower. You should pack up her stuff and keep trying her."

I found her suitcase and was able to fit most of her clothes in it. I used a Trader Joe's bag for the rest of her shoes and toiletries. After getting her things together, I telephoned her a third time and she actually picked up.

"Lauren," she snapped, "I'm working right now."

"You need to come get your things and your dog before I throw your shit out and take this animal to the pound."

"You better not do anything to Grant! You didn't even tell me exactly what day you'd be back. I'm at work now. Don't touch any of my stuff." She hung up.

At 10:45 p.m., Nina let herself in to find me sitting in the living room. James was in the bedroom with the door open. Grant began to bark, happy to see his owner. Nina stumbled a little when she walked in and dropped down on the chair next to me.

"Where have you been?"

"I had plans to get a drink at The Fish Market tonight. I left there before everyone else did so I could come here. When did you get home?" She spoke as if there was nothing wrong.

"Who were you with at The Fish Market?"

"There was a big group of us there for happy hour." She lit a cigarette and got up to head to the kitchen. "Want one?" she inquired over her shoulder.

"No, and I don't want you smoking in here," I told her in a state of disbelief at her blasé attitude toward everything. "I have a $6,000 lien placed against my condo because of that fucking dog. Why did you think you could bring him here? Why did you think it was okay to talk to Eric?" That betrayal was at the front of the line.

"What do you care about Eric? You have James. He's over you. You won, okay? You have the *film star*." She tipped the ash of her cigarette in the sink.

"I can't believe you didn't bother to mention you had a dog." I checked myself. I needed to bring some calming light into me before I decked crazy lights over there.

"I just got him. There's no one else to take care of him. He needs daily drops of Bach's Rescue Remedy to calm his Hyperactive Barking Syndrome. It's not his fault. He was with a family that had kids who poked him and kicked him, then the parents of those brats took Grant to the shelter where my sister volunteers. She sent me his picture and I knew," she took a drag of her cigarette, "I knew he was my canine soulmate."

Is she fucking insane?

She was completely calm, finishing her cigarette and then running water over the tip to put it out. She threw it in the trash. "I saved half of my steak from last night. I hope you didn't eat it." Her eyes rested on the dishes drying on the rack by the sink.

"Nina, you need to get your things and your dog, er, Grant, and leave. James and I want to go to bed. We've had a long, stressful day."

"I can call my friend tomorrow and see if she has the key to my old place, but I think she's in San Diego until Monday." Nina opened the fridge door and started pulling out her leftovers.

"What do you mean?"

"Jeanne has the key to my old place. I can't get in there 'til she gets back in town. Honestly, Lauren, what did you expect? Since I was staying all the way up here, I've doubled the amount of gas I have budgeted for each week. So I sublet my place to her and she went to San Diego with her boyfriend for the weekend. I was thinking about going, too, but I'm not sure if Grant would be okay by himself for a whole weekend. If you're interested in going, she has a three-bedroom place down there. James could go, too."

"Do you think you can go tomorrow? To San Diego? Or maybe get an extra key from your landlord?"

"All her stuff is there."

I rubbed my eyes. "I'm exhausted. You can sleep on the couch, but you need to walk Grant first thing in the morning and clean up after him."

She shrugged. "It's just a dog. It's no big deal. Go to bed if you're tired, then." As I walked to the bedroom, she called after me, "Hope you sleep well and say good-night to James for me!"

James turned his back to me.

The next morning, Nina was still sleeping on the couch when I woke up and made coffee. The dog started barking at the sight of me, and there was a fresh pee puddle on the kitchen tile. The noise woke Nina.

"I would have cleaned that up," she offered.

"I have a lot to do today. What time can you get your key from your friend? It's not a good time to have you stay on my couch and I need the dog gone."

She sighed. "Can I at least get a cup of coffee?"

I moved out of the way for her to pour a cup and she eyed the vanilla coffee creamer on the counter. "Did you go to the grocery store?"

"No."

"I bought that creamer!" She snatched it up with a light shake to feel it was almost empty.

And I lost it. "You bring a dog here who chews up the deck and carpet, talk to Eric, and smoke in my house, but you're giving me a hard time about fucking coffee creamer?!" I yanked the fridge door open and started pulling out all the food, not caring if it was hers or mine. "Take all your shit and leave. Now!"

"What is your problem?" she whined, tears instantly brewing in her eyes. "I don't have this condo or a caring boyfriend. I was there for you at the beginning and now that you have him, you don't care about me. It's like everything I did for you doesn't matter!"

I lowered my voice and changed my approach. "Nina, I appreciate you watching my place while I was gone, but right now, James and I need our privacy and rest. He has two premieres this month and it's a crazy time for him. I offered to let him stay with me so he could be away from the drama."

She checked and double-checked every room in my condo for her belongings. James took Grant for another walk while she lugged her things down to her car. While he was out, she made a few passive-aggressive comments about how I was catering to him. I didn't want to get baited into a fight, so I kept my mouth shut and went room-to-room searching every crevice of my condo after her. I had a gnawing feeling she would leave stuff here on purpose as an excuse to come back.

By the afternoon, her car was packed and Grant wiggled around in the backseat with all his nontoxic chew toys. They all still had their price tags on them.

"My key." I held out my hand. "If Eric was going to hurt me, would you let me know?" There had to be some level of girl code left between us.

"You are so self-centered! How would I know anyway?"

Apparently not.

It took a day or so for James to start talking to me without formality.

I brought up going to the police about Eric before he did and then I called Malibu PD to speak with a detective. The appointment with the detective was set for Tuesday after his premiere for *The Purpose.*

James was booked to stay at the W Hotel in Hollywood through the weekend so he could be close to all his movie premiere events. The day before he was supposed to check in there, I timidly asked him if he wanted to go alone.

"I don't want you here by yourself."

It didn't answer my question.

Then he put his arms around me and reassured me, "And I want you with me, even when you have a batshit crazy creature staying at your house."

"The dog or Nina?"

He laughed. "Both."

To my surprise, Matt had a stylist bring in a rack of dresses for me after we checked into the W. His suite was a revolving door of reporters, publicists, big yoga names, and friends of James all coming in to get a piece of him. I kept to the bedroom with the stylist for company.

"She'll need something in a current, hippie-type fashion, but nothing too Stevie Nicks," Matt instructed the stylist amidst all the commotion. He eyed my choice of wardrobe, jeans and a tank top. "Are those clogs?" He gave the stylist an exasperated look and walked out.

The stylist told me she thought James and I made a cute couple and that she loved dressing body types like mine. But when she caught sight of the scarring, she moved the dresses with cutouts to the back of the rack.

It came down to a one-shoulder, draped, eggplant dress that had a Grecian goddess feel to it, but with a modern twist since the bottom was a pencil skirt. She styled my hair in a loose topknot and gave me a pair of oversized chandelier earrings with amethysts.

When I walked around in the dress with nude heels for her to assess, she nodded in approval.

"James is going to love you in this," she gushed.

He's going to love it on the floor, I thought.

The red carpet went off without any issues. It balanced just the right amount of spontaneous sophomoric comedy and political correctness—a discussion about AIDS.

"Your scene didn't get cut, but your character has no name," Matt was quick to tell me as he pulled me back from James when the bulbs started flashing.

Tyler and Thom were already there when we arrived and they both looked smashing. The four of us have had quite a ride from this film.

While James was a step or two ahead of us, Tyler took my arm and pulled my ear close to his mouth. "What's the story with Nina?"

"Total shitshow, but I got her out," I said through a smile.

"I told you," he muttered as he let go of my arm. Only Tyler could say that without sounding like a complete ass.

The movie received a standing ovation, with many people in tears by the end of it, including me. I was so proud of James for giving such a profound performance and fantasized that he might even be nominated for an Oscar. We floated out of that theater.

chapter thirty-two

BATTLING SUPERMAN

A few times over the course of the evening, I looked around for Nina, but it wasn't until shortly after midnight that I spotted her. She looked enviable, wearing a royal-blue dress cut down to her navel with fabric draped perfectly over her boobs. For a brief second, I wished we could put the weirdness from our recent past behind us and simply have fun for one night, like we did when we first met.

That second was done and over as soon as I saw Eric standing next to her at the bar.

Matt was sandwiched between Scarlett and another young beauty when I interrupted their...conversation? Petting session? Whatever was going on in the dark corner of the room that I barged into.

"Look!" I pointed to Eric and Nina. "That's Eric with her. *Eric* Eric!"

"Where's James?" It was his first question and most important point. Matt shifted his focus and became all business.

"I don't know, I don't think he's in this room. Matt, we have to get them out of here, especially Eric, James—"

"Go find him and keep him occupied while I get security. Now, Lauren."

I froze, so he shoved me to get a move on. I bumped into a chair as I started off to find James.

From across the room, Nina lifted her glass in a toast and motioned for me to come join them. Matt grabbed a security guard and pushed his way through the packed room. All the crew was crowded around them. The door from the patio opened and a woman entered as James held the door open for her.

"This is Diane Forrester," he introduced her as I pulled up between them.

I almost tripped and caught James by the arm. "Hello." I tried to recover with a rushed, "Nice to meet you."

"James was just telling me how you ended up having a scene in the film doing a scorpion pose."

"Yes," I blurted out and stole a fast glance over my shoulder to see some sort of commotion going on near the bar.

James gave me a funny look and then his gaze followed the ruckus across the room.

There were two security guards standing over Nina in a heated discussion while she remained firmly in her seat. Eric was standing up behind her in full view. She pulled her VIP badge out of her purse and began waving it in the security guards' faces. Everyone around her, all those people we worked with on set, they all turned toward us.

James made a beeline for the bar in such a blur that his arm bumped Diane and knocked her off balance.

"I'm sorry," I apologized to her over my shoulder as I clambered behind him.

It took him less than ten seconds to clear the length of the room while Eric stepped up to intercept him. Nina was engrossed in her lengthy bitch session with security, clenching her VIP pass up for all to see.

Without a moment's hesitation, James punched Eric square in the face. Blood spurted from Eric's nose, but he came right back at James. Security guards were trying to get between them with no success. Both men were quick and strong. Eric's knuckles caught James in the cheek and knocked him off balance. As James tried to regain his stance, Eric kicked a barstool toward him. The velocity of James's rage was shocking when he retaliated. The two became intertwined, with James on top, mostly, for what felt like forever. In reality, it was about twenty seconds.

It took three security guards and two of the crew to break up the fight.

"Get him out of here!" Matt yelled even though the guards had Eric halfway to the door.

Eric's face was bloody and he writhed erratically. For a split second, our eyes locked. He wanted his blows to hit me, not James.

Nina reeled my way. "Are you happy now?" Another security guard tried to take her arm, but she violently pulled it out of his grasp. "Don't touch me!" Slowly, she collected her things before walking out the door with her head held high.

Thom popped out from nowhere and announced, "Show's over everyone. Go back to your drinks!"

Once James, Matt, Tyler, Thom, and I were secluded on the patio, James's fury resurfaced and he went for the door. Matt darted in front of him, barely in time.

James turned on me. "Lauren," he spat and yanked my arm to pull me up next to him. "What the fuck was he doing here?"

The side of his face swelled in the beginning of a shiner and the knuckles on his right hand split, allowing threads of blood to seep out from his raw skin. He panted, oddly reminding me of the passionate sex we had hours before the red carpet.

"I…" I crumbled. "I don't know! Oh my God, I'm so sorry. I don't even know what to say."

"Can you give us some privacy?" Matt asked Thom and Tyler as he moved slowly to come between James and me. For the first time since I met him, Matt looked at me with some compassion.

"I had no idea they would be here. I mean, I figured Nina might show up since the rest of the crew came, but him?" My voice started to shake.

"She's fucking crazy. The coffee creamer? C'mon, you didn't honestly think she would leave quietly?" The blood streamed out from the cut on his temple. "Damnit, Lauren!"

The tension was diffused by the patio door opening. Two of the security guards stepped out and took inventory of the three of us.

"It looks like his nose is broken, but other than that, he should be fine," one of them told Matt. "The girl's a real firecracker though, she was trying to get him to call the cops."

"Where are they now?" Matt asked.

"I dunno, her car? There's no way those two are getting back on the property."

Tyler returned with a bag of ice and draped it over James's right hand. I tentatively reached out to touch James's swelling temple but he jerked away.

"So now what?" James demanded.

The security guard looked from James to me and back to James. "That guy had no right to be here and he fought pretty hard. I think if you shut down the party now, we can just chalk it up as a bit too much to drink and maybe some jealousy?" He glanced my way again.

Matt took the hook. "Thank you, we'll wrap it up and go on our way. Thank you again for being so understanding. These things happen."

With the matter behind us, one of the security guards looked back to James. "Hey, boss, maybe I could get an autograph for the old lady?"

The next morning, the number of paparazzi outside the hotel seemed to have doubled and I assumed it was fallout from the fight last night, but then I saw LAPD. A uniformed officer placed James under arrest like we were in a dramatic movie scene. When he was formally charged with aggravated assault, he serenely offered his wrists in view of the cameras. With reverence, the officer cuffed him and paused for the shot of our hero sacrificing himself in moral righteousness.

James was neither surprised nor angry as he turned to the officer and asked, "Can I take her with me? They'll eat her alive if I leave her here."

Flashes from the sea of cameras popped off in all directions. Crowds of people closed in on the squad car as we pulled out toward the highway exit at an infuriatingly slow speed.

Dark sunglasses hid the panic in my eyes, but it took noticeable effort to keep my jaw relaxed. James put his bound hands over mine and mouthed the word "relax" to me.

Then to my complete shock, the officer in the front passenger seat pushed a small key through the grid separating us from them. "Can you take those cuffs off him?" he asked me. "Just put 'em in your purse 'til we get to the station."

While rubbing his wrists, James leaned forward and made small talk with both officers. The one in the passenger seat turned fully around to face James as they discussed *Clan* for the entire drive.

If either of them had asked me to snap a picture, I would have screamed.

chapter thirty-three

THE MORNING AFTER

They booked him, took his mug shot, and in complete Hollywood fashion, James shot his smoldering version of *Blue Steel* to the camera. His face ranged from bulging red welts to a busted lip, which made him look hot in a rugged and manly sort of way.

We were shown to a small interrogation room while we waited for James's lawyer. "It's just a formality," the officer explained. "I don't want to leave you out there with all those lookiloos."

Even though I was grateful for the privacy, it was tainted with resentment as I recalled my own experience of being held for questioning. Wanting to avoid a discussion that could easily turn south, I put my head down on the table to rest.

The door opening woke me and it was at that point that I realized this might not be a simple charge, the kind that would go away with lawyers and money. A male INS[13] agent entered the room with his badge up and ready for inspection.

I nodded to the INS agent in a way that let him know we recognized his authority and I told James, "INS. It's mandatory for your charge to be reported to them because you're not a US citizen."

"Should I wait for my lawyer?"

"Yes."

"She's right," the INS agent agreed. "I wanted to come in here and let you know we're filling out paperwork on your charge, but it's only because we have to. It's a formality. She knows that."

James's face fell.

"Basically, if you're found guilty of aggravated assault, you'll need to attend a hearing, an interview really. A panel of adjudicators will assess the seriousness of your crime and determine if you are a threat to national security."

"And if he is found to be such?" I asked.

---

[13] Immigrations and Naturalization Service

"They could take his work visa, but that's highly un-likely. Mr. Bayer, I can't guarantee the outcome of a po-tential panel, but in my nineteen years of experience, I've never seen anyone lose their privileges to make movies in the US just for socking a guy at a party."

"Do you know what happened?" James leaned in like they were drinking buddies.

I don't know the details," the agent replied, also lean-ing in.

"I still think you should wait for your lawyer," I ad-vised James. "No offense," I broke off to the agent.

"None taken," he said to me. Then to James, "You have a smart one here."

James's lawyer had already been briefed by Matt on the details surrounding Eric's harassment and theft. When he arrived, we were moved to a larger room so the lawyer, the INS agent, and two LAPD officers could all be present while James was questioned. The officers went easy on James, allowing him to constantly pause and confer with his lawyer. The lawyer presented my ev-idence of harassment, which embarrassed me to no end.

"Lauren, if you would have reported all this, there could have been a restraining order in place," one of the officers scolded.

"I know," I defended myself since no one else was there to do it. "There were a lot of complicated circum-stances happening during all this and the checks were cashed when I was out of the country. I have an appointment with a detective up in Malibu on Tuesday. Should we include her on this case? Because I'm ready to get started on the process and I want to press charges. At the very least, I'll need an official report to submit to the credit agencies."

"Keep your appointment," the officer sighed. "Right now, we need to finish questioning Mr. Bayer and get your statement as an eye witness. We have a few other witnesses from the party and we'll let him out on bail. If Mr. Merski chooses to press charges, things could be drawn out, but with all this documentation of harassment, chances are he'll shrink away."

Matt was waiting outside the police station to usher us past the wall of press into a dark car. Once he had our undivided attention, he turned to me. "You need to drop off the radar for a while."

I agreed with him to an extent even though I desperately wanted to stay with James. "What do you suggest?" I asked.

"You should go back to your condo in Malibu and pretty much stay there. Let him get through the press junket and premiere of *Clan* without this hanging over him. The schedule is tight enough as it is. He needs the focus to be on him, the movie, not *you*."

James popped his head up. "She can't stay in her condo alone, not with Eric around. She should go back

to New York with us tonight to finish the press for
Clan."

"There has to be a middle ground."

"We could get married," James said.

"What?" Matt and I exclaimed simultaneously.

There was a pause and I spoke first. "Is this something you have been thinking about, or did the idea just
come to you?"

"It was an eventuality. I was planning a more romantic proposal after the premiere, but it could be now or
then; the timing isn't important to me. I know this is
what I want." He lowered his tone, "Would you want
that too?"

Trying to have this conversation with Matt intently
listening was intrusive, but I knew it was part of the deal
if I wanted to be in James's life as a permanent fixture.

I nodded. "Yeah, James, I do want the same thing as
you, I think." But I still had to make sure of something.
"Is it too soon, though? I don't want you to feel like I
expect you to jump into a marriage right away. I'm happy
where we are...of course, I was hoping things would
progress to the next level."

"I think we both know that this is real."

Matt didn't bother to hide his disbelief. "So this is
the play then?" Matt half-demanded and half-told James.
"You guys are engaged? Congratulations? It's better than
her being your girlfriend, you know, punching a guy for

harassing your fiancée has a much more noble ring to it."
Matt didn't have as much use for the love we felt as he
did for the buzz our story created in the press.

"Thanks." James bypassed commenting on anything
Matt pointed out and looked to me with devotion.

"Where are we going now?" I asked them.

James made the decision. "Home," he told the
driver. "Drop Matt off first, and take us home to Lauren's condo in Malibu, please."

chapter thirty-four

THE REVIEWS ARE IN

"Superman was not so super. The stiff performance by British actor James Bayer lacked sophistication. If you need an escape from the holiday shopping, don't bother with Clan of Justice. *The only justice you could attain would be by forking over your ten dollars to see any other movie. The overdone and tacky costuming, coupled with Bayer's horribly delivered one-liners all appeared cheesy and forced."*

—*LA Times* Movie Review

"James Bayer's a heartthrob of a leading man for several B movies, and perhaps that's the top floor of the building in which he should have stayed. Cast as Superman in Clan of Justice, *his one-sided and, quite*

frankly, boring portrayal of the American icon is downright embarrassing. The other current "IT men" cast as Spiderman, Batman, and Aquaman were mediocre, but better than their British counterpart. BOMB."

—Rogerebert.com

"Even though James Bayer is physically the perfect specimen to play Superman, his inability to execute American-style lines is apparent. His best bet would be to swim back over the pond like Aquaman. Coincidentally, Rob Onion brought depth to the beloved Aquaman character; perhaps Bayer should take a page from Onion's book!"

—*USA Today* Movie Review

"James Bayer is the hottest ticket in town for his body, which will be in hot water if his contract isn't renewed for the sequel. Recent updates to his trial indicate a renewal might be the only contingency allowing him to stay in the US."

—*Hollywood Insider* News

"The numbers are in for your weekend box office hits. Unexpected front-runner The Haze *came in on top, grossing $22,635,037, followed by the romcom,* She

CATCH A FALLING STAR

Didn't Say it, But.... *as second with $11,566,400. Family-friendly Pixar movie* The Meanies *is still holding strong in third with $9,751,801. In sheer disappointment,* Clan of Justice *took a steep fall from the previous week's shallow opening and reports a mere $1,920,684 for this weekend. Ouch, so sorry to hear that for all you hot superheroes. Guess it's time to hang your costumes up, gentlemen. Back to you, Giuliana."*

—*E! News*, Thanksgiving Special
11/26/2009

chapter thirty-five

REMINICSENT

Both feet rested on the floor when I sat on the edge of the bed. Rhythmically, I pushed down on one foot at a time, letting the coolness from the laminate spread over the bottoms of my feet.

Ripples.

He vanished this morning without waking me. He's been isolating himself these days with early morning runs, wearing a black beanie and a long face. I couldn't bring myself to tell him everything I'd heard about his performance in *Clan*. Besides, there was no need to bring up any of the reviews, he already knew.

Matt started to communicate with me instead of James on certain topics in hopes I could soften the blow.

James had been waiting for a decision about his contract to come in, but I got the text first.

Matt: *No*
11/23/2009, 9:50 a.m.

Our engagement was a joke to most in the industry—that he would take up with a scandalous slut and then completely tank at the box office. It was the reviews about his acting that bothered him the most, I thought *(I hoped)*.

A couple weeks ago, we RSVP'd to Rob Onion's Thanksgiving soirée. But last night, James drank way too much and lashed out about his scathing reviews. I locked myself in the bathroom as I listened to him ranting in disjointed sentences interspersed with expletives, all the while repeatedly slamming something heavy down on the desk. I couldn't make out the object that bore the brunt of his force. There was a moment of silence and I reached for the doorknob, but then jumped like a wet cat, startled by the distinct sound of a laptop being thrown against a wall…and shattering. *Could he do that to us?*

I peeked in on him before going to bed to find him passed out sitting up in the chair with his head propped up clumsily on his hand. It looked as painful and uncomfortable as I imagined he felt on the inside.

When the morning light streamed in through the sheer curtains blowing from the open bedroom window, I wiggled my toes under the covers. The fresh air on Thanksgiving morning breathed some optimism through our condo.

Pushing the vision of him broken down in that chair out of my head, I went to the kitchen to brew coffee for me and boil water for his tea. When I pulled the Hydrocodone out to offer him one upon his return, there were only two left from the almost full bottle. Not wanting to deal with *that*, I reminded myself it could have been Nina.

The gust of wind that swept in angrily from the front door warned me of his dart to the shower. When the groan of the water pipes let up, I quietly brought him a cup of tea.

I sat on the counter by the bathroom sink with my feet dangling as the steam built up. He grunted heavily over and over, and then I heard it: the unmistakable intake of breath that occurs right before ejaculation. I bowed my head wishing I hadn't come in and the water snapped off.

"Jesus, Lauren, don't do that." He was irritable and his accent was thick.

"Why don't you come join me in bed?" I suggested coyly, letting my legs open on the counter and my robe fall down.

"I'm pretty sure you know I can't."

I left his tea next to the sink.

Lauren: *Hey, D...we're not going to Onion party, James is sick...can I come solo to ur place?*
11/25/2009, 9:15 a.m.

"Are you sure you don't want to come with me?" I asked when I popped my head into the office an hour later.

He got up and pecked me on the cheek. "No, you go. See you later, sweetheart."

A cozy thought of bringing him a wrapped piece of pumpkin pie teased my heart as I drove down the coast to Tyler and Thom's Buddha-themed Thanksgiving event.

I loitered there all day under lines of twinkle lights and prayer flags, faking how wonderful things were between us. A flash of the sparkling diamond with a glittery smile was all it took.

"No, the reviews weren't important. Yes, he's already bounced back. They wanted him for the next two films, but he's going a different route—one to showcase his range as a dramatic actor. It's really been his life's dream to be cast in more serious films anyway, not just the usual superhero blockbusters."

Thom nodded in fake approval as I recited my lines to all their star-fucker guests. I should have been a screenwriter because even I began to believe the lies I spewed. They actually tricked my spirits into lifting on the drive back.

The condo was empty when I got home—no note, no text. I indulged in a long, hard cry under a hot shower. After, I sifted through my nightstand to find a cold compress, my fingertips grazed the jagged edge of a thick piece of paper. I pinched it up to find a curled and torn photo.

In my mind's eye, I saw that same tailored black blazer I had maniacally shoved in a trash bag on my first day back to work here.

That jacket had been slung over the back of a barstool at Aceituna's in El Paso, a Coach purse hanging diagonally across it....

I had pulled that blazer and purse off my body and rolled up my sleeves, then I undid the top buttons on my shirt. Collin liked it when I exposed a bit of cleavage.

Then, I had freed the sticky bobby pins out of my French twist to let my hair down. I pulled my heels halfway out of the tight, black pumps to catch a breeze underfoot. I'd been trekking around all day in the Chi-huahuan desert—since 0700.

I had sat next to Collin as he shot the shit with our usual bartender for several minutes about fixing up some car. His hand found the small of my back and rested there.

After a couple drinks, I had moved in front of him, then leaned back, his arms and legs around me. This was standard. We usually stayed until last call on Friday nights.

Stop. Besides, I was only remembering the early days of El Paso.

If I kept this picture the bartender took of us on Cinco de Mayo wearing those stupid-looking sombreros, I'd just slip back into the "what could have beens." Before I could change my mind, I obliterated the picture in my shredder.

Dawn on Black Friday greeted me with untouched blankets and pillows on James's side of the bed.

The fact that I was too jumpy to send him a text after he'd been gone all night spoke volumes regarding the state of our relationship.

Unceremoniously, he came home at noon and we watched *Die Hard* on TV, snuggled up together on the couch. When I woke the last time, the TV was off, and he was staring off into space. I didn't want to break the spell of our intimacy, so I just remained in his arms until we turned in early.

"What do you think about going to Thom's class this morning?" James asked when I woke up the next morning.

I smiled.

Thom was over the moon to see us, especially to have *the* James Bayer front and center in his yoga class. Thom's enthusiam seemed to lift James's spirits.

The class was amazing. I felt our connection come through the sweat and intensity created on our mats. It was almost a sexual communion the way we were both breathing and making eye contact through the mirror at the front of the class. I desperately hoped this would carry over to the bedroom. Or anywhere.

After class, Thom invited us to get juice at a quaint place across the street. We crossed quickly in front of a stream of onlookers and cameras before ducking in and taking a seat in the back. Thom obviously knew the owner, because three raw pressed juices were set down in front of us while we were still looking at the menu.

James admired the large, glossy photos of elephants drinking from watering holes on the walls. "Where are these pictures from?" he asked the girl who set down the drinks.

"Africa, more specifically, the DRC," she replied. "Democratic Republic of Congo. The owner goes on a mission there every year or so to give ground support to the park rangers who are trying to maintain control over the illegal ivory trade."

"Is he here?"

"Yes, she is. Should I get her?"

A moment or two later, a no-nonsense looking woman with short hair appeared.

"This is Cindy Ludlow. Obviously, James Bayer." Thom still said James's name like he was about to stand up and salute.

"What can I do ya for?" she asked James copping a squat at our table.

"Can you tell me about the trips you take to Africa, to help the rangers?"

She explained to us how elephants were being brutally killed by the Sudanese militia and the Lord's Resistance Army rebels, called the LRA for short. The numbers were in the range of the tens of thousands of elephants per year. Through some contact, she had a connection to the rangers of Garamba National Park, where she assisted in combatting this horrific slaughter. When she traveled there with her partner, Janis, they patrolled the grounds with the park rangers. The best part of the experience was when they had the good fortune to help in the elephant rehabilitation centers.

Cindy was very liberal with her information and contacts, but near the end of our conversation, she warned,

"This was all fine and good, but it's too dangerous to go there now. The LRA is a brutal force, using children to kill both the elephants and humans. They dismember and destroy everything in their path. Janis and I don't go there anymore, but we still send plenty of money and strong, young missionaries from the West as often as we can."

He wore the same expression as he had when he sat across the table from me in the café on the ship.

We were going there. I could already feel it.

Just when we had my condo squared away, clean and organized with both our things perfectly meshed, he was ready to run away from the boring steadiness of life. Somehow, I always knew this was his true essence. No matter how many times he assured me that my life wasn't ordinary and what we had together would be enough, the nature of the beast took over and adventure beckoned.

"Do you have a travel agent who I could contact for some of the particulars? I don't know if it would be possible, but Lauren and I have discussed going on some sort of peaceful mission to work with and rehabilitate elephants. She's quite passionate about it." Upon referring to me, he reached over to center Ganesh on my necklace. Somehow, this was going to be spun as my idea.

I smiled with encouragement; I would take any optimism from him now, even if it meant traipsing off to another extreme "vacation."

Cindy looked from me to him and then to Thom. "Well, I do, but I don't know if this is the type of missionary work you're looking for. It's very rough and there aren't many women who would venture out into the field with these men. They're not amicable to some of our Western equalities."

"You went," James pointed out.

"It was less dangerous back then." She gave him a look of bewilderment as if she just realized he didn't see the differences between her and me. She laughed and patted him on the forearm. "Janis and I traveled with some younger, stronger men and women. Mostly men, but I think you can see why I might not come off the same as most women, especially a pretty one like your fiancée here. Sure, I can give you the contact information and you can ask all the questions, but you might really want to think this through very seriously before considering it to be a viable possibility."

A yoga class must have just ended across the street because a line began to form at the juice bar. Cindy said goodbye so she could get up and help the counter staff.

Thom asked James, "You know she swims in the lady pond, right?"

I giggled at James's surprised expression.

"Of course," he recovered.

Monday morning and not one career between us. He brought me a cup of coffee and then made love to me. It was the third time since going our yoga class and each time we fell deeper back into passion and connection.

I held him in my arms after he shuddered into my chest from an intense orgasm.

"I think we should go," he said while he was still inside me.

I nodded, torn between wanting to keep him locked up in my little condo and knowing that if I did, he would fly away.

"From Nunavut to Africa," he murmured in awe and hugged me tightly.

"It's a pretty dark place," I gently said. "You're not worried?"

"Yes, but we are bringing light there. We will be helping." He pulled out and rolled to his back.

"Maybe I'm being superstitious, but I want to give you the whole story before we totally commit to going there."

"What full story is that, sweetheart?"

"The full story of what happened to Collin."

e p i l o g u e

When the US began to seriously build up its forces back in 1990 along the Saudi/Kuwait border, one of Saddam's most trusted advisors, Sïad Masri, sought counsel on the leader's behalf far from any secure compound in Iraq. Sïad ventured out into the Iraqi desert alone, leaving behind any entourage or protective envoy.

The search for a mysterious, lone traveler in the cursed arid region, one who could slip in and out of view as if between dimensions, was Sïad's primary objective. It was not long into his trek before the lone one's vengeful vibrational match enchanted Sïad. This evil figure reeled the bloodthirsty advisor into IT's dark folds.

The contractual union between Sïad and this lone figure was silently witnessed by an other-worldly army of the same demons, known as the *Djinn*.

Sïad did not see the red ranks of hooded beings; they have the ability to hide themselves from the sight of

men. When Sïad departed, he sensed their cold stares
tethering him to the blood bargain he had just struck
with his newfound partner, the Messiah of the Djinn, the
red one known as Iblis.

During his journey back to the compound, Sïad considered how much detail from the blood bargain, if any,
should be revealed to Iraqi president, Saddam Hussein.

The Path of Least Resistance

Preview of Book II

PARADISE LOST: The statue of Saddam Hussein had just been toppled over in Firdaus Square located in downtown Baghdad, Iraq.
09 APR 2003

The human-like Djinn figure, Iblis, faded in and out of focus. It may have been a hallucination, for Sïad Masri had not slept in over four days. Many of the lightbulbs were burnt out in Saddam's remote palace that was currently being used as a hideout while Baghdad rioted. The chairs surrounding the mammoth ivory table remained covered. Dust had gathered on top of the thick, gold frames showcasing the immaculate portraits of the leader's sons, Uday and Qusay.

Saddam and Sïad had both been holed up in this palace for the past week with a handful of confidants plus several members of the elite Republican Guard. Upon witnessing the telecast of his own statue being toppled over, the leader stormed off.

Sïad found refuge alone in an unused dining area on the other side of the palace.

Goddamned Americans.

A slight red hue emerged, signaling the forthcoming appearance of Sïad's blood partner, Iblis. The hue of blood reflected off the aged skin stretched over its horrific face in the shadowed dining room.

"He didn't obey," Iblis hissed.

"Battle is your realm, Snake. Not proselytizing," Sïad snapped angrily at the figure as he flipped open a tiny, locket-like container that was soldered onto a woven copper and iron ring. He wore this amulet on his body at all times now. The image on the flat top of this encasement portrayed an ornate etching of a pentagram. After Sïad opened the lid, he tapped a decent amount of cocaine out upon the table's glistening surface and began to nervously cut a line.

Iblis bent away briefly in discomfort in response to this action. Djinn are weakened by iron, copper, and other types of metal.

Sïad snapped the locket shut without taking off the ring and snorted a four-inch line of coke right from the expertly carved table. Afterward, he tilted his head back and pinched his nostril shut to keep any lingering remnants of the drug within the lining of his nose.

Sïad's eyes reeled from the instant high as he regarded Iblis with disgust. "The Americans were not supposed to take that route!" he bellowed, slapping a hand down with intense force as he sprang to his feet. This caused his vision to blacken momentarily. Sïad shook his head to clear his sight, not sure if it was his company or the coke creating hallucinogenic trails off this ancient Djinn with whom he was now embedded.

"The plan was in place. I showed you." The reminder came in a voice barely above a whisper, for the Djinn never yell.

Past images arrived in Sïad's mind as if the vision was branded upon his brain's middle temporal region for all eternity.

For it was not that long ago that Iraq wished to claim victory over the US. Iblis went about to grant this wish by showing Saddam's most trusted advisor the anticipated path the Marines would take to Kuwait City. Certain this wish would come true, *Sïad advised Saddam to only prepare for the route Iblis showed him through a vision.* Every other path leading from Saudi Arabia to Kuwait was left unfortified, including the ones the Marines ended up taking at the last minute.

The charcoal smoke materializing in the dining room resurrected the memory of the night Sïad first witnessed this impossible and unfulfilled prophecy. A prophecy derailed by the US changing course at the last moment on the eve when Operation Desert Shield became Operation Desert Storm.

Sïad wanted to conceal the tremor growing in his throat as he furiously blinked his eyes and tried to formulate a rebuttal. He was at a disadvantage. The growing amounts of coke needed for him to achieve a high grew as the frequency of his use increased. He discovered that when the perfect amount of the stimulant was consumed, he existed in an equal vibrational match to his blood partner.

Sïad's demands for more potent cocaine became insatiable, as his belief that ingesting greater amounts of the drug elevated him to a dimension where he would eventually overcome his master. Excessive use of cocaine propelled him past the powerful high into madness, causing Sïad to go round and round in circles. As an invisible witness to many of these sessions, Iblis would interject irrelevant and confusing ideas into the advisor's head. Sïad acted upon these erroneous thoughts and subsequently cursed millions of Iraqi men with the results of his twisted conclusions.

Disgusting. Impressionable humans.

Sïad pushed away his desire to plead and roared instead. "Your prediction was wrong, you have tricked me! And now a chain of events, unseen even by YOU, has been set into motion. We are done!" Sïad spit on the floor in fury. "Null and void!"

Lingering among the dust in the crumbling palace ended for the Iblis. The blood curse upon Sïad was now fully enacted and set to be broadcast in disgraceful humiliation all over the globe. There was a sneer before smoke rose up from the floor engulfing Iblis into the ethers.

Saddam thinks he can hide.

The toxic stench of burning oil suffocated the elaborate room as Sïad found himself coughing, alone once more and questioning the reality of the encounter.

Recently, some of Saddam's inner circle had spied Sïad arguing out loud when no one else was in the room. Presumably, he was debating with himself. But any unbridled thoughts had by those subordinates—bearing even the most benign conclusions—were never voiced.

Sïad leaned over and snorted the last of his coke. This time, the china white powder actively burned his cilia as well as the extended membranes inside his beak. He clawed at his face, which launched a dusting of the snowy substance on the table's surface. Right in front of his eyes, particles of cocaine burned to crisp embers, leaving pinpoint holes of the darkest black ash in the ivory.

The charred marks blemished the table forever.

Blueprints were being drawn from a place that was as close as a pocket is to a pair of pants. The lone Green

Light—that indignant USMC Corporal who told his superiors to change the path US forces would take into Kuwait just one night before! This Corporal was the perfect snapshot of disgraceful arrogance rampant in Westerners. Revenge was to be laid upon young Corporal Collin Andrew St. Germain.

In a few years, when the majority of the US armor left Iraq, the red Djinni knew that dark forces could be strengthened and Iblis would gift the temporal remote viewing capabilities to a more humble, but fanatical, following. A small sect of the most radical believers in Afghanistan was currently growing, and they would be helpful in years to come. Those who were unyielding in their fundamental devotion to Allah, instead of a single, unbearable, human leader, would be easier for Iblis to control. After all, the hunger to foresee always crops up in those who will kill for their agenda.

If Iblis gave the Taliban the sight, the ability to see into future dimensions, they would happily execute revenge on the Green Light, Corporal St. Germain, *as well as any loved ones he may have.*

Catch a Falling Star

Reading Group Guide

For more information about *Catch a Falling Star* and *The Path of Least Resistance* visit <u>leahdowning.com</u>.

☐ The PROLOGUE takes place during the Afghan War when the number of troops deploying there was at an all-time high. IEDs (Improvised Explosive Device) were, and still are, the leading cause of death and dismemberment to US troops in Afghanistan.

- How has the IED threat become more prominent in our world today, both stateside and overseas?

- How has IED warfare contributed to the growing number of PTSD cases being reported when troops return home from deployment?

☐ Lauren is an outsider to the PuraYoga and film world when she travels up to Canada. Why do you think Tyler placed her in such an important position during the week-long training?

☐ Lauren's relationship with her body, food, and clothes seems to be intermixed. What are some clues in the story that tell us about her perception of her physical body? Why do you think she is so comfortable being in a bikini, naked, or in skimpy booty shorts in front of strangers, but yet seems to be very critical of herself?

☐ When Lauren and James are dogsledding with Genout and Pappa, there's emphasis on the mythology of the land. Superstitions are still kept and supernatural entities are revered.
What things do Genout, Pamela, and Pappa do that clue you into their beliefs?

- Is it possible that the Djinn entities are Sedna, just given a different name due to a different locale?
- What role do you think Iblis (also referred to as the red one, IT, or the Djinni master) plays in the story?

☐ James seems authentic in wanting to continue contact with Lauren after they return to the States. She has no faith in that, why?

☐ James tells Lauren that she "uses sex as a way to keep him both drawn in and pushed away at the same time."

How do Lauren's sexual relationships with James and Eric differ?

☐ Do you agree with Lauren's decision to keep her encounter with James (a foreign contact) concealed in her background investigation to have her clearance reinstated? What were her motives in bypassing that question?

☐ Lauren seems to have a hard exterior when it comes to her professional life, but not so much in her personal life. What are some examples of her toughness as an investigator juxtaposed to her weaker traits as a friend?

☐ Matt views Lauren as baggage. What are his motives for wanting her to drop out of the picture with James?

☐ Is Lauren divorced or widowed? Could she possibly still be married to Collin?

☐ Finally…what were your favorite Tyler moments?

Made in the USA
Middletown, DE
11 May 2022